Dragon's Dust

Part One

The Book of Seregon

Alfred Wohlmuth

Copyright © 1993 by Alfred Wohlmuth
Cover art, cover design, and interior illustrations by Alfred Wohlmuth copyright © 2016

All rights reserved. No part of this publication may be reproduced in any manner whatsoever without the prior written permission of the copyright owner.

ISBN 978-0-9981517-0-0

Published in the United States of America by Merlon Books

TABLE OF CONTENTS

1	SMILGA'S SECRET	1
2	THE MAP	15
3	THE CASTLE OF THAMEN	23
4	NOTOM OF THE MOUNTAINS	51
5	THE SERPENTS OF ELREIA	73
6	THE RUINS OF DWOR	93
7	GROK THE MIGHTY	119
8	THE BRINGERS OF EVIL	135
9	BACKSTABBED	151
10	THE SHEPHERD GIRL	169
11	THE FORBIDDEN VALLEY	185
12	SELLOCK THE WIZARD	211
13	A DIFFICULT DECISION	233

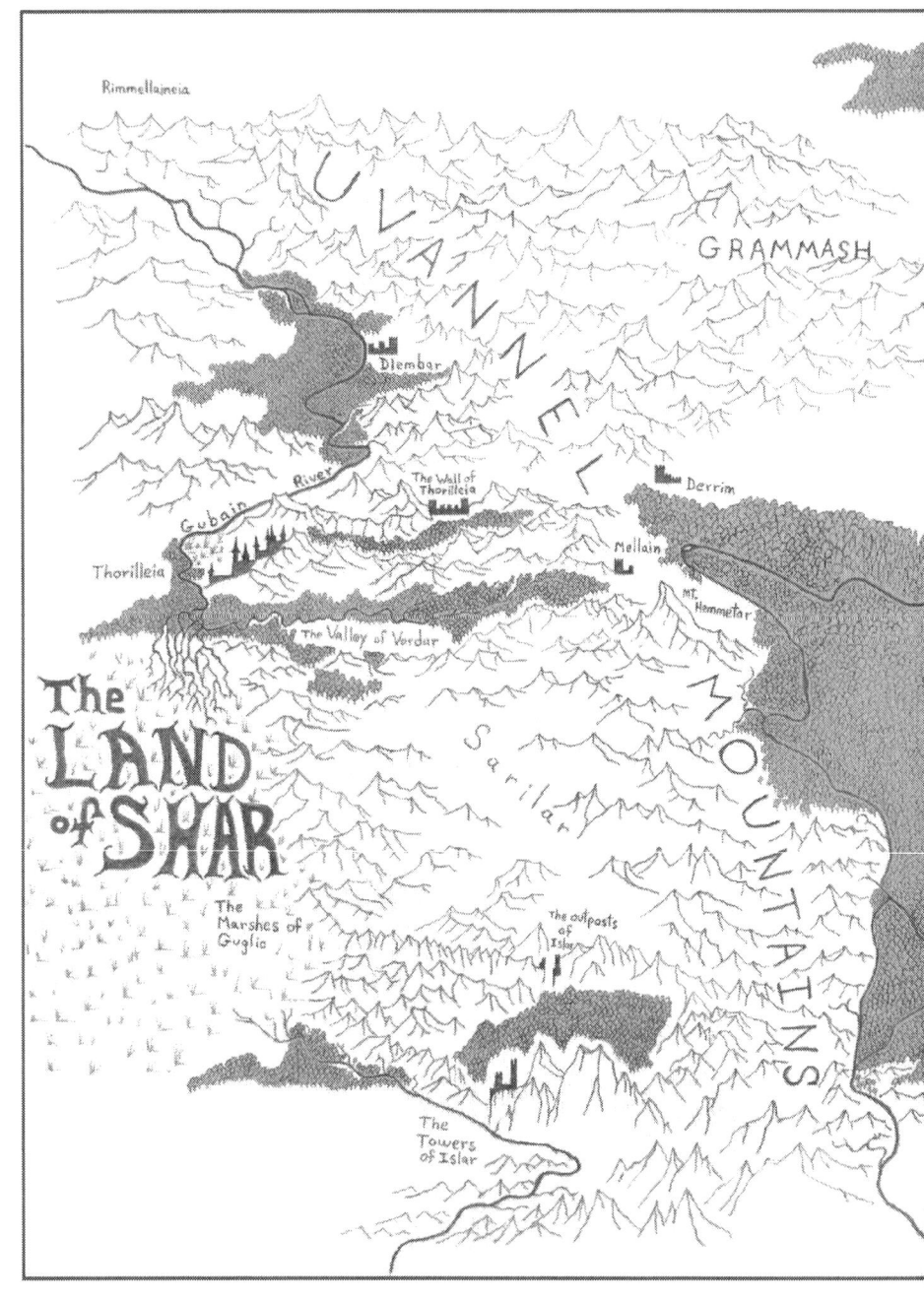

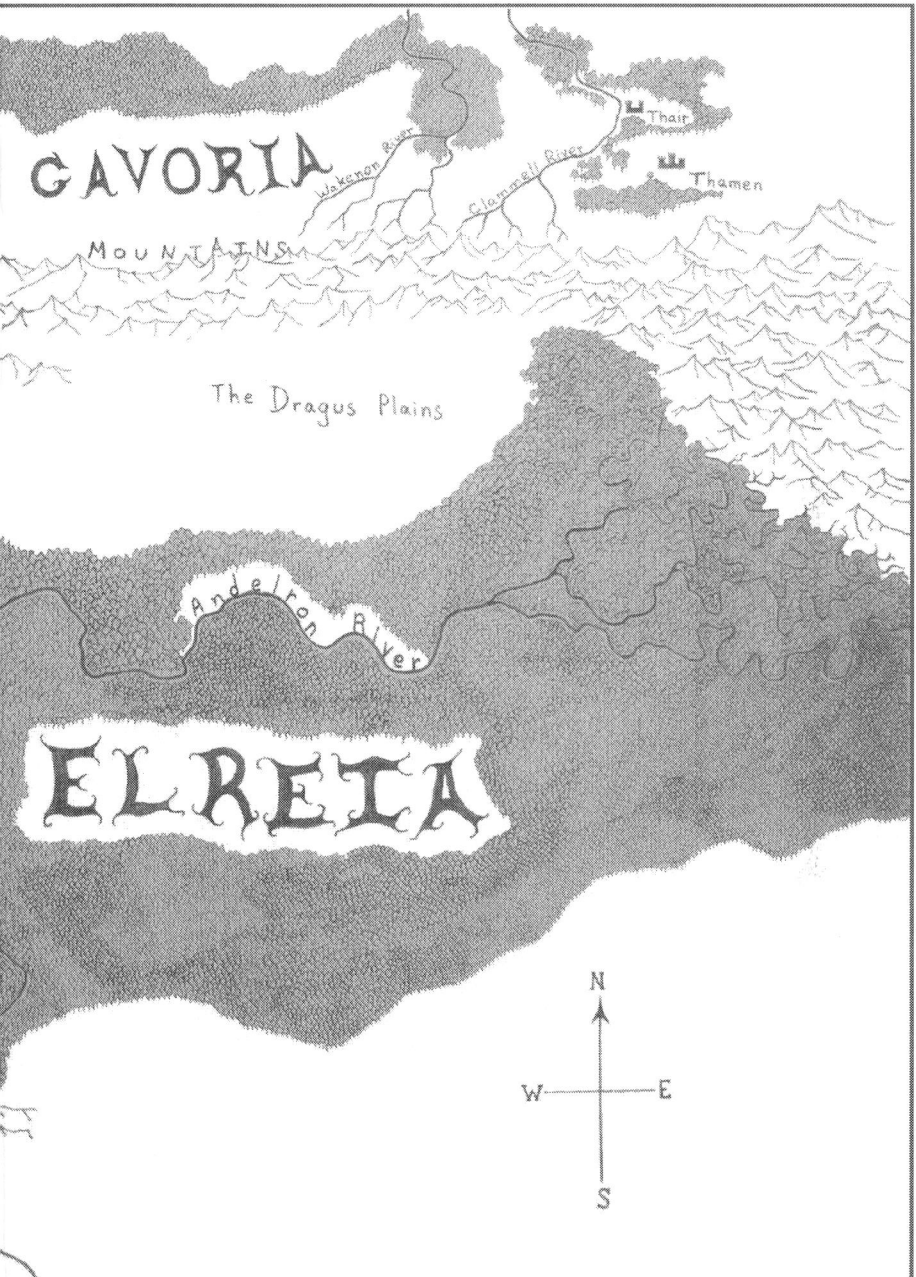

Chapter 1

SMILGA'S SECRET

Otok hid in the darkness of the woods next to a winding dirt road. As he leaned against an old, knotted oak, he peered through the trees at the moon suspended above a castle on a distant hill. The pale glow of moonlight silhouetted tall stone towers and cast eerie shadows as it cut through the forest. Gnarled branches drooped down from the contorted oak like monstrous arms with long crooked fingers.

Suddenly, something lunged at Otok from behind with a low menacing growl. It pounced on his back and grabbed him around the throat. Otok heard it growling into his ear as he bent low and leaned forward. He reached over his shoulder to get a grip, and with one quick jerk, sent the attacker tumbling over his head to the ground in front of him. The growl ended with a thud, which then turned to a quiet laugh of accomplishment.

"Caught you by surprise, didn't I?" said Gyank[*], who was lying on his back, propped up on his elbows.

"What kept you?" asked Otok. "I've been waiting so long, I wasn't sure if you were coming."

"I had to wait for the right moment to sneak away from the house without being seen. How about you? I hope your father didn't see you leaving, or we'll both be in trouble. You know how our parents feel about us going out at night to spy on the witch."

"Don't worry," said Otok. "I may not be as good as you at sneaking around, but I got away unseen."

Gyank hopped to his feet, and he stepped out onto the road as he brushed dead leaves from his shirt. He glanced down the road at the castle and caught a glimpse of a small bat as it flew over a dark tower

---

[*] Gyank rhymes with bank, the "y" is silent

in front of the moon. Then he looked in the opposite direction where a tangle of branches hung over the road in a giant arch, forming what appeared to be a dismal cave. Dim beams of moonlight piercing the mesh of twigs cast ghostly shadows at the entrance to this black tunnel of foliage. Standing side by side, they stared at where the road seemed to vanish into a dark hole.

Gyank turned to Otok, patted him on the shoulder, and said, "By the way, that was a good throw. Now come on, let's get going." He motioned with his hand for Otok to follow and they started down the road, disappearing into the darkness of the woods.

They had been close friends for as long as they could remember. Otok was big for his age, but he was not tall. He was a husky fellow, and stout enough to feel that he need not back down to anyone. Even so, he still looked like a boy, and he certainly had some more growing up to do. Among other things, he had a short temper that often got him in trouble. Unlike his stocky friend, Gyank was wiry, agile, and quick on his feet. He was a year or so older than Otok and a few inches taller, but he also looked young for his age. Because of their playful manner and youthful appearance, most adults viewed them as big children rather than maturing young men. Being in that strange realm between boyhood and manhood, they still took pleasure in play fighting and games of stealth.

Tonight they were going to test their bravery and skill by sneaking up to the witch's house deep in the woods. They had never been there before, but they had heard about the witch and the black magic she practiced. Stories around the fire at night usually focused on the witch when the storyteller's intent was to horrify. Most folks believed that she brewed strange elements in her caldron to conjure up things that were bizarre and unnatural. Few people ventured by her secluded abode because a deep-rooted fear kept them away.

Otok and Gyank had heard many tales, yet the most recent story being whispered among the villagers was too much for their curiosity to resist. A hunter, who strayed by her cottage while on the trail of a big buck, saw her shouting strange commands into the forest as if she were summoning evil spirits. He said she spoke in the tongue of the devil, and her harsh crackling voice sent the hunter fleeing for his life. By the next day, his story was being whispered among the children as well as the respectable people of the community—she was a witch, and a witch up to no good at that.

The hunter's story rekindled fear among the villagers and compelled Otok and Gyank to rendezvous at the knotted oak. Their plan was to find out what she was up to and return to the village alive to tell of their discovery.

The witch's house was nothing more than a small cottage, with a little vegetable garden off to the side. Surrounded by tall spruces, it stood alone in a tiny clearing. In the daylight, it probably had a wholesome look to it, but the dim glow from the moon gave it an eerie and threatening appearance.

Otok and Gyank crept quietly through the dark underbrush. They came to the edge of the clearing and peered out at the witch's cottage. The air was still, and the woods seemed unusually quiet as if even the crickets feared letting their presence be known. Lying on their bellies at the base of a huge spruce tree, they were completely hidden by the lower branches. The strong scent of evergreens hung in the night air.

Gyank broke the silence with a whisper, "Well, that's it."

"Uh-huh," replied Otok who was staring straight at the house without so much as blinking an eye. The curtains in the front window on the open porch were drawn closed except for a tiny space in the middle. The flicker of firelight could be seen through the curtains.

"What now?" Gyank asked quietly.

"I don't know. This was your idea."

"We must get up to that window. Do you think we can make it?"

"I guess so," said Otok.

The longer they lay in the grass outside the clearing, the more they recalled childhood stories about people who never returned after stumbling upon the witch's house at night. A deep fear grew within them as the silence thickened. Gyank took his eyes off the house, looked directly at Otok, and spoke in the softest whisper, "Are you scared?"

"No," said Otok who was deeply afraid, but refused to admit it for fear of ridicule.

"Let's go," said Gyank as he crawled out into the open on all fours. Otok was right behind him. With a stooping, rapid walk, they approached the cottage. But instead of staying on solid soil and moving around the house to get a peek into a window, they stepped onto the porch. The old, weather-beaten floorboards creaked and sagged as if to announce their presence. Stunned by the noise that pierced the silence, they froze and looked at each other. The expression on their faces confirmed that they should have known better than to make such a foolish mistake. They might as well have knocked on the front door.

Behind the house, a snoozing dog, much like a wolf, opened its eyes, lifted its head, and gave a quiet bark of uncertainty. The other dogs woke and their ears perked up to listen.

As soon as Otok and Gyank heard the dog, they ran off the porch, making even more noise and bolted across the clearing toward the woods. The sound of fleeing feet guided the animals to the intruders like a dinner bell. Four large dogs came flying around the front of the cottage in pursuit. Gyank was a few steps ahead of Otok, crashing through the underbrush. Low hanging branches smacked their faces, causing them to stumble. They knew that trying to outrun the dogs was useless, so after a short sprint into the darkness, they reached for the lowest branches of a big maple tree, and like two frightened squirrels, scrambled up the tree for safety. They were trapped and they knew it. The dark shapes below them barking and snapping at the air presented no immediate threat, but the sight of a small torch approaching from the direction of the cottage terrified them. The torchlight moved slowly, and as the witch came into view, she spoke in a demanding voice. It was a language strange to the ears of the two young men, and they listened in horror, expecting to be struck by a spell.

As she came to the tree, the dogs yielded back beyond the perimeter of the torchlight. The witch was dressed in black from head to toe like a widow in mourning. Her long white hair and her pale hands and face contrasted with her dark attire. She walked with a twisted and knotted cane, carved from a tree root. In her other hand, she held the torch from which a green and orange flame crackled and danced. It shed a sickly light on her wrinkled face and made her eyes glow so that one would think the light came from within.

She raised the torch up to get a look at her captives. Her cracked lips parted and the raspy voice of an old woman came forth. "What is to be done with them, Smilga?" Otok and Gyank clung to the tree while the witch replied to her own question. "Why, they're only boys up to their tricks. Only boys—yesss," she hissed. A barely perceivable smile came to her lips. It was an expression that made them feel like helpless prey, and they became even more afraid.

"Come down," she demanded, motioning with the torch, which caused the flame to wiggle. In the cool night air, they could feel the warm smoke rising up into the tree. Otok and Gyank didn't budge. They just tightened their grip and stared down at her, wondering what she was going to do to them.

"Don't be afraid," said the witch, trying to sound convincing. "My dogs won't hurt you." There was a long pause while she gazed up at them. The only sound was the crackle of the torch flame.

"Or, perhaps, it isn't the dogs you're afraid of."

Otok and Gyank looked at each other with surprise. Was the witch reading their thoughts?

"Afraid of Smilga?" she cackled.

Her laugh ceased abruptly. Then she looked down at her feet as if struck by a deep depression and quietly mumbled to herself. "They're not afraid of you, Smilga. They're afraid of the evil witch that stories are told about."

She suddenly looked up at them, her eyes opened wide and she shouted as if accusing them of a great wrong, "But the stories are not true! They're only the fabrications and lies of fearful people whose minds are closed to the truth." Her voice calmed, and she looked down again and muttered, "Why are people so afraid of someone who is different?"

The witch began mumbling to herself in a strange language. While she spoke words that neither Otok nor Gyank understood, they looked down at her and their fear vanished. As if her wicked powers had instantly drained away, she now appeared to them merely as an old woman. Without saying a word to each other, they climbed out of the tree. When they reached the ground, she looked at them, smiled and said, "It's not easy to accept a truth contrary to lifelong beliefs."

One of the dogs came forward into the light and growled at Otok. Before he could do anything, the old woman stomped her cane on the ground and spoke sternly in the strange language. The animal shrunk to the ground, its ears went back and it looked up at her, acknowledging her dominance.

"They won't hurt you," she said in a kind voice. "They're really good dogs once they know you. Come, we have much to talk about."

She turned slowly and walked back toward the cottage. Otok and Gyank followed. Once inside, the old woman extinguished the torch in a pail of sand near the hearth.

"Please sit down," she said.

The two companions glanced around the room. The only light came from the fireplace where a small but bright fire was burning. Next to the hearth stood a rocking chair, skillfully crafted from a rich, dark wood. In the middle of the room was a round, wooden table with four chairs placed around it. Otok and Gyank sat down while the old woman took a kettle from the fire and poured steaming water into a black teapot on the table. She took three cups from an open hutch and set them on the table. Then she sat down and leaned her cane against her chair.

"My name is Smilga. And what might you two be called?"

"I'm Gyank, and this is my friend, Otok."

"And what were you and your friend doing on my front porch?"

They looked at each other wondering what to say. The truth didn't seem appropriate, yet they couldn't think of a convincing excuse, and she wasn't going to be fooled by a poorly thought up lie.

"We came to spy on you," said Otok in a defiant voice, trying to make it sound as if it wasn't such a bad thing to do. "To find out what you're up to—to have an adventure."

"So, it's adventure you seek. I hope my dogs provided you with enough for one night. If you truly thirst for adventure, I might be able to accommodate you. But before we get to that, what did you mean when you said, you want to find out what I'm up to?"

Gyank responded to the question that was directed at Otok. "A hunter said he saw you summoning evil spirits with your magic."

"It's men like him who spread evil by telling stories that aren't true. He saw me calling for my dogs, and he ran as if a pack of wolves was after him. He's so sure I am a witch that his fear clouds his senses and panic governs his thoughts. I could have been singing a song and he would have acted the same way. So, you see, I don't have any evil powers. They're just stories told by ignorant, fearful people. What I do have is a great knowledge in the art of healing. The knowledge was passed down in my family for generations. Yet, no one has surpassed the skill of my great-grandfather."

Smilga glanced around the room as if someone had crept through a crack in the wall to eavesdrop. She leaned forward and spoke in a whisper, "He was not only a great healer, he was a wizard. He had many enemies, for people feared his power. Those who hated him called him an evil sorcerer, and those who befriended him called him an alchemist."

Leaning over the teapot, she lifted the cover and looked in. "I think it's ready."

She poured each of them a cup of deep brown liquid. They peered into the murky brew, but neither of them drank. Smilga watched with anticipation.

Then she spoke as if giving advice to her children. "Mistrust is an important quality for survival, yet we must trust someone or suffer a very lonely life." At that, she poured herself a cup and drank from it. Otok and Gyank began tentatively sipping the warm herbal brew.

"You two remind me of my youngest son, Bodan. He was young and strong when he left long ago. Bodan went in search of riches, glory, and most of all, knowledge." Smilga's voice turned to a whisper as she added, "A search from which he never returned." She looked at them with great intensity, the way one might do when reading someone's thoughts. "Are you willing to risk going on an adventure from which you may never return?"

"Of course," replied Otok as if it was a silly question, although truthfully, he was not sure at all.

Gyank said nothing. He just gazed at Smilga and slowly nodded his head, wondering what the old woman had in mind.

Smilga leaned toward them and extended her long bony finger. "If you're willing to risk your lives for wealth and adventure, then I might share a great secret with you. But first you must vow never to tell anyone what you are about to learn. Even if you choose not to venture out of this valley, you must swear to keep silent."

Overwhelmed with curiosity, Otok quickly responded, "Yes, we promise. We won't ever tell anyone. Your secret is safe with us."

Smilga turned to Gyank. "And you?"

"Yes ma'am, I promise."

"Gooood—very good," said the witch in a sinister voice.

Smilga took another sip from her cup and went to the fireplace where she sat in her rocking chair. The fire had burned down to a pile of glowing embers that cast a dim light about the room. As she sat next to the hearth, only one side of her face was illuminated; an eerie mix of orange light and dark shadow on her pale face made her look ghastly. She closed her eyes and started to speak. The words seemed to be written on the inside of her eyelids as she searched her memory for the ancient story.

"I was born in the Land of Shar, far to the south of the Grammash Mountains, but I remember nothing at all about it. My family had to leave when I was just an infant. When I was older, my mother told me stories of my great-grandfather and his life. As I told you, he was an alchemist. The king at the time was a good king, and my great-grandfather would give his services as an inventor and a healer. But the king died with no heir to the throne and the battle for power started. That's when we fled and traveled north to this valley. But before we left, my great-grandfather was accused of many evil deeds and he had to hide all his work and his writings. He would go down into the passages under the castle to hide from the witch hunters in the maze of tunnels. This is where I believe he hid all his books and potions."

Smilga paused to gather her thoughts and then went on. "He waited too long before trying to escape. He sent the rest of the family ahead and said he would catch up to them. It was later when my grandfather went back to find him that we learned he was killed. They burnt him for being in league with the devil—for being a witch. I was protected from the horror of it by my age."

"So, here's where I grew up, married, and had three children. All three of them were boys. They were much like you—strong, daring, and always looking for adventure, especially the youngest, Bodan. He went off years ago with my good wishes in search of the works of his great-great-grandfather. You see, although I was only a baby when my great-grandfather was killed, my parents made sure I knew the importance of his discoveries. That's why I agreed to let my son go after the secrets hidden in those passages far away."

They gazed at her with amazement until suddenly Otok caught onto Smilga's plan. Completely forgetting his manners toward elders, he spoke in an aggressive tone. "You want us to go searching for your great-grandfather's works and bring them back to you! That's it, isn't it? For what? So we can get ourselves lost or killed—like your son?"

Smilga quickly snapped back at him. "Be quiet and let me finish before you accuse me of sending you on a hopeless and fruitless mission." Smilga paused to regain her composure. "Yes, you may never return, but there's much to gain. There are many riches to be sought along the way. Gold and precious jewels lie hidden in long forgotten caverns in the mountains to the south. Kingdoms destroyed ages ago still have treasures to be uncovered by those daring enough to risk the journey."

Her rocking chair tilted forward as she leaned toward them. "Now, here's my proposition. I will prepare you with the knowledge you need for the journey. I'll tell you what landmarks to look for and what to avoid. You can keep whatever riches you may find by your daringness or by your fortune. Consider it payment for your boldness. For my knowledge and guidance, I ask only one thing as payment."

Otok and Gyank sat frozen, wondering what price Smilga would name. They figured she must want something of great value.

Smilga slowly rose to her feet, took her cane, and walked to the open hutch where many pretty cups and ornaments sat on display. Holding onto the edge of the hutch, she bent down and reached under its bottom. She appeared to be groping for something with her fingers. There was a distinct click, and a secret drawer on the side of the hutch near the floor moved slightly outward. She pulled the drawer open by grabbing the edges with her fingertips. Otok and Gyank were amazed how this hidden compartment was perfectly concealed by the intricate woodwork. Smilga removed an old book with a brown leather cover. She placed it on the table, unbuckled the leather strap that held it closed, and carefully opened it. The edges of the pages were brown and crumbling.

"This book belonged to my mother, and to her mother before her. Those who fear us would call it a witch's book of spells and potions. In truth, it's a book about plants. It tells which roots, herbs, leaves, and flowers are good for which illness. It also explains how to prepare each plant before it can be used to heal."

"What does this have to do with your great-grandfather?" Otok asked impatiently.

"He had a book just like this one, and I want it. That book is mine by right! It belongs to me, and I should have it!" She sounded as if someone was unfairly keeping it from her. "Mind you, it is not merely a book about plants like this one. No, it is more—much more."

There was something in her voice that made her simple request sound gravely wrong. What secret could be contained in that ancient book to make Smilga crave it so intensely? Perhaps it was worth more than all the riches she would gladly let them keep.

"What's in the book?" asked Gyank.

As if stunned by the question, Smilga froze. She fell into deep thought for a moment, and then said, "I'm not exactly sure."

Gyank looked puzzled. "Then why do you want it so badly?"

"I don't know what's in that book, but I do know it's something of great importance. Why would my great-grandfather give his life for it? Why did he refuse to give up his secrets even when they tortured him? My guess is that he was protecting more than his work. I believe he knew that anyone who found that book would become too powerful. I believe he made a great discovery before he died, and it rests somewhere in the secret tunnels under a castle in the Land of Shar."

The urge for adventure was growing within them, and the more they heard, the more their curiosity was aroused. The room was silent except for an occasional crackle from the glowing coals in the fireplace. Then suddenly, as if waking from a daydream, Otok blinked and came back to his senses. "This is crazy. You're talking about going into the wilderness, into the strange lands in the south. How can we expect to make such a journey and find a book we don't even know exists?"

"Do you think I'm foolish enough to tell you all this if I didn't think you could do it? You have many things working in your favor that my son didn't. First of all, there are two of you. You can help each other in countless ways. One can sleep while the other watches for danger. You can care for each other if sick or injured. It's very different from traveling alone. Besides, anyone who can get right up to my front steps without waking my dogs has a good chance of avoiding many dangers that others would encounter."

Examining the old discolored pages in front him, Gyank said, "This book is written in a strange language."

"Yes," said Smilga. "It's written in the ancient language that was spoken in the Land of Shar. And so is the book you will search for."

"Then how are we to know it from other books?"

"It looks just like this one, so I was told. But there's one way to know for certain." Smilga turned to the inside of the cover and pointed to the book. "It bears this symbol. This is my great-grandfather's mark."

On the inside of the leather cover was the rough outline of a man dressed in robes. His arms were stretched upward over his head. In one hand, there appeared to be a stone, and in the other, a torch. The figure stood in a cloud of smoke. It was just a simple drawing, yet they stared at it as if it would give them the answers to all their questions.

"Find the book with this symbol and bring it to me. I will translate it."

Gyank looked up from the book and sat back in his chair. "This is certainly much to think about."

"Yeah," said Otok in a dreamy voice, as if held in a trance while his eyes remained fixed on the symbol.

Looking directly at Smilga, Gyank said, "I think we should go home and give this whole thing some thought."

Smilga leaned toward them ever so slightly, like a cat getting ready to pounce and spoke in a tone of voice that made goose bumps run up their necks. "Yes, you do that. You go home and think about all this. But may you suffer tenfold the tortures of my great-grandfather if you disclose what you've heard here tonight. Tell it to no one. For if the wrong ears learn what you know, there may be horrors unleashed for which you would be to blame. Remember your vow."

"Our word is good no matter what the stakes," replied Gyank

proudly.

"Then be off. No one is to know where you've been tonight. You will return tomorrow evening, and I will expect an answer."

Chapter 2

THE MAP

As Otok and Gyank walked away from Smilga's cottage, daydreams about finding great wealth and discovering wondrous secrets ran through their minds, and they didn't speak until they were almost home. When they got back to the knotted oak, Gyank grabbed Otok's arm and pulled him so they faced each another. "Do you suppose she was telling the truth about her great-grandfather and the book?"

"I guess so," said Otok. "Remember the look on her face when she talked about the book?"

"I sure do—it was frightening. She couldn't have been faking the whole thing. There must be some truth in it. Why would she bother telling us all that anyway? Unless she wants to send us off to get killed."

"I think she's telling the truth. And I think there is a place called the Land of Shar, and secret a book, just like she said."

"Then you think we should go?" asked Gyank.

"I'd really like to know what's in that book. Besides, Smilga said we might find riches. If we do, then we'll live in comfort for the rest of our lives, and our families will want for nothing."

"That reminds me," said Gyank. "What will our parents think about us going off on our own? We can't just leave without letting them know. But no matter what, we can't tell them about the book, or that the witch had anything to do with us leaving."

"You're definitely right about that," agreed Otok. "And we better get home before they notice we're gone."

"Let's go then," said Gyank. "And don't get caught sneaking back into your house."

"Don't worry. I can sneak around just fine if I have to."

At that, they parted and crept back to the village, each by a different path so that if one were caught, he wouldn't give the other away.

~ ~ ~

The next night, they met at the knotted oak tree again.

"Did you get away unseen?" asked Gyank.

"Yes, but it doesn't matter anymore because I spoke to my pa."

Gyank looked concerned. "I hope you didn't mention the witch or her book."

"No, I told him that it was time for me to go out into the world and seek my fortune."

"What did he say?"

"He said that I was a man now, and I could go if that was my decision."

"My father said pretty much the same thing. So now it's up to us. I say we tell Smilga that we'll do it. I still have my doubts about her, but we just can't let this chance go by."

"I agree," said Otok. "This might be our only chance to strike it rich, and discover a wizard's secret worth dying for."

"Then let's go and tell Smilga."

When they arrived at the witch's house, she was sitting on the porch waiting. Her dogs were lying around her chair. One of them lifted its head and barked. Smilga slowly extended her hand, signaling the dog to stay. Otok and Gyank walked up to the porch and just stood there looking at her. She seemed to be in a trance as she stared straight ahead and didn't acknowledge their presence. Her long white hair hung straight down both sides of her head, framing her wrinkled face. Her eyes were open, but they did not move or even blink. It looked as if she had died sitting up with her eyes open.

"We'll do it," said Gyank, breaking the silence.

Smilga snapped out of her trance and looked at them. "As I expected." She slowly got up from her chair, and said, "Come, we have things to do."

Smilga made a motion with the back of her hand as if to push a mosquito away from her face. The dogs responded to this hand signal by getting up and slowly walking off the porch in single file. As they disappeared around the side of the cottage, Smilga led Otok and Gyank inside and closed the door. "Sit at the table," she said as she went to the open hutch. Smilga bent down, opened the secret drawer, and took out an old piece of paper that was folded many times. She unfolded it and laid it out on the table. It was a map with sketches of castles and mountains far beyond the territory that Otok and Gyank were familiar. In fact, the entire range of their travels was marked by a tiny sketch of a minor castle in the north.

Smilga sat down at the table and said, "This map was made by my grandfather. It's all I have left to show the way south to the Land of Shar. My grandfather was not a mapmaker, but he pieced together this map based on other maps he had seen; whatever he wasn't sure about, he guessed at. So this map isn't perfect, but you'll find that his guesses are not far from the truth. There may be more or less distance between places, but I assure you they are all there."

Smilga pointed to the map and said, "Here's where we are, the Kingdom of Thair. To the south are the Grammash Mountains, steep and rugged. And there's no way around them. Yet, there is a narrow footpath that leads through the mountains to the Great Forest of Elreia. This is the way you must go. If you fail to stay on the path and go too far west, you may find yourself in the Dragus Plains. The plains are hot, dry, and barren, and they stretch for hundreds of miles. Avoid them at all costs."

Smilga ran her arthritic index finger along the mountains. "As you can see, if you stray too far east, the mountain range grows thick. There are many more miles from one side to the other, and it will take much longer to find your way across—if you get across at all. The mountains are very dangerous. Many have been known to die wandering among the peaks."

"How will we ever find that footpath?" asked Gyank. "It would seem that's the only way to get across the mountains safely."

"Take the main road leading south out of this valley. In a few days, you'll come to a small village under the rule of a castle to the east." Smilga pointed to the castle of Thamen on the map. "Here you will seek a man named Trenden. He's the cobbler. Tell him, and only him, that you spoke to me, and that I've sent you on this quest. He knows the mountains well, and he should be able to help." Smilga paused. "If he still lives."

"If he still lives!" said Otok.

"No one said this journey would be easy. I've done my best to plan a route for you, but if things go amiss, you'll have to rely on your wits and your luck to find the way."

She gazed at them for a moment and then drew their attention back to the map. "Once you've gotten across the mountains, you'll be in the Great Forest of Elreia. In some places, the undergrowth is so thick it's impassable. But where the forest isn't so dense, you may find Erifs."

"What are Erifs?" asked Gyank.

"The native people of the forest. They have strange beliefs and customs, but they're not a bad people. Even so, as travelers in a strange land, you should be wary of everyone. Be careful who you talk to and what you say. Most of all, don't speak of the book. In fact, don't even tell anyone where you're going. There are many who would follow you and kill you if they knew what you were after."

Smilga looked down at the map. "Now, there are many trails in the woods and many lead to dead ends or other dangers. Whether you find a trail or not, you must make your way southeast to the Andelron River, which flows west for many miles before it heads south. Follow the river. It will lead you to the Uvannel Mountains where it makes a sharp turn, as you can see, and goes southeast. Here's where you must leave the river and head west to the mountains bordering the Land of Shar. The best way to know when to leave the river is to look for

Mount Hemmetar. Its peak is much higher than any of the surrounding mountains, and it should be easy to spot from a long distance off. In fact, you should be able to see it from the river."

Smilga studied the map in silence for a moment. When she spoke again, she sounded concerned. "I don't know how my family got across the Uvannel Mountains, but it's up to you to find the passage they used, or find another way. Remember, the mountains hold many dangers. Most of all, beware of the Voraks. They are the barbarian warriors of the mountains, and they're an evil race. Once across the mountains, you will be in the Land of Shar. It's a dreadful place where death strikes without warning. You must be alert at all times."

Smilga suddenly grew quiet and gazed at them intensely as if scrutinizing their strength of character. After a long uncomfortable pause, she looked down at the map, put the tip of her yellowed fingernail on a tiny sketch of a castle with pointy towers, and said, "Now listen very carefully. This is the castle of Thorilleia. My great-grandfather lived here, and somewhere in its underground passages lies the book we seek."

Looking up from the map, Smilga said, "My great-grandfather's name was Seregon. Although, I doubt anyone would remember him—it's been so many years since his death, but none of that matters. Just remember, it is here that you must go—the castle of Thorilleia. And you must somehow find your way into the darkness of those secret tunnels."

It was clear that once Otok and Gyank headed out on their quest, they would be completely on their own. They stared at Smilga waiting to hear more, but she was silent.

"Is this all you can tell us about our journey?" asked Gyank.

"I'm sorry, but that's all I know. I was only a child when I made the journey, and I don't remember it. I only know the stories told to me by my family years later."

Smilga put her hand on the map and slowly pushed it in front of Gyank. "Take the map. It may help you. Besides, I have no use for it anymore. If you don't succeed, then my hope of recovering the book will be gone." With great emphasis, she said, "Use your wits. Before your journey has ended, they will prove more valuable than any map or advice I could give you."

Gyank picked up the map, folded it carefully and placed it in an inside pocket of his shirt. "We'll do our best to find the book."

Smilga pointed her finger at them and said, "Along the way, there will be chances to find riches. They are for you to keep if fortune brings them to you. Whatever treasures you find will be your reward for taking this journey."

"At this point, we're more interested in that book," said Gyank.

"The book is mine!" snapped the witch. "And don't you forget it!"

"Don't worry," said Gyank, a bit startled. "We'll bring it to you. But we also want to know what's in it. I think it's only fair."

"I suppose so," said Smilga calmly, after realizing how nasty she had just sounded. Tilting her head slightly, she smiled warmly and added, "First get the book."

"Don't worry about that," said Otok with confidence. "If the book is there, we'll find it."

"Good. There's one more thing to do before your preparation is complete. Come, I will show you."

Pushing down on the arms of her chair, Smilga slowly stood up. She took her crooked cane and moved toward the door. Otok and Gyank followed her outside to the vegetable garden on the side of the cottage. The moon was bright and they could see the plants in the garden quite well.

"This is kir," said Smilga, pointing to a leafy plant. "It's not common around here, but you may find that it is abundant in other lands. It is the food of travelers and warriors. It can be eaten leaf, stem, and root. Kir gives lasting endurance to travelers long after weariness would have claimed them. It also gives strength for battle." Smilga picked a leaf, tore it in half, and handed it to them. "Taste."

"It tastes sweet," said Otok with surprise.

"Yes, and it will keep you on your feet, so remember what it looks like. Now this is goplic," said Smilga, pointing to a thorny bush. "It quenches the thirst of travelers in dry lands."

She got down on her hands and knees and began to dig with the end of her cane. She pulled a long thick root from the base of the bush and shook it furiously, causing dirt to fly off in all directions. "Here, take it. Snap the root in half and suck on the inside."

Otok did as Smilga requested. "Sour," he said, making a terrible face.

"Yes, sour, and extremely good for thirst. Someday you may be happy to taste that sour root. Then there's smeatle," said Smilga, showing them a plant with long slender leaves. "This may prove to be the most valuable of all. Smeatle is a plant used in many healing potions. Take the leaves, score them with a knife so the juice can ooze out, and wrap them onto any open wound with a cloth. The wound will heal quickly and without a scar. This smeatle plant has not bloomed yet, but when it does, the flowers are a beautiful bright yellow. They can be boiled into tea and sipped slowly to drive out almost any fever or disease. If you're able to recognize this plant, it may save your life."

"Thank you for everything," said Gyank.

"No need for thanks," said Smilga. "Go and seek your fortune. I wish you luck—and remember, use your wits."

The two companions headed across the clearing toward the woods, leaving Smilga standing alone in her tiny garden. She kept looking in their direction as if there was one more thing she had to tell them, but just couldn't think of it at the moment. Only after they disappeared into the darkness of the forest did Smilga break her stare and head back into the cottage.

They walked in silence as if a heavy burden had been suddenly thrust upon them. The feeling that they had accepted a great responsibility weighed on them so much that the hike back through the woods seemed to take no time at all. When they reached the knotted oak, they stopped and looked at each other.

"What do you think?" said Otok. "Tomorrow morning? Right at this spot?"

"That sounds good. And bring anything you think might be useful."

They departed and went back to the village by separate paths as they did the night before. They couldn't help but wonder what treasures might be found, and what dangers they would encounter. Yet, most of all, they were fascinated by the prospect of discovering the powerful and mysterious secrets of a mighty wizard.

Chapter 3

THE CASTLE OF THAMEN

The next morning, Otok came down the road carrying a pack full of gear. With a bow in one hand and a quiver slung on his shoulder, he approached the knotted oak. Gyank's pack was leaning against the tree next to his bow and quiver, but Gyank was nowhere in sight. Otok knew that his friend wasn't far off and was probably stalking him.

Scanning the forest nearby, Otok spoke in a loud voice, "Alright Gyank, come on out."

Just as Otok finished his sentence, Gyank dropped out of the tree and knocked him to the ground. They scrambled to their feet and faced each other. Otok tossed his bow aside and pushed his quiver from his shoulder as Gyank lunged at him, driving him back against the tree. Gyank had him pinned for a moment, but Otok quickly turned the tables by locking his hands together around Gyank's waist and lifting him clear off the ground while squeezing him in a viselike grip.

"Alright, you win, you win," said Gyank, gasping for air while his feet dangled above the ground.

Otok released him, and Gyank took a step backward.

"I could have killed you if I wanted to," said Gyank as he removed a small hatchet from his belt. With one quick stroke, he let it tumble through the air. The head of the hatchet sunk deep into a dead stump across the road, making a dull noise as it came to a sudden stop.

"Not bad," said Otok, picking up his bow. "But watch this." He nocked an arrow and drew back on the bowstring, putting a deep bend in the heavy bow. It took a good deal of strength to hold perfectly still while he aimed. Then he let the arrow fly, striking the stump only an inch or two above the head of Gyank's hatchet.

"Excellent shot!" said Gyank.

As they went across the road to retrieve their weapons, Otok asked, "Did you bring the map?"

"It's right here in my shirt," said Gyank, patting his chest.

"I brought everything I might need," said Otok, "extra clothes, bed roll, coils of rope, water skins, cooking gear, and plenty of dried foods."

Gyank reached into a side pocket of his pack and took out a tiny tinderbox. "Otok, look at this," he said, opening the rectangular metal box that fit in the palm of his hand. Inside was a finger thick piece of metal along with two pieces of flint. The rest of the box was stuffed with brown clumps of extremely fine plant fibers that had the consistency of cotton.

"This is a fast and easy way to start a fire," said Gyank. "And the lid fits so tight that you can dump it in water and the inside will stay dry."

"I bet that will come in handy on rainy days."

Gyank squeezed the box closed, and as he was putting it away, he said, "I always keep it in this side pocket of my pack so I can find it even in the dark." Gyank flung his pack onto his back, grabbed his bow and quiver, and they headed down the road.

It was a sunny day in the spring when Otok and Gyank set out on their quest to find the book. Traveling south out of the Valley of Thair, they walked leisurely under a cloudless sky and spoke of good fortune. The air was cool as they hiked through the woods and out into vast open fields separated by sparse groups of trees. As they continued south, the land sloped gently upward and downward in an endless sea of hills, like long shallow waves in the ocean.

When the late afternoon sun began to cast long shadows on the green slopes, they headed toward a little hill off the road to the east. It had a few fir trees on it, and they knew the pine needles would make a soft bed. After laying their packs down under a tall pine tree, they collected a few dead branches and made a small fire, just big enough to cook their evening meal. As dusk approached and the fire burned low, Gyank looked across the hills at a dark line of trees on the horizon.

"Maybe we can make it to that forest by tomorrow," he said. "I bet that's where we'll find the village with the cobbler named Trenden."

"If he still lives," said Otok without blinking as he stared into the embers of their dying fire.

"We'll soon find out."

The sky grew dark and filled with stars as they rolled out their blankets and went to sleep.

~ ~ ~

The next morning, Gyank was up and preparing breakfast while Otok was just beginning to stretch and yawn.

"Come on Otok, we have a long way to go today."

Otok sat up and looked around as if he was expecting to find himself at home in bed.

"Breakfast is ready," said Gyank.

After a quick meal, they packed their gear and were heading south along the road. The day went by quickly, and by late afternoon the road had led them into the forest. They could no longer see for miles. The woods closed in on all sides and they walked in silence along the dirt path that wound its way through the shady forest. They kept looking ahead to see what was around the next bend, but each turn only revealed another section of dense woods. Eventually, darkness caused them to settle down for the night, and they set up camp a short distance off the road. But this night, they didn't fall asleep as easily. The forest seemed less friendly than the wide-open fields.

Despite their uneasiness, the night passed quietly, and the following morning they continued along the road. By afternoon, they had gone much deeper into the forest and had become accustomed to the stillness of the woods. They walked without concern for what might be ahead until they heard voices coming from around the next bend in the road. The trees blocked their view, but they were certain that the voices were coming closer. The sound of men talking was mingled with the dull clap of horseshoes on the dirt road. They stopped and listened.

"Do you think we should hide?" asked Gyank.

"Why should we? We didn't do anything wrong."

Moments later, they were spotted by one of four armed guards on horseback. He whispered to the others and they stopped talking as they approached. Riding four abreast on large warhorses, they blocked the road from side to side. Each was clad in chain mail over which they wore brightly colored garments. They had shiny metal helmets, and long swords dangled from their belts. As they brought their steeds to a halt, the one who appeared to be the leader spoke. "Who are you? And what are you doing on this road?"

As Gyank answered, he tried to sound and act older than he was. "I am Gyank, and this is my friend, Otok. We are simple travelers."

"And who are you?" asked Otok.

"That's none of your concern. Just answer the questions, and answer them quickly—if you know what's good for you."

"We're not looking for trouble," said Gyank, "We're just travelers heading south."

"Is that so?" said the leader, leaning forward in his saddle while looking down at them. "Do you know where this road leads?"

"I know there's a village south of here," said Gyank.

One of the other men spoke casually to the leader. "Seems to me that they're just a couple of boys wandering about where they shouldn't be—probably runaways."

"Yes, I think so," agreed the leader as he and two other guards dismounted. "A couple of runaways who nobody would bother about if they never came back. And what might they be doing with bows in the king's forest? Hunting the king's deer perhaps? The penalty for this crime is rather severe, but I think we should go easy on them. They'd make good stable boys for the king's guards."

"Wait just a minute," said Otok, as his temper began to flare. "I'm not accustomed to being falsely accused of a crime by someone who won't even tell me his name. And I'm not going to be a stable boy for anyone!"

The leader stepped in front of Otok. He was a head taller, and with an angry expression on his face, he said, "I don't care what you're accustomed to." He turned to his fellow guards and commanded, "Seize these outlaws!"

Gyank was the quickest to react to these words. He jumped backward, pulling the bow from his shoulder as two guards rushed forward to grab him. He jabbed the tip of his bow into the stomach of one man, causing him to bend over and clutch his belly. Before Gyank could make another move, the second guard caught hold of the bow and yanked it from his hands, pulling him off balance.

At the same time, the leader grabbed Otok by the arms, but he soon paid for underestimating the strength of the young man who he jostled roughly. Otok ripped free of the man's grip with one quick motion. His large hand recoiled back to his shoulder, and he drove the heel of his open hand up into the face of his attacker. There was a crack as the leader's nose broke. He stumbled back, but Otok advanced, slamming the heel of his hand repetitively into the man's only vulnerable spot, his face. Blood dribbled over the man's lips and dripped off his chin as he fell back into the horses, causing them to rear up. The man on horseback was nearly thrown, and he fought to regain control of his steed. Gyank was on the ground trying to fend off two guards while Otok rushed to his aid. He grabbed one of the guards by the shoulders and pulled him backward. The man fell to the ground with a crash that whipped his head back and caused his helmet to fall off. Otok grabbed the other guard by the foot and dragged him off his friend.

Gyank jumped to his feet. "Let's get out of here!"

They turned toward the woods and bolted, but one of the men on the ground grabbed Otok's legs and tripped him. Gyank stopped to help as Otok rolled onto his back to fight off the man clinging to him. They saw the leader approaching with sword in hand. He was furious and his bloody face made him look terrifying.

"Gyank, run!" shouted Otok while twisting to break free. "Get out of here! Run!"

Gyank fled into the woods. The guard on horseback spun his steed and gave a sharp kick, causing the horse to spring forward. Otok struggled to his feet, and with a mighty shove, pushed one of the guards into the leader. As the horse passed in pursuit of Gyank, Otok caught hold of the rider's foot and held on. The man reached down to break his grip as Otok was dragged along next to the horse. But Otok's hands were quick as well as strong. He grabbed the rider's wrist and pulled him out of the saddle. As the man tumbled to the ground, Otok was nearly trampled by the hooves pounding the earth next to him.

Otok had no chance. In an instant, three guards were on him, and when the leader put his sword to Otok's chest, the struggle was over. Otok felt utterly beaten, but he was glad that at least Gyank had escaped.

~ ~ ~

When Gyank stopped running, he was deep in the forest and completely alone. The only sounds were his heaving breath and pounding heart. He sat on a fallen log to rest and to think. He was lost, but he knew the general direction of the road, and that's where he needed to go to save his friend. Gyank looked at his bow. In all the confusion, he managed to pick it up before he fled. He had only planned to use it for hunting or to defend against wild animals, but now he wondered if he would need to use it against people. He certainly didn't want to kill anyone, but he would if he had to. He took his quiver off his back, and to his dismay, most of his arrows had fallen out in the struggle. Of the twelve he started with, only four were left.

"I'll just have to make them count," he said to himself.

Gyank stood up and headed back. When he got close to the road, he slowed his pace and approached with great caution. Listening intensely, he quietly stepped onto the road and looked in both directions. He walked to the spot where they had encountered the guards hoping to find some of the arrows that had fallen from his quiver, but they had taken everything. The only thing left was the tracks. From the look of them, they had gone back the way they had come, and Otok was with them. His footprints had a wide gap between them, which indicated that he was running. Farther down the road were spots where Otok's footprints vanished, and in their place was a trail of smooth dirt. Gyank grew angry imagining his friend tied to a horse and having to run in order to avoid being dragged along the road. He quickened his pace, and by dusk the forest ended and Gyank found himself looking at rolling hills of farmland and shady meadows. Far off to the east was an enormous castle on top of a steep hill. A road wound back and forth through the surrounding countryside and led up to the front gate. Gyank figured that they must have taken Otok to the castle. But he had no intention of following the road—he would only be caught. Instead, he left the road and cut across the sparsely wooded hills. Whenever possible, he walked among clusters of bushes and trees in an attempt to remain unseen.

 As Gyank approached the outer wall of the castle, he stopped under the cover of a group of trees and looked at the massive stone structure. It seemed risky to scale the wall, yet Gyank had to find a way to get inside. He waited until it was dark and then searched the outer wall. He found a few spots that were climbable, but none would take him all the way to the top. After hours of this discouraging work, Gyank gave up and crept into a dense clump of vegetation. He crawled under a thick bush to be sure he was completely hidden and pulled a blanket around his shoulders. It was difficult to fall asleep. And when he finally dozed off, his sleep was restless and uneasy.

 The next morning, for some unknown reason, things didn't seem as bad. The situation hadn't changed, yet Gyank knew that one way or another, he was going to get Otok out of that castle. He hadn't the foggiest idea how, but since any plan would have to be executed under the cover of darkness, he had the whole day to come up with one.

Thinking about how they got themselves into this mess, his thoughts shifted to Smilga. She said to seek out a cobbler in the village along the south road under the rule of a castle to the east. If this was that castle, then the village shouldn't be much farther down the road. With renewed hope, Gyank made his way back to the road and headed south. He had not gone far when he came to a fork in the road. Although the roads curved through the rolling hills, it was clear that the left branch led to the castle while the right continued south.

Soon Gyank was passing through fields of young crops. Corn, rye, wheat, and beans were just beginning to break the soil. The road also ran along apple and peach orchards. It was much too early in the season for fruit, yet these blooming orchards provided a place to hide when people or guards on horseback came down the road.

Eventually, the road led to a tiny hamlet. Old wooden cottages were scattered about the perimeter while the main road was lined with shops and stores. Gyank walked down the main road toward the village square. It was impossible to avoid people, so he tried to act as if he belonged there. This strategy was useless because, in a tiny hamlet such as this, everyone knows each other, and Gyank stood out anyway. He got some curious stares, but there seemed to be nothing hostile about the townspeople.

Gyank felt a sense of relief when he saw a little cobbler's shop in the square. He quietly walked into the shop and looked around. The smell of fresh leather permeated the air. An old man sitting at the workbench was hammering a nail into the sole of a boot that he held between his knees. He hadn't noticed Gyank enter the shop.

With a forced smile, Gyank said, "Good afternoon, sir."

Startled, the man looked up. "Oh, hello. Can I help you?"

"Is your name Trenden?"

"Yes, my young lad. And who are you?"

Gyank sat down in a chair by the door and sighed with relief. "Thank goodness I found you."

"Who are you? And how do you know my name?"

"A witch told me about you. She sent me to find you and said that—"

By the expression on the man's face, Gyank knew he had said the wrong thing.

"Now you listen to me, young man! You sneak in here, startle me out of my skin, and then claim to be on a witch's errand. So if you don't start explaining right now, I'll have you seized and questioned."

Gyank was struck with fear and he jumped to his feet. His only chance to get help had turned into a nightmare.

"Please, don't call out," pleaded Gyank. "I'll tell you anything. Just don't call for the guards."

Realizing how terrified Gyank was, the man tried to calm him. "Don't worry, I won't call out."

Gyank slowly sat back down. "I'm sorry. I didn't mean to startle you. I was just so relieved to find you. My friend was seized and taken away by horsemen in armor. I was hoping that you could help me."

"I see," said the cobbler, glancing out the shop window to see if anyone was nearby. "Things like this are not uncommon here. But you still haven't told me who you are and how you know me."

"My name is Gyank, and I come from the Valley of Thair where I know an old woman. She isn't really a witch, but people think she is."

"That's a serious thing to think," said the cobbler. "It could cost the old woman her life."

"Well, Smilga told us to look for a cobbler named Trenden because he could help us find a passage through the mountains."

"Hold on a minute, one thing at a time. Now, who is Smilga?"

"Smilga's the witch … uh … mean the old woman. She said you would know her."

Gyank was slowly realizing that he might be telling all this to the wrong person, and fear started to creep back into his mind. "How many Trendens are there in this village?" he asked suspiciously.

"Just me," said the old man. Then the expression on his face changed as if he suddenly realized the obvious. "I was named after my father."

"Where's your father?"

"He's been dead for years."

Gyank looked down at the floor and slowly shook his head in despair.

"Things aren't all that bad," said Trenden. "I don't know of any passage through the mountains, but I'm not a bad fellow. I just had to be wary when you first came in here. One has to be careful you know. As I said, what happened to your friend is not uncommon. The king's guards do as they please around here."

Trenden noticed that his words weren't making Gyank feel any better. He thought for a moment as he watched Gyank stare at the floor. Then, as if coming to a decision, he said, "If some old hag told you that a cobbler named Trenden would help you, then I won't make a liar out of her. I may not be my father, but then again, who is?" Trenden chuckled at his own joke.

Gyank looked up at him. "You mean you'll help me?"

"That's what I said, my boy."

"But my friend was taken to the castle, and you could be arrested for trying to help me rescue him."

Trenden smiled. "That is if we get caught. I don't plan on getting caught. Besides, it's about time someone did something about these guards. The king himself doesn't know about some of the terrible things they do."

Gyank was delighted to have found someone willing to help, and he stayed with Trenden for the rest of the day. When evening came, they closed the shop and went to Trenden's little cottage on the outskirts of the village. Once inside, they closed all the shutters and lit some candles. Then the two of them sat at the table to devise a plan.

"I want to do it tonight," said Gyank.

"One night is as good as the next as far as I'm concerned. I realize you want to get your friend out as soon as possible, so tonight it is. Sometimes I take my wagon up to the castle to sell boots to the noblemen. I haven't been there in a while. That's how you'll get inside."

"I was thinking of scaling the wall," said Gyank.

"Scaling the wall?" said Trenden with surprise. "An experienced mountain climber wouldn't try it. Besides, even if you did manage to get over the outer wall, then you'd have to tackle the moat."

"The moat?"

"I guess you didn't realize the castle is so well fortified—well, it is. Within the outer wall is a grassy field that is often used for jousting, and then just before the second wall is the moat—about twenty or so feet across. Beyond the second wall are the living quarters, the stables, and a few small courtyards before you get to the third wall."

"The third wall!" said Gyank, as his eyes grew wide.

"Yes, there are three walls before the inner castle where the king lives, but most likely, we won't have to worry about the third wall. My guess is that your friend is being held behind the second wall. That's where the guards live. I'm sure your friend is not in the dungeon. That would only be the case if he were a prisoner of some importance. I bet the king doesn't even know that your friend is being held. It's more likely those guards took him to work as a servant."

"That's right," said Gyank. "Just before the guards seized us, they mentioned using us as stable boys."

"If that's the case, then your friend is probably in or near the stables, which are between the second and third walls. But before we go anywhere, I must know if you have any stalking ability. Can you move silently and disappear in shadows when necessary?"

Gyank responded as if it were an insulting question. "I've practiced such skills all my life; yet, I've never put them to such a test. But that doesn't matter. I don't let my friends down. I'll do whatever I must do to save Otok."

"Good. Then here's the plan. We'll rig up leather straps underneath my wagon so that you can suspend yourself. Before we get to the main gate, you'll crawl under the wagon and get into the straps.

The wagon has low hanging boards on both sides that will keep you out of sight. Once we get inside the main gate, you must not let go. There's too much open space and no place to hide. Wait until we get across the drawbridge and the moat. Then the rest is up to you. Pick a good time to drop to the ground. The wagon will just keep rolling. You must stay out of sight, find your friend, and free him. Then get back to a spot along the way we came in. This way you can jump into the back of the wagon when I'm on the way out. They don't check wagons on the way out, only on the way in. So if you and your friend are under the canvas in the back of the wagon, you shouldn't be noticed. But stay still and be quiet until I tell you it's safe."

Gyank was amazed at the brilliance of the plan. "That sounds like a great idea. It should work like a charm."

"It should. But remember, you must find your friend and get to a good hiding place so you can get back on the wagon. If you miss the wagon, it will be up to you to find another way out." Trenden looked straight at Gyank and said, "Remember this, if anything begins to look rotten, use your head. There are high stakes here. Those guards are not fools—we could be walking into a trap. The men who took your friend might be expecting you to try to rescue him. There would be nothing I could do if you were caught. So just remember, once you drop off the bottom of the wagon, you're on your own. It's up to you to save your friend. Do you understand?"

"Yes, I understand," said Gyank, knowing that Trenden was putting himself at great risk to help him.

"One last thing, if you don't get back to the wagon in time and must find your own way out of the castle, come back here to this house. Just be sure that you're not followed. Now, do you know what you're supposed to do? If there are any questions, ask them now. Once we start, there will be no talking."

"I understand everything perfectly."

"Good, then let's start preparing our equipment. First of all, let me get you some clothes."

"But I have clothes."

Trenden didn't respond. He just walked over to a large chest by the foot of his bed in the other room. He brought out two dark garments, a shirt with a hood and a matching pair of pants. "Try these on for size," he said, tossing them over Gyank's arm.

Gyank held the outfit up and noticed there was something strange about the material. It was unlike any fabric that he had ever touched. It was soft and flexed easily, yet it seemed very strong. He moved around the room to see it in a better light, but couldn't figure out what color it was. First, he would guess black. Then he held it close to his face and thought it was dark green or even a deep dark blue. He draped it over a chair and stood back from it. Then it seemed to be brown. The more Gyank looked at it, the more he wasn't sure.

"Well, put it on already," said Trenden impatiently.

"What color is it?" asked Gyank, with a puzzled look on his face.

"I don't know," answered Trenden as he swept the shirt off the chair. "I don't think you or I will ever know for sure. And if you really want to wonder about it, watch this."

Trenden started to gently shake the shirt, sending waves down the fabric. As Gyank strained his eyes to focus on the wiggling material, a faint pattern became visible. There seemed to be a barely noticeable design of uneven spots and wavy thick stripes. Still, Gyank was not sure if they were really there, or if his eyes were playing tricks on him.

"That's very strange," said Gyank, mesmerized by the pattern that seemed to appear and disappear as the fabric moved.

"Yes, it is," said the cobbler with a smile as he tossed the shirt to Gyank. "I gave up trying to guess its color or its pattern a long time ago. Now stop admiring it and put it on."

Gyank put on the pants first and then slipped the shirt over his head. It fit loosely.

"It's not tight," said Trenden. "That's good. You have plenty of room to move."

As Gyank tied the laces that closed the front of the shirt from the chest to the neck, Trenden eyed the garment up and down and said, "This is a strange outfit indeed. Not only can't you guess its color, this fabric is dull and it doesn't reflect any light." Trenden's voice lowered to a whisper. "It's made of the same substance the night is made of—darkness."

They looked at each other, frozen in a long pause. Then Trenden went on, "It was my father's. I don't know where he got it. My father made boots for a living, but he was a mountain climber at heart. He knew the mountains well and sometimes he would travel beyond them to other lands. He brought this back from one of his trips. Whoever he got it from told him that it makes the wearer almost impossible to see at night in the woods. I don't know about that, but it's great for sneaking around and hiding. It should help you a great deal tonight."

Trenden thought for a minute and said, "It would also be wise to take some rope."

"I have rope," said Gyank.

"Is it mountain climber's rope?"

Gyank produced a coil of rope from his pack and handed it to Trenden who inspected it. "This is good rope, but not the best." Trenden stepped into the other room and returned with a thin coil. "This is the stuff you need—strong, light, easy to handle, and it won't cut your hands. Next, you don't want to burden yourself down, but you must take everything you need, like a hammer and chisel."

"Why would I need that?"

"I'm sure your friend isn't sleeping in the king's bed. They probably have him chained up for the night in one of the stables. You'll need tools to free him."

"Of course," said Gyank, realizing he should have thought of it himself.

"I suggest you leave your bow here. It will only get in the way. Besides, you'll be in much more trouble if you shoot someone."

"How about my hatchet and my knife?"

"The knife is good, but what would you do with the hatchet?"

"Well, I can throw it pretty good."

"Throw it?" said Trenden with a smile. "That's an interesting skill. If you feel it might be useful, then take it."

After a quick meal, they rigged up the wagon with leather straps to carry Gyank between the axles. Gyank emptied all his gear out of his pack, except for the tinderbox, and took only Trenden's rope along with a hammer and chisel. Dressed in Trenden's stalking clothes, and with his knife and hatchet hanging from his belt, Gyank climbed on the back of the wagon and got under the canvas. Trenden sat in the driver's seat and softly snapped the reins to get his old mare moving. The rickety cobbler's wagon began slowly rolling down the road toward the castle in the quiet darkness of the evening.

Trenden halted the wagon a safe distance from the main gate and glanced around. Without looking back, he said, "It's clear—get under the wagon."

Gyank strapped himself in and held on. The road was bumpy, and even though Trenden went slow, it was by no means a smooth ride. Gyank twisted his head to see where they were going, but all he could see was the lower part of the horse's legs and the bottom of its hooves. He knew they were at the gate when the wagon came to a stop.

The gate consisted of a stone arch with tall rectangular towers on each side. Dark slits in the stone alternated up the towers, and from within these black crevices, unseen archers could take aim. Directly above the arch, a small, square tower protruded from the wall. The path of the wagon was barred by a heavy portcullis.

"Who goes there?" cried a voice from above.

"The cobbler," called Trenden, looking up at the tower above the arch. He tried to see the man he was speaking to, but all he could see were two dark rectangular holes in the stone.

"What business might a cobbler have in the castle at this hour?"

"A messenger was sent to fetch me this afternoon. He said that one of the noblemen would like to purchase a pair of boots."

"At this hour?" questioned the voice from the dark opening in the tower overhead. "Why are you so late?"

"A wheel on my wagon was broken and it took me hours to repair it."

"No one is to pass the gate after dark. Come back tomorrow."

Gyank's hope faded, but he was unaware of Trenden's ingenuity. He clung to the bottom of the wagon and listened while he learned a clever trick.

"Well, it's all the same to me," said Trenden casually. "Now I can go home and rest. The messenger said those boots were needed tonight, and I'm already late. If there's any disturbance about it tomorrow, I won't be to blame. So if you would kindly give me your name, then I'll be off."

There was a pause.

"Open the gate," the man cried.

Creaking noises echoed from within the wall as metal gears turned, hoisting the gate upward. Trenden sat patiently while the spear-like points at the bottom of the portcullis slowly crept up in front of him. From a distance, it looked like the teeth of a giant monster, yawning in the dim light. The wagon passed under the portcullis and came to a stop inside the wall. The guard on duty approached the wagon. "Is it boots alone that you carry?"

He yanked aside the canvas in the back of the wagon, revealing wooden boxes of all sizes. Trenden didn't even bother to turn and watch.

"Alright cobbler, you may pass," said the man, waving him onward. "And be sure it's only boots you leave with," he added as Trenden started pulling away.

Trenden wondered if the policy of checking wagons had changed since his last visit to the castle, but there was nothing he could do about it now.

Once again, Gyank tried to look ahead. He twisted as much as he could in the straps, but he could see nothing in front of the wagon, only the legs of the old mare as she plodded across the jousting field. After what seemed like a long time, the wagon rolled over a wooden platform. They were crossing the drawbridge. The sound of hooves clapping against wooden planks echoed loudly above the dark moat.

Gyank knew he had to let go of the wagon before they reached the third wall, yet if he dropped to the ground at the wrong time, he could find himself lying face up in the middle of a courtyard as the wagon rolled away. This thought plagued his mind and he began to sweat. There was no way for him to know when it would be safe to let go, and time was running out.

Suddenly, the ground went completely black. Gyank figured they must be passing under an arch. Taking advantage of the moment, he lowered himself to the ground and let go of the straps. The wagon rolled on, leaving Gyank lying face up in the middle of the road. He flipped onto his belly and realized he was under an arch in the third wall. Without making a sound, he quickly stood up and flattened his back against the inside of the stone arch. Looking toward the inner castle, Gyank could see the wagon moving steadily onward. When he looked in the opposite direction, he saw a maze of stone buildings and wooden houses separated by narrow streets. It was a village within the castle walls.

To Gyank's horror, a group of guards was walking toward him, talking and laughing as they approached. Gyank froze and held his breath. He was sure they would see him. Yet they walked right through the arch without noticing the dark shadow pressed against the wall. Gyank took a deep breath and exhaled as he watched them disappear around the corner of a building. He looked both ways and darted from under the arch to a stone building nearby. Creeping in the shadows of the narrow streets, Gyank used his skill as never before. Tonight he was not playing with Otok—he was doing this to save him.

It seemed like hours before he eventually came to a long wooden building. It was the stable on the west wall of the castle grounds. A large sliding door had been left ajar, and Gyank slipped through into the darkness. It was pitch black inside and he bumped into one of the wooden stalls. He could hear and smell the horses, but he could see absolutely nothing. Using his hands to feel his way around, he went from stall to stall, calling his friend's name in a whisper. Gyank came to the other end of the stable with no success. He sat down in a pile of hay and tried to fight back the feeling of hopelessness. If Otok wasn't in the stable, then Gyank had no idea where he could be, and if he didn't find him soon, he would miss the wagon and be stuck within the castle walls.

As Gyank wondered how long Trenden could stall by riding around the castle grounds, an idea came to him. He carefully pulled open the stable door and peeked out. When the time was right, he slipped out of the stable and around the side of a stone building with thick ivy vines running up the wall to the roof. Gyank figured that if he could get up there, he would have a view of everything between the second and third walls. Light shined from windows on both sides of the street, but no one was outside, so he began to climb. He held onto the vines where he could, and where they were not strong enough, cracks in the stone wall provided sufficient hand and footholds.

Minutes later, Gyank was on the roof looking down at the maze of dark buildings. Then all hope vanished when he saw the wagon moving slowly toward the drawbridge. He could have gotten to it, but that would mean leaving Otok in the hands of the castle guards. Gyank suddenly thought back to what Trenden had told him: "Once you drop off the bottom of the wagon, you're on your own. It's up to you to save your friend."

The sight of the wagon rolling toward the drawbridge would have caused most people to give up. Gyank was different. The hopelessness of the situation toughened him, and he clenched his fists in anger. He would find Otok and make those guards pay for what they did.

Looking across the rooftops, his eyes were drawn into the distance where he saw a stable against the east wall. Scanning the sea of buildings, he concluded that this was the only other stable between the second and third wall, and that's where Otok must be.

Gyank sprang into action. He climbed down the vines so recklessly that he almost fell. He ran back into the stable, pulled together a pile of straw, and kneeling down in front of it, he took his tinderbox out of his pack. He placed a small clump of plant fibers on top of the straw and struck the small metal bar with the flint. Sparks flew into the clump of tinder and it caught fire. Gyank put a handful of straw over the tiny flame and set it afire, illuminating the walls of the stall nearby. He quickly twisted together a handful of straw to use as a torch and stuck it in the flames. The dry stalks ignited instantly and he hurried to the other side of the stable, opening every stall with a horse in it as he went. At the far end of the stable, he threw the handful of burning straw onto a pile of hay in an empty stall, setting it ablaze. Then he pushed the sliding door open wide and ran out of the stable yelling, "Fire! Fire! There's a fire in the stable!"

Piles of straw and hay blazed brightly as smoke billowed and spooked horses fled out of the stable. People came running from all directions, and as the commotion grew, Gyank slipped through the streets unnoticed and headed for the stable by the east wall.

~ ~ ~

Otok was awakened by shouts coming from the street. He stood up in the darkness and began to move toward the door, but he was stopped short by the chain that held him to the wall. His hands had been shackled together, leaving him just enough slack to work a shovel. At night, he was chained to a stall by an additional chain attached to the one that bound his hands. Otok realized there was a fire and that everyone would be rushing to it. This was his chance to escape, and he didn't know when, or if, he would get another. He was well aware that he couldn't break the chains that held him, but perhaps the wooden planks of the stall might give way. In the darkness, he took hold of the chain with both hands and placed one foot up on the wall. Otok leaned back and put his entire body into the effort. Grunting and straining, he pulled on that chain until tears came to his eyes. He could feel the wooden board bending, yet it was strong and it held. As soon as he eased off on the chain, the board went back into its original position. Otok gathered his strength and pulled again. This time, he took his other foot and placed it so that he had one foot on each side of the bolt connecting him to the wall. The strain between his legs pushing on the wall and his powerful arms pulling on the chain held him in a horizontal position above the floor. His teeth clamped shut, and in the darkness, his face was contorted by the strain on his body.

There was the sound of cracking wood, and Otok fell hard on the stable floor. The chain whipped back and struck his head with a glancing blow. Otok hardly noticed it. He went to the door and looked out into the courtyard. People were running everywhere, and in the background, he could see flames jumping from the roof of the stable in the distance. Holding the loose chain in his hands, Otok ran out into the courtyard and headed for the drawbridge.

~ ~ ~

As Gyank approached the stable on the east wall, he caught sight of his friend running toward the drawbridge and took off after him. Gyank had almost overtaken him when Otok stopped abruptly. A group of guards was hurrying across the drawbridge on their way to fight the fire. They spotted Otok with chains dangling from is hands and charged toward him. As Otok spun around to run back the way he came, he could hardly believe that the shadowy figure coming up behind him was Gyank.

"This way!" shouted Gyank.

They ran up a stone stairway leading to a tower adjoining the east wall. At the top of the steps was a heavy wooden door. It was unlocked and they ran through it into a short hallway, slamming the door on the guards behind them. Otok threw his body against the door and braced his legs. Gyank was next to him, pushing with all his might. The muffled sound of fists pounding on wood echoed through the door. Two benches lined the hallway, a small one, and a long heavy one.

Gyank grabbed the small bench, wedged it against the door, and leaned on it to hold it in place. Thinking quickly, he took off his pack and pulled out the hammer and chisel.

"We can't hold it much longer!" cried Otok.

"We won't have to," said Gyank, taking the chisel and using the hammer to wedge it between the stone floor and the bottom of the door.

Not sure if the chisel would hold, Otok held firm while Gyank tried the door at the other end of the hallway.

"It's locked!" said Gyank, tugging on the door furiously.

"We're trapped! And this chisel won't hold much longer," said Otok, leaning hard against the door.

The pounding on the door sounded more organized as if the guards were combining their strength with each blow. That gave Gyank an idea. "Grab hold of this bench," he said while picking up one end of the heavy bench and tucking it under his arm. Otok did the same with the back end and they charged at the door.

One well-placed shot next to the lock caused the door to fly open into a long corridor. They dropped the bench, and as they ran down the hall, Gyank spoke in short bursts. "This hallway runs along the second wall—I'm almost sure of it. We must get to the top."

They came to another door, and once through it, they were outside and at the bottom of a long, stone staircase that ran to the top of the wall. There was no handrail on the side of the staircase opposite the wall, just a steep drop to the stone floor below.

"This is it," said Gyank, charging up the steps two at a time.

The stairs led to a small, stone platform, slightly wider than the walkway that ran along the top of the wall. The only thing on the platform was a big, open barrel of stones that were to be thrown from the wall if the castle was under attack. The top of the wall had huge, stone blocks that alternated up and down so that soldiers could throw rocks or shoot arrows, and then duck behind one of these merlons to hide. Gyank stuck his head in the gap between two merlons and looked over the top of the wall. It was a long way down to the moat.

"Here they come!" shouted Otok, looking back down the stairs. He took a wide stance at the top of the steps and held the chain with both hands, letting the end with the bolt and a chunk of splintered wood dangle in front of him.

Gyank pulled the rope from his pack and tied it around one of the merlons. Then he tossed the coil of rope over the wall and watched it unravel as it fell. Unfortunately, it didn't reach all the way down to the moat.

The guards ran up the steps with their swords drawn to meet Otok as he began to swing the chain in a big circle, building up momentum. The first man, caught by the surprising strength and swiftness of Otok's blows, was knocked off balance and he fell to the stone floor below. He landed with a crash and lay motionless. As soon as he fell, two more guards took his place at the top steps. Otok whipped the chain around in such an erratic fashion that the guards couldn't get near him without being struck. The young powerhouse stood his ground. When the guards tried to rush him, he caught one in the head with the bolt at the end of the chain, causing him to fall back on the men behind him. Another was stripped of his sword when the heavy links of chain smashed his hand against the wall. Otok blocked the entire stairway and no one could get by him, nor could Gyank come along side to help. Even if he could get near the top of the steps, he had no weapon to use against swordsmen.

Gyank scanned the guardhouses and courtyards below. They had attracted much attention, and many more guards ran toward the stairs to give aid. Gyank knew he had to do something to help Otok. Glancing around to see what was at hand, he noticed the barrel of stones standing next to the wall. Grabbing the lip of the barrel with both hands, he threw his weight back in an attempt to topple it over, but the barrel hardly budged. It was just too heavy. With Otok struggling to hold off the guards, and a mob of men racing toward the bottom of the steps, Gyank gathered his strength and violently threw his weight back, yanking at the top of the barrel with all his might. It tipped slightly and then settled back to its original position.

"Hold on, Otok!" he shouted as he pulled stones out of the barrel as fast as he could, letting them drop carelessly to the floor. Guessing that the barrel was light enough, he once again yanked hard on the rim. The barrel began to tip, and just when Gyank thought it wouldn't go over, it fell. Jumping out of the way to avoid stones as they rolled out, he got down low behind the barrel and pushed hard. It moved slowly but gradually picked up momentum as stones tumbled out from the open end.

"Otok! Look out!" he shouted.

Glancing back, Otok saw the barrel rolling up behind him, and threw himself against the wall, pressing his back to the stone. Gyank guided the barrel to the top of the steps and gave it a final shove as it rolled past Otok. For a moment, the guards weren't sure if they should try to stop it, or just turn and flee. But once the barrel reached the top step, nothing could stop it. The guards closest to it put their hands up in vain as the barrel rolled over them. The men behind them turned in panic and fled down the steps. But there was no way to avoid it. The speed of the barrel dramatically increased as it bounced down the staircase, crushing and smashing everyone in its path. The barrel broke open half way down the steps, and stones bounced and tumbled all the way to the bottom. Some of the men jumped off the side of the staircase, but the stones followed them, hopping and scattering in all directions. The entire stairway was littered with stones and fallen guards moaning in pain.

"Let's go," said Gyank. "Over the wall."

Otok hopped up on the wall and started climbing down the rope. Gyank was right behind him. They quickly lowered themselves down the wall until they came to the end of the rope. Then they let go and splashed into the dark murky moat. Otok had trouble swimming with the heavy chains, but Gyank helped him across the moat where they climbed out of the slimy water.

"To the gate," said Gyank as they ran. "If we get through it in time, we just might catch the wagon."

"What wagon?" asked Otok between gasps.

Gyank didn't answer. He was a few steps ahead as they ran across the grassy jousting field. The gate was closed and the guard on duty called out. "Halt!"

They ignored the warning and ran for the steps that led up to the platform where the guard stood. The man picked up his crossbow, cranked the bowstring back, and loaded a bolt. He took aim and fired at Gyank who was almost to the bottom of the steps. As soon as Gyank saw the man taking aim, he dove to the ground. The crossbow bolt flew over his back and sunk deep into the dirt by his heels. Otok was not far behind. He hurdled his prone friend and charged up the steps. With no time to reload, the guard dropped his crossbow, drew his sword, and rushed down the steps to meet the boy in chains. Otok whipped the chain up at the man, striking his helmet as it wrapped around his head and neck. With one might tug, Otok pulled the man off his feet and sent him crashing to the ground.

Gyank shouted up the stairs, "Get to the wheel that opens the gate!"

Otok ran up the last few steps to the platform, took hold of the wooden spokes sticking out of the wheel, and began to crank up the portcullis. Moments later Gyank was with him, pulling and tugging frantically on the wheel. As the gate crept up, they glanced back at the castle. The glow of fire reflected off buildings behind the second wall and illuminated a cloud of black smoke rising up to the sky. They suddenly caught sight of armed men on warhorses charging across the drawbridge.

"Hurry!" yelled Gyank as they grunted and strained, pulling even harder on the wheel. Once the portcullis was up, they locked the wheel in place. The horsemen were closing in fast as they sped across the jousting field.

"Get through the gate!" shouted Gyank. "I'll try to slow them down!"

Otok raced down the steps and jumped the last half dozen to the ground. He landed on his feet and fell forward. Cupping the loose chain in one hand, he put his other hand down to catch his balance as he took off for the gate like a sprinter.

Gyank pulled the hatchet from his belt and began to hack wildly at the thick rope that held the gate open. The rope snapped and Gyank bounded down the steps with hatchet in hand. The sound of spinning gears and grinding metal reverberated through the towers as the weight of the portcullis pulled it toward the ground. Gyank charged at the closing gate with the horsemen right behind him. He dove headfirst and rolled under the gate just before the spikes on the bottom edge of the portcullis slammed to the ground. The horsemen closest to him couldn't stop quick enough to avoid crashing into the portcullis. Otok and Gyank didn't look back. They just ran as fast as they could down the road, leaving the horsemen trapped within the castle wall. Ahead of them, they could barely make out the shape of a wagon creeping along the dark road.

"That must be Trenden," said Gyank, gasping for breath.

"You mean the cobbler that Smilga told us about?" said Otok, panting heavily as he ran. "He's alive? And you found him?"

"Not exactly ... can't explain now ... we must catch that wagon."

Sprinting down the road, they caught up to the wagon and hopped on the back. Trenden didn't know he was being chased, and turned his head in surprise. When he saw Gyank, he faced forward, snapped the reins, and gave a quiet yelp. The horse picked up the pace, and as they sped down the road, Trenden shouted back to Gyank, "If the guards know you've escaped, there's no way we can outrun them. Their warhorses will be on us in no time."

"Don't worry," said Gyank. "I did something that should slow them down."

"What's that?" asked Trenden.

"I locked the gate with them inside."

"That was clever. Even so, don't think it will stop them. There are other exits from the castle, and they'll soon be searching the countryside for you."

When they arrived at Trenden's house, he hopped off the wagon and said, "Follow me, quickly." He led them to a small shed on the side of the cottage where he had an anvil and some tools. He freed Otok of his chains, and as he hid them under the cottage, he said, "If the guards find these, I'll be in big trouble. Now wait here. I don't want you dripping that slimy moat water in the house. If the guards come here looking for you, that might give me away. In fact, as soon as you're gone, I'll have to move those boxes around in the wagon to hide the wet spots."

Trenden rushed into the house and came out a few minutes later with his arms full of equipment.

"Gyank, here's your bow and all your gear."

As Gyank stuffed his things into his pack, Trenden handed Otok a sack bulging with supplies. "Here are some other things you might find useful on your journey. You don't have much time, so listen carefully. If you travel all night, you'll be far beyond the borders of Thamen by daybreak, and the guards won't search outside their own realm. But you can't take the road. It will be patrolled and blocked off in places. There's a trail leading south through the woods. Not too far along the way, there's a stream where you can wash up and fill your waterskins. Remember, don't stop until you see the dawn. It will take that long before you're a safe distance away."

"Thank you," said Gyank. "I wish there was something we could do to repay you for all your help."

"There is something you can do—get out of here and escape. You'll find the trail just beyond those trees." Trenden pointed to the woods. "Now go. Get out of here."

"What about your stalking clothes?" asked Gyank.

"Keep them!" said Trenden urgently as he glanced down the road to see if anyone was coming. "I have no use for them, and I'm sure you will. Take them and go."

Otok and Gyank headed south along the trail at a good pace, stopping only at the stream to wash and fill their water skins. Before dawn, they were far away from the castle of Thamen.

Chapter 4

NOTOM OF THE MOUNTAINS

The companions walked wearily along the trail until they saw the predawn light in the eastern sky. They were exhausted, and even though it was morning, they lay down next to a fallen log to sleep. Otok lay on his back looking up at the leaves waving slightly in the breeze. Gyank sat next to him with his back against the log and his legs extended straight out in front of him.

"Thanks for coming after me," said Otok sleepily.

"Coming after you?" said Gyank. "What makes you think I went into that castle and risked my life to get you? I went in to retrieve my arrows." Gyank tried to sound convincing, but he wasn't doing a good job of it.

"So, where are the arrows you risked your life for?" asked Otok, turning his head to look at his friend.

Gyank didn't answer. He just tried to hide the smile that was beginning to grow on his face.

"Well, where are the arrows?" asked Otok as he reached over and shoved Gyank on the shoulder just hard enough to knock him over.

They giggled at each other until Gyank sat up and looked at his quiver. "Speaking of arrows, we only have four left," he said, handing his quiver to Otok. Then he handed Otok his bow. "Here, take my bow. You're a better shot than I am. And when we use these arrows, we'll have to make them count."

"I'm afraid there are other things we'll miss more than bows and arrows. All my gear is lost."

"We'll just have to do with what we have. And speaking of that, let's take a look at what Trenden packed for us."

Gyank opened the sack that Trenden had given them. Inside he found two coils of rope, a knife in a sheath, and some spikes specifically designed for mountain climbing. There was also quite a bit of dried fruits and meats. This type of food was favored by travelers because it would keep a long time and provided good nutrition.

After examining the supplies, they fell into a deep sleep and didn't wake up until late in the day.

~ ~ ~

When Otok woke, Gyank was leaning over him, shaking him gently. "Wake up," he said. "We have a long way to go before we reach the mountains. I suggest we get going and hike for at least a few hours before it gets dark."

They had something to eat and headed south along the trail. The deeper into the woods they went, the more the trail was overgrown. Gradually, it disappeared altogether, and they found themselves walking in a zigzag pattern to avoid large patches of thorns and briars. The sun was getting low in the sky and dusk grew near.

"Do you have any idea where we are?" asked Otok.

"No, but it really doesn't matter. We have to go south, and if there's no trail, then we'll make one. As long as we keep going south, we'll find the mountains sooner or later."

"It's going to be getting dark in a little while," said Otok, pushing a branch aside so it wouldn't smack him in the face.

"Yes, I suppose we should start looking for a place to set up camp."

They settled down by the base of a huge beech tree and built a small fire to cook supper. After they were done eating, Gyank gave one of his two blankets to Otok and then took out the map. He could hardly see it in the dim light of their dying fire, but he looked at it anyway. They soon fell asleep and dreamt of the book and the secrets it might hold.

The next day they continued south. By dusk, the woods thinned enough for them to see steep, rugged mountains looming ahead through the trees. The sky was bright orange behind the majestic snow-covered peaks in the distance, and long, thin, purple clouds floated above the mountains while an eerie gray mist drifted at their base. Neither of them had seen much of anything outside their own valley, and they were awestruck by the vast mountain range stretching before them. The forest dwindled to small brush mixed with clusters of evergreens, and the terrain became rocky. They found themselves climbing a steadily rising slope, and their breath grew shorter as they labored onward.

Gazing up at the towering peaks, Gyank said, "Look at the size of those mountains."

"And we have to get across them," said Otok, wiping the sweat from his forehead with the back of his hand.

"We have to find the path Smilga told us about."

"It's getting too dark to start looking now."

"You're right. Let's settle down for the night, and we'll look for the path tomorrow."

They set up camp at the base of a huge boulder and were up early the next day, climbing rocky slopes higher into the mountains as they searched for a path. Although there was some vegetation on the slopes, the loose stone made progress slow. In some places, the incline was so steep that their hands reached the ground in front of them, and they often grabbed hold of a tree branch or small bush to pull themselves up.

"This is rough," said Otok.

"Yeah, and those cliffs at the top of the slope are straight up and down. Even if we can't find Smilga's path, we need to find some kind of trail." Gyank pointed at a group of boulders to their left. "Maybe we should work our way over to those rocks. We might find something. At least it's better than fighting our way up to those cliffs."

There was little shade, and they were hot and sweaty by the time they reached the boulders. Dwarfed by these massive stones, they stopped and rested for a moment.

"Look!" said Otok. "There's a path over there."

"Where? I don't see it."

Otok pointed along Gyank's line of sight at a ledge that hugged a vertical stone wall farther off to their left. "See, it runs along the side of that cliff."

"You're right, there is a path over there, or at least a ledge. Let's go."

They climbed down between the boulders and found a small trail leading up through the rocks.

"This must be it," said Otok, excited about their discovery.

"It's a path alright, but there's no way to be sure if it's the one Smilga told us about—not unless Trenden's father was here."

"It doesn't matter. It's still better than trying to climb the wall back there."

"You're right about that. Let's follow it."

The trail ran along the base of the cliff between the boulders and it gradually climbed up to the ledge, which angled steadily upward. Soon they were high above the steep slope, and they could see for miles. Behind them, the dark green of the forest stretched into the distance, and before them were endless cliffs and mountain peaks they had yet to cross. From a distance, they looked like two insignificant little specks, inching their way across the face of the mountain. They walked single file next to the cliff because a loose stone near the edge of the trail could send them tumbling to their death on the boulders far below.

They hiked along the ledge for hours, watching the rocky ground below rise up toward them only to drop off sharply again. They had found an easy way through the steep and rough terrain, and they were moving along at a good pace until the path abruptly ended. The ledge had collapsed, leaving a wide gap in the trail.

"A dead end," said Otok.

"Sure seems like it."

They sat on the ledge and carefully peeked over the precipice to look straight down at the rocks far below. The vertical drop made them dizzy. Then they looked across the gap where the path continued. It seemed that there was no way across, especially for two inexperienced mountain climbers.

After thinking in silence for a while, Gyank said, "We have to go back the way we came. I remember seeing a spot where we could climb down into a ravine. Then we can walk past the broken section, and look for a place to climb back up."

"I guess we don't have much choice," said Otok.

They headed back, and when they came to the spot Gyank had picked out, neither of them liked what they saw—a fifty-foot drop to the top of a rocky ravine.

Otok looked over the edge. "You mean we have to climb down there?"

"I don't like it either, but I don't see any other choice."

They took out a coil of rope and one of Trenden's climbing spikes. Gyank drove the spike into a crack on the ledge using the back end of his hatchet. He tied a loop in one end of the rope, and put it around the spike. "Wait for me to get to the bottom before you start your climb," he said as he pulled the rope taut and began to lower himself down.

Soon both of them were at the bottom of the cliff, looking up at the ledge. Gyank took the rope and made a big whipping motion with his arm, sending a wave up the rope. He repeated this motion a couple of times until the loop flopped off the spike and the loose rope fell down upon them.

"That's one spike gone," said Gyank. "But we still have the rope."

"Yes, and let's hope we don't need it for a while."

They were now standing on one side of a deep ravine. The footing on the steep incline was not good, and they leaned toward the cliff to keep their balance. Gyank coiled the rope and put it back in his pack while Otok looked ahead at the rocky slope they had to cross. It was made up entirely of broken slabs of stone, loose rocks, and sand. There was no vegetation to hold onto, so they used their hands to balance as they made their way along the slope. Progress was slow and difficult, but eventually they were looking up at the broken ledge high above them.

Breathing in gasps, Otok stopped for a moment and stood up straight. "If we don't get back on the path, we'll never get across these mountains."

"We're almost to the other side of the broken ledge," said Gyank, concentrating on where he was putting his hands and feet. They had gone only a few more steps when they noticed their efforts were causing the rocks below them to roll down into the ravine, and as the stones and gravel below them moved, the slope above them also began to move. They stood still, waiting for the sliding stones to come to a halt, but it was too late. They had started a series of events that they couldn't stop.

"Landslide!" shouted Gyank as stones and gravel came rolling down toward them.

They ran across the slope to avoid the oncoming slide, but the ground above them moved, chasing them as they fled. Rocks, broken slabs of stone, and gravel tumbled down the ravine, and the ground below them began to slide. Caught in the midst of the avalanche, they fought to avoid being buried by the moving earth. Somewhere along the way down into the ravine, they lost consciousness and they were helpless.

~ ~ ~

When Otok awoke, he had a terrible headache, and before he moved, or even looked around, he wondered if he had broken any bones. The sun was low in the sky and he was shaded from its direct rays by the long shadow of a mountain peak. When he tried to move, he realized that he was buried up to his chest in sand and stones. He pushed the stones off him and struggled to get free of the remaining earth that held him in the ground. He was badly bruised, but he didn't seem to have any broken bones.

As he crawled out of the rubble, he wondered where Gyank was, and if he was still alive. Otok stood up and began searching for his friend, wandering back and forth across the barren landscape calling Gyank's name. The avalanche had created a fairly level field of rocks and sand, yet it was difficult to walk on the shifting stones. Looking ahead rather than where he was stepping, Otok stumbled and fell. Undaunted, he got up and kept searching, only to fall again.

Aching all over and with his head pounding, he staggered about the rocky wasteland. Beyond the shadow of the mountain, he saw what looked like an arm among the rocks. He rushed over and found Gyank buried up to his chest with only one arm sticking out of the ground. He was not moving, and a stream of dried blood ran from his forehead to his chin.

"Gyank! Are you alive? Can you hear me?"

There was no answer. Otok fell to the ground in front of his friend and started pulling the stones away from his chest. While pushing handfuls of sand and gravel to the side, he heard a sound behind him. It wasn't loud, but it was distinct, the sound of one rock toppling onto another. He quickly turned his head to see what it was. To his horror, there were two mountain lions moving toward him among the rocks. He reached to his shoulder to grab his bow, but it wasn't there. It had fallen off during the landslide. Thinking quickly, he turned back to Gyank and kept digging as fast as he could, trying to get to the hatchet tucked in Gyank's belt. He frantically pulled armfuls of gravel away from his friend's body until there was a deep hole. Then he reached down, pulled out the hatchet, and jumped up to face his attackers. With the hatchet in one hand and a fist-size stone in the other, he stood in front of his helpless friend, still half buried in the ground.

Working as a team, the mountain lions encircled their prey as they positioned themselves to attack. Otok's head was pounding, and his bruised body ached when he moved, but he wasn't going to wait for the cats to lunge, so he hurled the stone and it bounced in front of one of the cats, causing the animal to jump back. Crouching in a posture ready to leap, the mountain lion wrinkled its snout, showing its fangs, and let out a roar that ended in a long threatening growl. Otok picked up another stone and threw it. This time he hit his mark. The stone struck the cat on the shoulder and bounced off with a thump. As Otok stooped to grab another rock, the second mountain lion charged and leapt into the air. Otok turned to face the beast just as it pounced on him. He lost his footing, slipped into the hole he had dug, and fell on his back with his leg stuck in the hole next to Gyank. The cat opened its paws wide and sunk its claws into Otok's shoulder while its gaping jaws came toward his neck. Grabbing the cat by the throat with his free hand, Otok held the beast back as he violently hacked up at it with the hatchet. The cat let go a wild, piercing screech and jumped off sideways.

Before Otok could get his leg out of the hole, the other cat lunged through the air and landed on his back. Otok twisted to throw the animal off, and to his surprise, the cat flopped to the ground next to him. Otok raised the hatchet to strike down on its skull, but the cat lay dead on the ground, the fletching of an arrow shaft was sticking out of its neck.

Otok didn't hesitate to see where the arrow had come from. He quickly pulled his leg out of the hole and turned to face the wounded cat crouching nearby. The animal was bleeding, but this only seemed to make it fiercer. It growled and then charged. But before the mountain lion reached Otok, its stride broke and it stumbled. An arrow had pierced its rib cage, and the beast roared and squirmed violently on the ground before it died.

Blood ran down Otok's arm from the claw wounds in his shoulder. His bruised body was so weak that he collapsed to his knees as the bloody hatchet slipped from his hand. He put his head against Gyank's chest, and as he heard the thump of Gyank's heartbeat, he felt a heavy hand on his shoulder. Otok looked up and saw what appeared to be a giant standing over him. The setting sun was behind the man, so only his dark silhouette was visible.

"He's alive," whispered Otok, with tears in his eyes.

"We must get him to my camp," said the man in a grim voice.

As the man knelt down and began to widen the hole, Otok realized that he was not a giant. He only appeared that way because Otok had been looking up at him. Yet this hefty man had a broad chest and was considerably taller and heavier than Otok. Although his beard was graying, he had a head full of wavy brown hair. He was dressed in animal skins, and slung across his back was a heavy recurve bow made of horn and a hide quiver full of long arrows. He wore homemade leather boots with straps crisscrossed up to his knees, and an animal-skin pouch dangled at his hip.

Digging side by side, they worked in silence. As soon as Gyank was unburied, the man reached into the hole and gently touched each of his limbs.

"Checking for broken bones?" asked Otok.

"Yes," said the man while concentrating on what he was doing.

He carefully slid the pack off Gyank's back, and ever so gently, lifted him out of the hole. Cradling Gyank in his arms, he stood up and said, "Follow me." Then he headed across the rocks.

Otok pulled Gyank's pack out of the hole and followed in the man's footsteps. Although the mountain man was carrying a limp body, he moved across the rocky terrain with ease while Otok struggled to keep up as they weaved between boulders and past stunted evergreens. Otok looked at his blood-drenched shirt and thought it strange that the man paid no attention to it. As he followed, Otok pulled a cloth from Gyank's pack and did his best to bandage his wounded shoulder.

After a short hike, they came to a wide, level spot surrounded by mountainous cliffs. In the center of the barren landscape was a campsite consisting of a small lean-to made of hides and sticks, a few skins stretched and drying on wooden frames, and a circle of stones containing the ashes of a dead fire. The man gently placed Gyank in the lean-to on some hides. Hanging from one of the sticks supporting the lean-to was a pouch filled with water. The man wet a cloth and wiped Gyank's forehead.

"Will he be alright?" asked Otok.

"We will see," said the man, wiping the dried blood from Gyank's face.

Once he was done, he stepped out of the lean-to and said, "Stay here. I'll be back."

He headed back the way they had come, and when he returned, he was carrying the two dead mountain lions, one draped over each of his broad shoulders. In his hand were Otok's bow and quiver.

"I believe you dropped these," he said, tossing the bow and quiver on the ground near Otok.

"Thank you," said Otok, reaching to pick them up. "Well, that's the end of the arrows," he said as he looked into his empty quiver. Otok glanced at the man and noticed he was not paying any attention to him as he laid the dead cats out on the ground.

"What are you going to do with them?" asked Otok.

"I waste nothing," the man answered abruptly as he pulled out a knife and started to skin one of the cats. "I didn't want to kill them, but I had to, or else let them kill you and your friend. So the best I can do now is to make good use of them."

"They're mountain cats. I don't even think they're edible," said Otok. "Besides, we should let them rot for trying to make a meal out of us."

The man stood up and looked straight at Otok. His stare was piercing and Otok looked away. "How dare you speak of such wonderful animals that way?" He pointed his bloody skinning knife at Otok and seemed to get angrier as he spoke. "Have you no respect for other living creatures? If you wouldn't have been so careless, your friend would be awake right now, and these cats would be alive."

Otok knew the man was right, and he felt ashamed about what he had just said. He sat on the stony ground in silence and didn't look up. The man noticed his reaction and went back to skinning the cats, and as he did so, he began talking to the dead animals under his breath.

"I'm sorry for killing you. Your death is on their hands. They have no business being in the mountains if they can't take care of themselves." The man suddenly looked at Otok, and in a curious tone, he asked, "What are you doing in the mountains anyway?"

"We're on our way to—" Otok stopped himself, but it was too late. The man knew he was hiding something.

"You're on your way where?"

"Nowhere. We're just crossing the mountains—exploring."

The man gave Otok an angry stare.

Otok looked right back at him as he tried to justify himself. "And if we are going somewhere, why should I tell you? I don't know you. I don't even know your name."

The man stood up tall and approached Otok. He was a big man and he appeared formidable. Standing in front of Otok, he proudly declared, "I am Notom, man of the mountains. Who are you?"

Otok stood up and stuck his chest out, trying to look proud. "I am Otok."

"Who's your friend in the lean-to?"

"That's Gyank, my closest friend."

"And the two of you are crossing the mountains for no reason at all," said Notom suspiciously.

Otok didn't respond, and after a brief pause, Notom turned his attention back to skinning the cats. Otok sat down and rested his aching body. His shoulder wound was throbbing and blood had soaked through his improvised bandage.

"Looks like I was right," said Notom, pointing at Otok's arm. "You don't even know how to take care of yourself." Notom put aside his skinning knife, knelt down next to Otok, and unwrapped the bandage. "These wounds are deep," he said. "I'll have to tie them up."

He went to his pack, which was in the lean-to next to Gyank, and took out a small wooden box. In it was a metal needle and some hair from a horse's tail. He told Otok to look the other way and began to stitch the wounds closed. As if to demonstrate his toughness, Otok watched every stitch without flinching. Once the wounds were closed, Notom wrapped them with a fresh bandage.

"Rest," said Notom, as if giving an order. "When I'm finished with the cats, I'll make a fire and cook something to eat."

Otok nodded his head and lay back on the ground. Using Gyank's pack as a pillow, he propped up his head and kept an eye on Notom. Otok couldn't figure out this strange man of the mountains. He was clearly helping them, yet he was cold and distant. Each time Otok tried to start a conversation, he received a gruff response, and Notom went back to whatever he was doing.

It was dark by the time they finished eating. Notom looked up at the moon and said, "Rain tomorrow. You better sleep in the lean-to."

"Thank you for all your help," said Otok.

He didn't get a response, but he wasn't expecting one. He crawled into the lean-to next to Gyank and fell asleep.

~ ~ ~

The next morning when Gyank woke up, he heard the sound of rain above his head. He opened his eyes and saw that he was in a lean-to made of animal skins. The sound of water dripping off the back of the lean-to mingled with the soft patter of raindrops on the roof. Otok was lying next to him sound asleep. He went to wake him but suddenly realized that he ached all over. It took him a moment to turn his body toward Otok, and then he nudged him. "Otok, wake up."

Otok rolled over and opened his eyes. "Gyank, are you alright?"

"I'm badly bruised, but I'll be alright. Where are we?"

"We were saved by a mountain man named Notom. We're in his campsite." Otok lowered his voice to a whisper. "But there's something strange about him."

Otok lifted his head to see if Notom was nearby, and Gyank struggled to push himself up on one elbow. When they looked outside the lean-to, they saw Notom sitting on a boulder not far away. He was hunched over with his arms folded and a hood pulled up over his head.

They couldn't tell if he was sleeping in that position or just sitting still.

"You see what I mean?" Otok whispered. "He's sitting out there in the rain. And it doesn't seem to bother him in the least. He must have been there all night."

"What's so strange?" said Gyank. "This lean-to isn't big enough for the three of us. Be thankful he let us stay in here. Otherwise we'd be out in the rain."

"I am thankful," said Otok. "Still, he's a strange kind of fellow. I think he lives in these mountains. He saved us both, but he's not very friendly. I think he's suspicious of where we might be going."

"You didn't say anything about the book?" asked Gyank in a whisper.

"No. But he knows we're up to something."

"If he saved our lives, he can't be that bad. And if he's willing to let us stay in his lean-to, we should just be grateful because right now I'm in no condition to travel."

"If we're going to do any more climbing, I'm in no shape to travel either," said Otok as he pulled the blanket down to reveal his bandaged shoulder.

Gyank's eyes opened wide. "What happened?"

"I got clawed by a mountain cat while you were knocked out. Notom killed the cats, helped me dig you out, and then carried you here."

"Dig me out?"

"You were buried up to your armpits."

"Maybe that's why I ache so badly."

Otok went on to tell Gyank the whole story. Soon after, they closed their eyes and fell back to sleep while listening to the rain on the roof of the lean-to.

~ ~ ~

For the next few days, Otok and Gyank stayed in Notom's camp and rested. During that time, Notom didn't say much. He didn't ask any questions about why they were in the mountains, or where they were going. He was mysteriously quiet and frequently stared off into the distance as if in deep thought. Although he provided food and let them sleep in his lean-to, they were suspicious of him and his motives. It didn't make sense that he would do so much for them, yet not act more friendly. His comments were usually short and rather odd, which left them guessing at what he meant. When they asked for an explanation, his reply was usually just as puzzling. It seemed as if his peculiar manner was a way to get them to think for themselves. As time went by, they grew more accustomed to him and their suspicion diminished.

After several days of rest, their aches and bruises were gone and Otok's shoulder was healing nicely. Even so, they preferred to stay with Notom a while longer. They sensed his vast knowledge and wanted to learn as much as they could from him, even if it meant dealing with his odd ways. After much debating, they decided to trust him with part of their secret. One morning after breakfast, they sat down next to him by the dying fire.

Gyank spoke first. "Notom, we're grateful for all you have done for us. We've had a hard time telling you that. We're not used to someone as quiet as you and, at first, we didn't trust you very much. But we are truly thankful."

Notom sat quietly. But this was nothing unusual. Looking at him through the wispy smoke from the smoldering ashes, Otok said, "After everything you've done for us, we feel that we should at least tell you where we are going. I think we owe you that."

They stared at Notom's expressionless face and, as always, they had no idea what he was thinking. Then a smile came to his lips and a joyful expression caused his whole face to wrinkle up. "You have just made all my efforts worthwhile. If I've won your trust, that is indeed an accomplishment. And just out of curiosity, I would like to know where you're going. Not many people would risk crossing the mountains."

They hadn't expected such a friendly reaction from a man who had been so cold and quiet all this time. They looked at each other with surprise, and then Gyank said, "We've left our home in the north to seek our fortune. We're headed south in search of riches and adventure."

"That's right," added Otok. "And we plan to travel all the way to the Land of Shar."

The smile suddenly left Notom's face, and he shook his head.

"What's wrong?" asked Gyank.

"You have no idea what you're getting yourselves into. The Land of Shar is perilous. There are dangers in that region of the world that you cannot even imagine." As if giving a grave warning, he said, "Go home."

"Is that all you can say?" said Otok. "Go home?"

"We thought you might be able to help us," said Gyank.

"I will help you the best way I know how. And that is to advise you to go home. If you can't handle yourselves in these mountains, how can you expect to survive in the Land of Shar?"

"We can do it," said Otok. "We're tougher than you think."

"We realize it will be dangerous," said Gyank. "But we're going anyway, and we hoped you might be able to help in some way. Perhaps you could show us the way through the mountains."

"Getting through the mountains is the easy part. Then you will have to cross the Forest of Elreia and it is plagued with dangers. Packs of large wolf-like creatures prowl those dark woods."

"We're not afraid of wolves," said Otok.

"These are not merely wolves. They are a species of their own, and they're the beasts of nightmares and folklore. Most people call them Elreia wolves, or black wolves because their fur is black as night, but the people who live in that forest refer to them as wacoba. They roam the great forest, hungry for the taste of flesh, appearing without a sound as if by black magic. Some folks say they're bewitched by mysterious dark forces and that the piercing, gray eyes of the wacoba can cast a spell on a man, rendering him helpless."

"Those kind of stories don't frighten us," said Otok.

"Elreia wolves are only one of many perils you might have to face in the great forest. Then you must cross the Uvannel Mountains, the harshest of all mountain ranges. You will have to survive a gauntlet of dangers before you even get to the Land of Shar." Notom paused as if a thought suddenly occurred to him. "It seems that someone has misled you about how difficult this trip will be. Who told you about the Land of Shar?"

"An old witch," said Otok, as if that would justify it.

"A witch?" said Notom with surprise. "I should have known it was something like that. I suppose she's also the one who sent you on this journey."

Before Notom made any other assumptions, Gyank interrupted. "The villagers think she's a witch, but we know her better, and she's just an old woman who's been falsely accused."

"Don't be so gullible. She obviously tricked you. They do that you know. A witch would find a strong lad or two and get them to feel sorry for her. Then she'd talk them into doing all sorts of tasks for her. Let me ask you, is she getting anything out of this journey of yours?"

They were suddenly struck by the possibility that Notom might be right, and Otok's anger grew at the thought of being fooled. They all fell silent, and when Notom saw their reaction, he said, "So what did she promise you? And what small price did she ask for herself?"

Otok and Gyank were too shocked to answer. They just sat looking at the pile of ashes that was once their breakfast fire. They had not planned to tell Notom anything about the book. They were only going to tell him that they were seeking their fortune to satisfy his curiosity. Then he might help them across the mountains. But the thought of being tricked made them boil inside.

Without another word, Notom stood up and walked over to the lean-to. He lifted the waterskin and took a sip.

Otok burst with anger. "Notom's right! She tricked us! Whether she's a witch or not, she has us out here risking our lives to get the book for her! Do you remember how she demanded that we give her the book no matter what else we might find along the way?"

Gyank stared at the pile of ashes. "I can't believe she would do this to us. We're doing her bidding as if we were her slaves. That book must be very valuable."

"She won't get away with it!" shouted Otok. "We'll get that book! We'll find out its secrets! Then we'll go back to her and see just how badly she wants it!"

"You'll do no such thing," said Notom, standing by the lean-to. His bow was strung and an arrow was nocked. Otok and Gyank were sitting with their backs to him as they looked over their shoulders. He could easily shoot either one of them before they could do anything.

"You innocent young fools. I knew it would only be a matter of time before you would slip up and say too much. I was patient and it paid off. So, the book does exist, and it's in the Land of Shar. It will be mine now. And there's nothing you can do to stop me from getting it. You've come to the end of your journey. I'm sorry it has to be such a wasteful end."

Notom drew back on the bowstring and aimed at Otok. The cold look in his eyes was piercing, and time seemed to freeze. All Otok could think of was how the mountain lions fell and squirmed at the will of Notom's bow. This skillful archer would not miss, and Otok knew it only too well, but he'd rather die fighting than take an arrow in the back. With incredible speed, he spun around and dove at Notom's legs, knocking him backward into the lean-to. The supporting sticks snapped and the entire structure collapsed under his weight. For as big as he was, Notom was surprisingly quick. He scrambled out of the rubble and faced Otok. His legs were flexed, his hands open, ready to grab or block. Otok threw a punch at his head. Notom caught the fist, threw a kick into Otok's ribs, grabbed hold of his upper arm and flipped him to the ground.

All along, Notom had one eye on Gyank. He saw him pull the

hatchet from his belt when Otok charged, but Gyank had no chance to throw it because Otok was in the way. Instead, he ran up to Notom and took a swipe at him the moment Otok was thrown to the ground. Notom ducked under the hatchet as it sliced the air. With one swift step, Notom was too close for Gyank to take another full stroke. Yet Gyank tried and got his elbow caught under Notom's armpit. A knee came up sharply into Gyank's stomach, and he sunk to the ground, gasping for air. Notom ripped the hatchet from Gyank's hand and turned to face Otok who was just getting to his feet.

"Come on boy. Let's see what you're made of," said Notom, flipping the hatchet from one hand to the other.

Otok charged. Odds meant nothing to him when he was in a fight, and he would have done the same if Notom had a battle-axe. Otok caught hold of his wrist and pulled the hatchet down to the side. Their other arms locked together and they leaned into one another, stalemated. Otok squeezed Notom's wrist with all his might. The grip on the hatchet began to loosen, and it fell to the ground. At that instant, Otok knew he could overpower his much larger opponent. With one mighty effort, he drove the powerful mountain man back toward the broken lean-to. Notom quickly stepped aside as he yanked Otok downward and stuck his leg out. The young powerhouse tripped over Notom's leg and went flying head first into the rubble.

Notom stood ready to take on whoever got up first. Otok lay stunned in the debris of the lean-to, and Gyank was still on the ground, trying to catch his breath. After a brief pause, Notom relaxed from his fighting stance, and said, "Looks like you had enough. I must say, not bad for a couple of boys."

Gyank stood up holding his stomach. It was obvious that Notom had no intention of killing them. Otok crawled out of the broken lean-to. "How could you have missed me?" he said, referring to the arrow that should have pierced his chest.

"Very simple—I didn't shoot. As a matter of fact, I hardly had enough time to toss my bow aside before you came charging at me with your head down. Gyank would have noticed it if he didn't look down to pull out his hatchet."

"What about the book?" asked Gyank. "Don't you want it for yourself?"

"I don't know anything about your book, nor do I care. You see how easy it was for me to trick you into dropping your guard. A few clever words and I let you do the rest. If I wanted to kill you, the both of you would be stretched out right now. I just wanted to prove a point. Only I didn't expect Otok to rush me. I hope the bruises you got from this experience taught you something. You have no idea what you're up against. So I'll tell you again. Go home!"

With a calm resolve, Gyank said, "We're going to the Land of Shar—with or without your help. We are thankful for all you've done for us, but we best be on our way." He turned and went to get his pack. "Come on Otok, let's get going."

As Notom stood there quietly and watched them collect their gear, he realized something about these boys that until now had not been apparent. Although they looked like youngsters, they didn't act like it. They were committed to their quest, and serious about fulfilling it. After a moment of thought, Notom stopped them. "Wait. Don't be so hasty. Let's sit down and discuss this. Maybe there's something I can do to prepare you for what's ahead."

Gyank responded in a humble tone of voice, "Notom, we'd be very grateful if you helped us in any way. You live in the mountains. I'm sure there's much we can learn from you."

Otok nodded his head. "This is definitely true. And we want to learn whatever we can to help us survive."

"And I will teach you what I know," said Notom.

They sat down around the ashes of the fire and told Notom the whole story—from Smilga's book and map to the secret passages under the castle of Thorilleia. Notom listened intensely. He hadn't heard such a story in a long time, and when they were done, he was still unsure of Smilga's motives. Perhaps the lie he made up to trick them wasn't too far from the truth. On the other hand, he thought maybe Smilga was sincere. Either way, he still maintained that they should give up the journey and go home. But since they insisted on going, he decided to help them as best he could. He agreed to lead them across the mountains, and they were delighted to have him as their guide. Yet Notom planned to aid them in a way far greater. He was well aware that the road beyond the mountains was a perilous one, and he did far more to prepare them than they realized.

He taught them the skills of mountain men, how to stalk, hunt, fish, and trap. They had some previous knowledge of these skills, but with Notom's guidance, they improved and sharpened their abilities. They learned how to climb and use ropes. He showed them better form with the bow and gave Gyank a few pointers on how to throw his hatchet. Otok was concerned about having an empty quiver, so Notom showed them how to make arrows. Having been familiar with only metal-tipped arrows, they were amazed when Notom showed them how to make arrowheads out of stone. Whenever they came to a place where obsidian, flint, or agate could be found, Notom was sure to give them a lesson in flaking arrowheads and other primitive stone tools. He taught them how to straighten sticks to be used as arrow shafts, how to tie the arrowheads in place, and how to attach the fletching.

Notom had a wealth of knowledge about so many things that would be useful on a dangerous journey, and he was keenly resourceful. He could take whatever was at hand and make use of it in ways that most people would never think of. But most of all, he taught them how to fight. Of course, they already knew how to fight, but not the way Notom did. He showed them his stance and how he shifted his weight from one foot to the other. He demonstrated how to use an attacker's force against him, and how to get someone in a hold while avoiding being struck by a weapon. Notom instructed them on how to use a simple staff as a deadly weapon. And when it came to battle, he knew all the tricks of doing combat with multiple opponents. Many afternoons were spent practicing these fighting skills. Sometimes they fought with bare hands, and other times sticks with blunt points were used as swords, axes, or spears. They were unaware that Notom's style of fighting was very unorthodox. They were equally oblivious to the fact that this would give them a big advantage against anyone trained in conventional forms of combat. Even well-seasoned fighters would find their movements and tactics unpredictable.

As the companions practiced, their skills grew. And when they became confident, Notom would defeat them with a new technique just to keep them humble. He felt that overconfidence in battle was dangerous. Otok and Gyank enjoyed learning everything that Notom taught them, yet they truly did not grasp the value of the training they received.

In the weeks it took to cross the mountains, a strong bond had grown between them, and they were not looking forward to parting. Still, the time had come, and they headed down a pass early one morning, knowing that they would part by late afternoon. As they hiked down the slopes, Otok and Gyank tried to think of reasons why Notom should go with them on the rest of the journey. But Notom had his mind made up, and when it came time to say good-bye, he stuck to his decision.

"Won't you reconsider coming along with us?" asked Gyank.

"No, my life is here in the mountains. You are young and you have learned well."

"I wish we could pay you back in some way," said Gyank. "We're truly in debt to you."

"Don't think of it that way," said Notom, trying to teach them one last lesson. "You owe me nothing. Someday you will be in a position to help someone else. Do it because it's the right thing to do, not because that person will pay you back in some way. If all people thought like this, we would live in a happier world."

Notom looked down the slope at the vast forest below. "You have a difficult task ahead of you, and I wish you good fortune. Someday you may come back this way, but it will never be the same. Both you and I will be different. A year from now, the people we are today will be gone forever, and they will never exist again. Time changes all things. Even the great mountains are at its mercy." He turned and looked up at the rugged mountain peaks illuminated by the late afternoon sun. "May the spirit of the mountains always be with you, my friends, and may our paths cross again."

He smiled at them and walked away. As they watched him disappear behind a cliff, they suddenly felt a great loss. They stood in silence for a while until finally they picked up their gear and headed down the slope. Looking to the south, they could see a dark, dense forest stretching endlessly in front of them. They were entering the country of Elreia.

Chapter 5

THE SERPENTS OF ELREIA

As they descended the slopes into the forest, the cover of the trees blocked their view of the mountains behind them. Gyank pulled the map out of his shirt and unfolded it. "I wonder if Notom took us through the same passage that Smilga told us about."

Otok looked over Gyank's shoulder at the map. "Does it really matter? We have to go southeast to get to the river anyway."

"I guess you're right," said Gyank. "As Smilga said, trail or no trail, we must head southeast."

The late afternoon air was cool and pleasant in the shade of the woods as they made their way through the trees. It had taken several weeks to cross the mountains, but since they had lived off the land while traveling with Notom, they still had most of the dried meats and fruits that Trenden had given them. They only had one bow. But now Otok had a quiver full of stone tipped arrows on his back. Gyank had his sheath knife that he brought from home, so Otok wore the knife that Trenden had packed for them. As for the rest of the gear, they made the best of what they had.

The Forest of Elreia in late spring was full of color, and they hiked for days without difficulty. But as they went deeper into the forest, they noticed the woods were getting thicker and their progress was slower. Eventually, the vegetation became so dense that they had to take turns using Gyank's hatchet to hack through the vines and branches blocking their way. One would chop a narrow path and the other would follow. It wasn't long before their progress came to a halt. They were both exhausted and their muscles ached from hacking and slicing all day long. It was getting near dusk and the thick canopy of leaves above them blocked the sunlight. The forest seemed to close in behind them. In an attempt to get through the woods with the least amount of cutting and chopping, they had strayed to the west. Aside from knowing that they had to go southeast, they were completely lost. They had no idea where they were, or how much farther they would have to go to get out of the tangle of dense undergrowth. Tired and lost, they sat down among the twisted foliage to think over their situation.

"What next?" said Gyank in disgust. "Just look at the mess we got ourselves into. We can't even see a few yards ahead."

Long slender leaves hung down all around them and stuck to their sweaty bodies. Pulling leaves off his face and neck, Gyank said, "It seems as if these sticky plants are trying to smother us."

Otok sat quietly and rested. The plants didn't seem to bother him as much, or maybe he just wasn't showing it. Suddenly, Gyank froze. He slowly looked up at the giant plant hovering over them as he reached out a hand to get Otok's attention. "Otok, look. Look at this plant."

Otok tilted his head back to look up at the plant drooping all around them. Dangling above them were big yellow blossoms.

"Look at those flowers," said Gyank. "This must be a smeatle plant."

"The leaves are the right shape, but it's too big. Don't you remember how small the smeatle was in Smilga's garden?"

"Maybe her plant wasn't full grown. Or maybe they just grow much bigger here because of the soil. But this is certainly the same type of plant Smilga showed us. These leaves are exactly like the ones in her garden. They're just bigger, that's all. And she did say that it blooms with bright yellow flowers."

Gyank cut off some leaves and put them in his pack. Climbing up to pick the flowers, he looked ahead through the thick growth of vines. Below him, he saw a small clearing and what appeared to be a tunnel through the underbrush.

"Hey, Otok, get a look at this. There seems to be a tunnel over here. I can't be sure, but that's what it looks like."

Otok climbed up next to him. "That's what it looks like alright. Let's go and see."

They pushed their way through the brush and jumped down into the clearing. The weeds and grass had been trampled down, and the foliage had been pushed back in a circle. On one side of the clearing was a hole through the dense underbrush. Almost perfectly round and about two feet in diameter, this hole had not been cut, but rather pushed open through the heavy growth by some creature. As soon as Gyank realized this, he pulled the hatchet from his belt, and looking up into the trees, he said, "Otok, better nock an arrow."

"I'm way ahead of you," said Otok who had already done so.

Gyank spoke quietly. "This clearing was made by a creature of some kind, and so was that tunnel."

Holding his bow sideways in front of him, Otok slowly squatted down with his arrow pointing at the dark hole. "Maybe we should check this tunnel."

"It's getting dark," said Gyank, glancing at the dimming sky through the trees. "I certainly don't want to spend the night in this den. I don't want to explore that tunnel either. But if we're going to get out of here, I guess that hole is the easiest way. I don't know about you, but I can't hack my way through this wall of brush any longer."

"Well, if it's either use the tunnel or cut our own, then I'm with you. Let's try the tunnel before it gets any darker."

Otok placed the arrow back in his quiver, slung the bow on his shoulder, and pulled the knife from his belt. Gyank figured that if he had to fight on his belly, a knife would be more effective than a hatchet, so he tucked the hatchet back in his belt and drew his knife. Otok went into the tunnel first. Lying on his stomach, he squirmed his way into the hole. After taking a last look at the clearing, Gyank went into the hole head first after his friend.

The tunnel wound its way through the underbrush avoiding the trunks of large trees, yet it was amazingly easy to move through. They were continuously crawling downward, and after a while, the ground became damp.

"We must be getting close to water," said Otok, turning his head to look back at Gyank even though the tunnel was too dark and narrow to see anything behind him. Farther down the tunnel, Otok stopped and said, "I was hoping this was an abandoned tunnel, but now it seems that we're not so lucky."

"What do you mean?"

"When you get up to where my head is, take a look at this track in the mud."

Gyank crawled up to the spot and saw a reptilian looking track as big as a man's hand. It had three toes pointing forward and one back. The impressions of the toes had small deep holes in front of them, indicating the creature was armed with long claws. As they crawled along the tunnel, it got so dark that they could hardly see a few feet in front of them. Soon it would be completely dark and they would have to feel their way forward. But then Otok whispered with excitement, "I see light ahead."

They squirmed to the end of the tunnel, and once outside, they realized it wasn't as dark as they had thought. It was dusk and the sun was just setting, but in the tunnel, the thick vegetation had blocked out the dim sunlight.

They found themselves standing on a clump of wet moss at the edge of a small pond with their backs leaning against a dense wall of entangled vines. There wasn't even enough room to walk single file around the pond without sliding on the mud. On one side, a tiny stream led into the pool, and on the other side the water dribbled out through the vegetation. The pond itself was still and murky, and a layer of green slime covered most of the surface.

"We're not much better off here than where we were," said Gyank. "But at least we're by a stream. We could follow it. Maybe it leads to a larger stream and eventually to the Andelron River."

As they scanned the forest surrounding the pond, they noticed the tunnel that they had come down was not the only one leading to the pool. A number of similar tunnels of various sizes led into the slimy water. Looking at these dark holes in the foliage, Gyank said, "This is not good. We have to get away from this place before the sun goes down. Whatever these things are, I don't want to face them in the dark."

"Neither do I. But which way do we go?"

Otok had a good point. The impenetrable forest closed in on the dismal pool, and the only way out was to crawl along the streams at either end. In order to do that, they would first have to go into the murky water.

Gyank looked toward the end of the pond where the sound of water quietly gurgled through a gap in the foliage. "Let's try to make our way to the stream flowing out of this pool of muck."

They put their knives back on their belts and worked their way along the side of the pond by hanging onto the brush that grew along the edge. The orange glow from the setting sun faded, leaving only pinkish-purple clouds to shed light on their progress toward the stream. In the dim light, neither Gyank nor Otok noticed tiny bubbles coming to the surface of the pond. Moments later, a reptilian creature poked his nostrils up through the green slime to sniff the twilight air. Only inches below the surface, a large dragonlike head slowly glided across the pool. As Otok and Gyank approached the outgoing stream, they noticed the water was shallow and clear.

"Look down there," said Otok who was a few steps ahead. "There's something white on the bottom." Holding onto a branch, Otok moved closer. "It's a skeleton!"

"Are you sure?" said Gyank, clinging to a vine with both hands as he leaned out over the water to get a better look.

Otok turned his head to answer and saw a pair of scaly green claws slowly breaking the surface of the water as they reached for Gyank's ankles. "Gyank, look out!" he shouted.

It was too late. The creature grabbed Gyank's legs just above his boots and pulled him off balance. But Gyank didn't topple into the pool, he held onto the vine and dangled above the water as the creature pulled violently, trying to drag him under. A reptilian head sprang up out of the scum, and a long muscular neck wrapped coils around Gyank's body, working its way up to his chest as the claws climbed up his legs.

Otok pulled the knife from his belt and held onto a branch as he reached out over the pond to stab at the scaly coils engulfing his friend. Like a snake wrapping around a mouse, slimy coils of the serpent's body quickly covered Gyank up to his chest. Otok's feet slipped in the mud as he stretched, and the point of his knife barely scratched the creature's hide. Gyank gave a painful groan as the coils tightened. His grip on the vine loosened and he fell into the water. The prehistoric beast thrashed its huge tail back and forth and disappeared into the murky depths, dragging Gyank along with him.

Otok clenched his knife in his teeth, pulled the bow off his shoulder, and braced himself against the vegetation lining the pond. He quickly drew an arrow from his quiver, laid it across his bow, and took aim at the spot where Gyank had been pulled under. But he didn't shoot. He couldn't risk hitting Gyank, and he stared wide-eyed at the enlarging circle of ripples where Gyank had disappeared.

Suddenly, he noticed v-shaped ripples made by the wakes of many other serpents moving silently just under the surface of the water. These ripples all pointed to the spot where Gyank had been dragged under. Otok pulled back on the bowstring and fired an arrow into the center of one of the wakes. The unseen creature wriggled and twisted fiercely as it broke the surface, displaying its yellow-green belly. Otok didn't pause to watch the creature struggle. He nocked another arrow and let it fly. It struck another one of the terrible serpents, and again there was a display of violent thrashing. Otok quickly fired two more arrows, and both of them hit their mark. The creatures rolled and splashed and jerked their bodies erratically while coils of scaly hide popped above the surface, trailing long strings of green algae.

Otok frantically scanned the water for his friend, but Gyank was nowhere to be seen among the churning brown water and clumps of green slime. Otok could no longer take aim on any fixed target. He threw down his bow, took the knife from his teeth, and without hesitation, dove head first into the swirling water.

~ ~ ~

Gyank felt the tremendous strength of the creature as it pulled him to the bottom of the pond. As he fought to hold his breath, he thought to reach for his hatchet or his knife, but it was useless. His weapons were covered by giant coils of scale and muscle. In fact, he felt his hatchet being pressed into his side by the tightening grip of the monster. Since his arms were above his head when the creature attacked, they were not entwined by serpent's body and waved freely underwater.

Gyank felt the presence of other creatures trying to get a grip on him as if he was a morsel of food being fought over by a school of hungry fish. Yet they didn't bite at him. Their intent was to grab and pull him from each other. In an attempt to keep its prey away from the other serpents, the monster that held Gyank in its grasp moved to the shallow end of the pool where the stream flowed out. As the creature twisted and rolled, Gyank was thrust into the muck on the bottom of the pond. He felt something long and hard pressing against him. At first he thought it was a dead branch. Then he realized it was a bone—a human bone. It was part of the skeleton that Otok had seen just before the attack. The powerful creature suddenly jerked its body, pushing Gyank through the bits and pieces of bone that formed the skeleton. That's when somewhere deep in the mud, Gyank's hand fell upon an unusual object. He thought it might be the smooth round part of a leg bone, but it felt cold and metallic. Gyank closed his hand on it just as the creature shifted and yanked him out of the muck. The object that he had grasped slid up out of the mud much easier than he expected. At that moment, Gyank realized what he had picked up. It was a sword.

A rush of strength ran through his body. He was no longer helpless. If only he could hold his breath just a few seconds longer. Gyank pulled his arm as far away from himself as he could to get the point of the sword on the coils covering his chest. Then he stabbed. Gyank was amazed at the speed with which the serpent let go and wriggled away from him. It was as if he had struck the creature with a blacksmith's red-hot poker.

Gyank planted his feet on the bottom and thrust himself upward, and although his boots sunk down into the mud, he found himself standing in water that only came up to his armpits. He took a couple of deep breaths as he spun his head in a circle to get his bearings. To his horror, Otok was gone.

In the midst of the splashing and foaming, he suddenly saw his friend's head pop up for a breath and then sink under the water again. Otok was wrestling with several of the creatures as their serpentine bodies struggled to envelop him, but he had his knife and was slashing and stabbing wildly. As Gyank pulled one foot out of the mud to step forward, he felt the stiff neck of a creature wrapping around his legs. He lifted the sword high in the air and let it fall. It sliced through the water and deep into the monster's flesh. The water turned red with blood as the serpent wriggled away. Otok's head popped up again, he whipped the hair out of his face, took a breath and went under, still fighting and stabbing.

"Hold on Otok!" cried Gyank as he headed for the spot where Otok was pulled back under. With each step, Gyank fought to lift his foot out of the thick muck on the bottom of the pond, and he took long strides to avoid being knocked off balance. He slashed at the ugly brown water in front of him whenever part of a green scaly body broke the surface. And each time a creature grabbed him under the water, he thrust the sword down and felt the beast squirm as the water turned red. Amidst the swirling water, Otok popped to the surface again, gasping desperately for air. Gyank was close by and put his new blade to work.

Being careful not to cut his friend, he stabbed a creature as it twirled its body around Otok. The monster instantly released him and darted away underwater. Clinging to each other and gasping for breath, they fought their way toward the edge of the pond while hungry serpents slithered into the shallows after them. The long thin sword sliced through the air and cleanly severed the dragonlike heads of the serpents. Splashing through knee-deep muddy water, they threw themselves against the thick vegetation and clung there, breathless. The remaining creatures slithered out of the pond and disappeared into the dark tunnels. The water calmed as the last ripple worked its way to the edge of the pond and vanished. Still breathing heavily, they rested with their backs pressed against the foliage. The woods around them were silent except for the gentle sound of water trickling in the stream nearby. The dim light that lingers after sunset was fading and it would soon be dark.

"That was close," said Gyank.

"For a minute, I thought you were gone for good."

"For a minute, so did I," replied Gyank, lifting his pants leg to examine his wounds. The creature's claws left long scrapes that burned from the filthy water.

"Where did you get that sword?" asked Otok.

"It must have belonged to the man that died here. I picked it up out of the mud by the skeleton. Here, take a look," said Gyank, handing him the sword.

Otok examined it. "This is certainly a special sword. It must have been lying at the bottom of this pond for ages. And look at it—not a spot of rust or anything."

Otok was right. It was a long sword in perfect condition. The blade was slender yet strong and was made from an unusual bluish-sliver alloy. The hilt was skillfully crafted from dark steel, and looking at it more carefully, Otok said, "Hey Gyank, did you notice the design on the hilt?"

"No, let's see."

Gyank looked at the handle. A design of intertwining snakes was engraved in the hilt. "I wonder if it means anything." Examining the hand guard at the top of the hilt, Gyank said, "There's something written on it. But I can't make it out. These are strange letters—it must be a different language."

Otok looked at the engraved words. "It's probably the name of the sword. I've heard that all great swords have names."

"Is that really true?" asked Gyank, wondering if he had made a great find.

Otok shrugged his shoulders. "I don't know, but I suppose it could be. Those words could be its name written in the language of the people who made it."

Admiring the weapon, Gyank said, "Whatever its name is, I'm going to call it Serpent Blade. Not only does it have snakes engraved into its hilt, but the serpents of this pool jump from its touch as if it was fire." Gyank sliced the air a few times. "I don't know anything about swords, but this thing is so easy to handle, and it fits comfortably in my hand."

Otok reached over his shoulder to count the arrows in his quiver. "Better hang onto that sword," he said. "We will need it. Most of my arrows are at the bottom of the pond, and I have no intention of going in to get them."

Otok waded through the mud to get his bow and slung it over his shoulder. Gyank tucked the sword in his belt, and together they walked through the shallows toward the stream. It was covered in vegetation, so they had to crawl in the water to get under the overhanging branches. Less than a foot deep, the stream was cool and clear, yet they dare not drink from it. They had gone only a short distance before darkness forced them to stop. Cutting back the undergrowth beside the stream, they cleared a place to sleep. As they lay still in their little nest, they wondered if the serpents might come for them in the night. Neither of them spoke of it, yet they both listened intensely for the slightest sound of movement in the surrounding darkness. Gradually, they drifted off into an uneasy sleep, Otok clutching his knife and Gyank with a hand on the hilt of his sword.

~ ~ ~

The next morning when Gyank awoke, he felt dizzy. His head ached and when he tried to sit up, the dizziness became so intense that he couldn't help but fall back down. Then he felt the pain in his stomach. He put his hand up to his forehead. He was sweating and burning up with fever.

"Otok," he groaned.

As Gyank slowly stretched his arm out to wake his friend, he heard a voice. "Why don't you let 'em sleep?"

Gyank sat up quickly to see who had spoken, but it was useless, and he fell back down again.

"Take it easy," said the voice.

A man dressed in the drab clothes of a simple worker stood up and stepped around so Gyank could see him. He had a big belly that Gyank noticed as he looked up to see the man's face. The chubby fellow smiled warmly at him.

"Who are you?" asked Gyank.

"Opus is the name."

"How long have you been here watching us sleep?"

"Not long. Listen, you better lay still and let me take care of you. You have a sickness of some kind."

"I guess it's no wonder," said Gyank. "After all that terrible water I swallowed."

"Looks like your friend has the same thing you have," said Opus as he squatted down and gently touched Otok's head. "Yup, you both have a fever. And for the moment, you're both going nowhere. I'll be right back. You just lay still and rest."

Opus got up and disappeared into the dense forest. Gyank was amazed how easily he moved through the tangle of vines and branches. Unable to do much else, Gyank lay back and closed his eyes. A short time later, Opus returned with a bowl in his hand.

"Here, drink some of this," he said, lifting Gyank's head while tilting the bowl. Gyank didn't even have a chance to ask what it was before he took a sip.

"Now lay still and rest. Don't worry about anything. I'll watch out for you."

Gyank was dizzy and in pain, but he still had to ask, "Why are you helping us?"

"Can you think of a reason why I shouldn't?"

"No, not a one." said Gyank as he closed his eyes. He didn't know why he felt safe with this man sitting next to him, but he did.

~ ~ ~

For the next day or so, Opus came and went, bringing them bowls of warm broth, and every time Gyank or Otok awoke, Opus was there to comfort them. Soon they were well enough to sit up and eat a solid meal.

"That'll do it to you alright," said Opus. "You drink swamp water and you're bound to get one sort of sickness or another."

Otok gave him a funny look. "We didn't exactly sit down and have a cup full. We were attacked by giant serpents of some kind."

"If that's the case, then I'm surprised to see you at all. Those creatures are very dangerous. Everyone's afraid of them."

"And rightfully so," said Gyank. "It was very kind of you to nurse us back to health. Who are you? Where do you live?"

"I'd be happy to tell you. But couldn't you to tell me something about yourself first. You're the ones who seem to be far from home. You must have stories to tell. And I've been holding my questions because you were sick."

"Of course," said Gyank. "But first, I must say that we're very thankful for all your help. I wish we could give you something in return. Unfortunately, right now we have nothing of value."

"Not so," said Opus. "Everyone has friendship and kindness to give. And they have the greatest value." Opus smiled. "More than gold and gems. Besides, I don't want payment for helping you. So tell me, what brings you here to fight serpents?"

"I assure you," said Gyank, "we didn't come to fight serpents. As you guessed, we're far from home. As for the rest of our story, there isn't much to tell. We come from up north, beyond the Grammash Mountains, and we've encountered many dangers. None of it is of any real importance."

"So, why did you leave home at all? There must be some reason for your journey."

Although spoken in a friendly way, Opus's pointed question caught Gyank off guard. And while he paused, Otok proudly declared, "We are adventurers. And we left home to seek our fortune and test our luck and our skills."

"Just what I always wanted to do," Opus said cheerfully. "I'd like to hear more. But now I suppose it's my turn to tell you something about myself." Opus hesitated, and there was sadness in his voice when he spoke. "There's a reason I left you in the forest and didn't bring you to my home. It's because I don't have a home. I live in a small village not far from here, but I certainly wouldn't call it home. I don't have a family. In fact, I don't even know where I was born. When I got old enough to ask about such things, the people I live with told me that my parents died when I was an infant, and they raised me as a favor to my mother and father." Opus looked down at the ground. "My parents must have been terrible people to have friends like these. They work me like a horse and treat me like a slave. For all I know, they could have kidnapped me when I was little and made up that story about my parents. Or I could have been abandoned. I really don't know. I guess it doesn't matter much now."

"Why do you stay with them if they treat you so badly?" asked Gyank.

"I've given it much thought. I don't have a single friend in that village. Most of them are thieves and cutthroats. I've often considered heading off into the forest on my own. I just never did it. I don't have anywhere to go."

Otok ruffled his brow. "A place to go or not, I would have left long ago. And I would have left them some bruises to remember me by as well."

"I guess you think I'm older than I really am. I may look older, but I bet I'm about the same age as you," he said, looking at Gyank.

It was true. Opus was quite a bit younger than he appeared. Although an inch or so shorter than Gyank, he had the features and the voice of someone much older, and his chubby build also made him seem more mature.

"I've always looked older," said Opus. "I guess in some cases it could work to my advantage. But getting back to what I was saying, I didn't bring you to the place where I live because they would have taken everything you had, and thrown you out, and then yelled at me for bringing you there. So I didn't tell anyone. I just spent as much time with you as I could."

"Opus, you should be proud of yourself," said Gyank. "You are incredibly kind and cheerful for someone who has such problems."

"I try not to let things get to me. But you're right. I should leave, and I was going to. But it's dangerous to travel the forest alone."

Gyank nodded. "After being attacked by those serpents, we know that just as well as anyone."

"You said that you're seeking your fortune, but where exactly are you headed?"

"We're headed for the Andelron River," said Gyank.

"Sounds great!"

"What do you mean, 'great'?" said Otok. "It's a long and dangerous journey."

"I guess we just look at it differently. I've lived under bad circumstances for so long that a chance to go down the Great Andelron River is something I can't pass by."

"Wait just a minute," said Gyank. "Who said that you were

coming with us down the Andelron?"

Opus frowned. "Why won't you let me go with you?"

Otok and Gyank glanced at each other. They really had started to like him, and they certainly could use all the help they could get. But it wouldn't be right to lead him into the Land of Shar unknowingly.

"If I'm finally leaving those wicked people, and you're headed for the Andelron, I don't see why we can't travel together. It'll be safer that way for all of us. Besides, I know how to get to the Andelron."

"We could find it on our own," said Otok. "We're planning to follow this stream."

"This stream does eventually meet up with the Andelron," said Opus. "But first it leads into a swamp that's miles across—with plenty of those nasty snakes. I know a much easier way." A hint of a smile appeared on Opus's face. "It's far better than trying to make it through the swamp."

Gyank glanced at Otok and said, "We'll have to talk it over."

"Of course," agreed Opus. "You go right ahead. I'd do the same if I was you."

Otok and Gyank walked a short distance upstream. Although the gentle sound of running water muffled their voices, Gyank still spoke in a whisper. "We can't tell him about the book, but I think it's safe to join up with him. What do you say?"

Otok responded just as quietly. "I say we take him along, and when we come to the Land of Shar, he can go his own way."

"I was thinking the same thing."

They walked back to where Opus was waiting. "You're welcome to join us," said Gyank. "We decided that you'd make a good traveling companion."

"Thank you so much. You won't regret taking me along. I promise. Just let me go back to my shack and pack a few things. It won't take long." Opus's excitement suddenly turned to concern. "There may be trouble. If someone sees me leaving, they may try to stop me."

"We'll go with you," said Otok confidently. "Nobody is going to stop you from leaving. We'll make sure of that."

Walking in single file, Opus led the way along hidden trails in the dense forest. Otok and Gyank were amazed that they didn't need to hack their way through the vegetation. Soon the forest thinned out and they were on a heavily used path. They could see cottages ahead of them through the trees. As they walked down the main road, people stopped their work to stare coldly at the strangers.

Opus leaned toward Gyank, and in a low voice said, "It seems that your sword is getting just as much attention as you are. Not many people own swords around here. Some of them would pay a nice price for yours, while others would slit your throat for it. Unfortunately, your weapon is more likely to start a fight than prevent one. In any case, you can't hide it, so try to ignore the stares." Opus paused. "But be ready to use that sword."

They turned down a small path leading to a cottage with an old, weather-beaten shack next to it. "This is my master's cottage," said Opus. "I sleep in the shack. Wait out here. I'll go in and gather my things."

As Opus went inside the shack, a man poked his head out a side window of the cottage. A moment later, he stormed out of the cottage with an angry look on his face, rushed into the shack and started shouting.

"Seems like Opus is in trouble," said Otok.

"Yes, but let's not make too much of a fuss. I don't like the looks we got coming down the main road."

Through the open door, they saw the man grab hold of Opus's arm. Opus ripped free. "Let go of me, Norg! I'm leaving! And you're not going to stop me."

The man shouted back at him, "I am your master! You leave and I'll hunt you down!"

Gyank stepped through the doorway, drew his sword, and pointed it at the man's chest. "Opus wants to leave," said Gyank. "I think you should let him go." Without looking away from the man, he spoke to Opus. "Finish packing—we're getting out of here."

Opus's master was fuming, but he didn't move. "I'll remember you and your friend," he said, pointing to Otok who stood outside the door, keeping a lookout. "And when I come to get Opus, I'll make you pay for your foolish bravery. I have friends, and you won't get away with this."

While the man glared at Gyank, Opus quickly finished stuffing some clothes into a sack. He rolled up a blanket as fast as he could, wrapped a cord around it, and flinging the sack on his shoulder, he said, "I'm ready. Let's go."

Standing by the door, Otok said, "Come on, it looks clear."

Opus slipped out the door while Gyank held the man at bay a few moments longer before darting out of the shack. They ran to the back of the cottage where a trail led into the woods.

"Norg is not the type to make false threats," said Opus. "I suggest we move quickly."

They hurried along the trail, looking back often to see if they were being followed. After hiking for hours without seeing or hearing any sign of pursuit, they came to a halt. Gyank took out his map and looked at it. "That village isn't even on this map."

Standing next to him, Opus glanced down at the map, and said, "That map won't do you much good. It's not detailed enough. It doesn't show any of the hundreds of trails that run throughout the forest. But don't fret. I don't even know them all. In fact, I only know the trails close to my village, except of course for this trail."

Gyank gave him a suspicious look. "How is it that the only other trail you know is the one we need to take?"

Opus smiled. "Everyone knows the way to the Andelron. In my isolated village, the only way to get goods is from traders along the river. The path to the Andelron is well traveled. No one would dare go any other way. It's too easy to get lost. At least that's what everyone says. I've actually never been to the river."

Otok took a step closer to Opus in a threatening fashion. "What do you mean, you've never been there? You said that you knew the way."

"I do," Opus said. "But I never said that I've been there." Opus could tell they were skeptical, and he tried to reassure them. "I may have never taken this trail, but it doesn't matter. People come and go this way all the time. It's the only safe way to the river. There are no forks in the path, or anything like that. You just stay on the trail and you can't go wrong." Opus could still see the doubt in their faces, and he spoke with absolute certainty as he pointed to the ground. "This is the trail to the Andelron River. We are on it. Now let's go."

With that, Opus turned and walked down the trail. Otok and Gyank looked at each other for a moment and then quickly caught up to him.

"You're very persuasive," said Gyank.

"I've always been a good talker. I guess it just comes naturally to me."

"It's good to be so convincing," said Otok. "We could have used you a while back when some guards had us cornered. Next time, we'll let you do the talking."

Opus laughed. "That's fine with me, as long as you back me up when I run out of words."

~ ~ ~

It was late in the afternoon when they sat down by the side of the trail to rest. Opus opened his sack and pulled out something wrapped in a cloth. The bulging material seemed as if it was filled with stones. He opened it and said, "While I was scurrying to pack, I managed to throw these in with my clothes. Want some hard biscuits?"

"We did have plenty of food," said Gyank. "But it was doused in the same water that made us sick, so we dumped it all. I'm sure it was spoiled."

"I would have tossed it," said Opus. "Better to go hungry than get sick again."

"You're right about that," said Otok. "I'll have biscuit if you don't mind."

After gnawing on rock hard biscuits, they hiked for a few more hours. At dusk, they stopped and set up camp a good distance off the path to avoid being seen if anyone came along the trail. Since their only food was a handful of biscuits, they rationed themselves one more each and settled down to sleep for the night.

Pulling his blanket around himself, Gyank said, "I wonder if that man will really hunt us down like he said."

Lying on his back looking up into the trees, Opus said, "His name is Norg. He's the one who told me stories about my parents. They were probably all lies. He was always mean to me. I suppose that's why I didn't turn out to be hateful like him. Whatever he was like, I wanted to be just the opposite, so I looked at him as an example of the kind of person I didn't want to be. I know it sounds odd, but it was my way of dealing with the hardships he put me through. And he despises my happy outlook on life. In fact, he's always insisted that I call him 'Master.' I guess it's because he wanted to keep me in my place."

"Well, you're rid of him now," said Gyank. "That is, unless you think he will hunt us down."

Opus rolled on his side. "I really don't know. I've never run away before. I told you he doesn't make false threats, but it would be quite a chore for him to track us down. Although he did like the idea of having me work for him like a slave. All he ever gave me was a place to sleep and enough food to keep me from squawking."

"I bet that took quite a bit of food," said Otok jokingly.

Opus smiled. "I guess I always found a way to eat more than my share."

With that thought in mind, they fell silent and went to sleep.

Chapter 6

THE RUINS OF DWOR

The next morning when Gyank awoke, Opus was gone. His sleeping gear was still there, but Opus was nowhere in sight. Gyank nudged Otok to wake him. "Get up. Opus is gone."

As Otok sat up and rubbed his face, they heard something coming through the woods. It was Opus.

"Where have you been?" asked Gyank.

"I've been looking around, and I've found something very interesting. Come on, I'll show you."

Otok and Gyank followed him through the woods to a flat boulder embedded in the earth. The exposed part of the stone was level with the ground. They stood around the chunk of rock and stared down at it.

"What's so interesting about this rock?" asked Otok.

"Look at the grooves in it," said Opus, pointing at two parallel grooves that ran across the entire stone. "It looks as if these grooves have been worn down by carts and carriages rolling over this rock for ages. Also, notice the way the trees grow around here." Opus extended his arm, pointing with his open hand. "There aren't any big trees along this stretch. All the older trees are either to the left or to the right. I bet this was once a road. And it must have been a major road at that. It was wide and it must have carried much traffic for this stone to be worn out the way it is."

"Now that you point it out, you're right," said Otok. "You can actually see where the road used to be by the way the young trees and brush grow in a line."

Gyank glanced toward the sun to get his bearings. "This road heads south. Now the question is, should we go back to the trail that we know leads to the river, or should we follow what's left of this ancient road?"

"I say we follow the road," said Opus. "It's heading in the same general direction. If Norg were hunting us down, he'd never expect us to stray from the trail. And I'll bet no one has gone this way for years. Who knows what we may find?"

"I'm with Opus," said Otok. "This road must lead somewhere. Besides, as long as we keep going south, we'll eventually get to the river. And Opus is right—it's a good way to throw someone off our trail."

"Then the road it is," said Gyank.

They went back to the campsite, grabbed their gear, and were soon hiking along the remnants of the ancient road. Although severely overgrown, they could still follow the road because the surrounding forest was filled with huge trees. The Great Forest of Elreia was indeed very old, and the thick trunks on either side of them guided them through the woods. For the most part, the road went straight south, and they covered much distance before they had to stop for the night. With only a few biscuits to share, they went to sleep hungry. The dark woods made them uneasy, and they were awakened often by the nocturnal sounds of the forest.

The next few days went by slowly. Opus's biscuits had run out, and the anticipation of where the road would lead them was overpowered by their hunger. Yet neither their curiosity nor their hunger was satisfied as the forest revealed nothing but tall dark trees, many of which were centuries old. They plodded along in silence until finally something caught their attention. Standing among the young trees ahead was part of a broken stone arch stretching out over the road. As they approached, they came to the edge of the woods and saw the massive stone ruins of an ancient city. They entered under the broken arch and began roaming through the streets of what was once a great city hidden in the depths of the forest. Trees and bushes grew up through stone foundations of wooden houses long gone. Other ancient structures added to the feeling that no man had tread there in ages. As the party walked among the ruins, they thought of the great wealth and effort it must have taken to build such a place. A feeling of mysterious loss came to them, and they wondered what could have brought this great city to an end.

When they came to the city's main square, they saw a road lined with stone statues leading up to the ruins of a castle. Each statue was an amazing work of art, and the years of erosion couldn't hide the skill of the craftsmen who carved them.

The companions walked past statues of great warriors and beasts of all kinds as they went up a slight incline to the outer wall of the castle. Clearly not intended as a defendable stronghold, the castle looked more like a palace built to demonstrate wealth and power. Numerous ornate steeples that had disintegrated over the years laid in crumpled ruin about the structure, and chunks of broken marble were scattered everywhere. Entering through the outer wall, they suddenly came within view of the Andelron River, which ran along the far side of the castle at the bottom of a steep hill. From where they stood, they could see sunlight sparkling off the great river as it snaked gently through the surrounding forest for miles in both directions.

"That's it!" shouted Otok.

Opus's bottom jaw fell open and he gasped. "I've known of the Great Andelron River all my life, yet I never imagined it was so magnificent."

After marveling at the wondrous view, they found a small stone building with a slate roof still intact and decided to use it for their camp. It was near the ruins of the castle and was one of the few places that provided shelter.

As they laid down their equipment, Gyank said, "Now that we made it this far, we should start thinking about heading down the river."

"What's the rush?" asked Opus. "We just got here. These ruins are begging to be explored. I'm sure there's fish in the river. After we've had something to eat, we'll search for treasure. There's bound to something of value left in this city."

"I'm not so sure it's a good idea to stay here long," said Gyank. "There's something about this place that makes me uneasy. I can't explain it—it's just a feeling."

Otok gave him a funny look. "There's nothing wrong with this place. It's just an old city."

"Perhaps you're right," said Gyank. "But we still have to give some thought to getting down the Andelron. I think we should build a raft."

"Good idea," said Opus. "Then we'll explore the city. But first let's catch some fish."

"I'm all for that," said Otok. "And with all the brush growing around here, I'll bet there's rabbits about. We should set some snares."

They went down to the river, cut some straight sticks to be used as spears, and waded into the shallows. After spearing a few fish, they made a small fire on the riverbank to cook their catch and were soon collecting logs for a raft. They planned to use Trenden's rope only to lash the frame of the raft. Flexible vines would be used to tie down the rest of the logs. This way they could save most of the rope but still have a solid raft that wouldn't come apart easily. They worked hard, yet progress was slow, and it was near dusk by the time they finished constructing the frame. When they realized that building a raft was going to take longer than expected, they left the unfinished raft on the bank and climbed back up the hill to the campsite.

As the sun fell low in the sky, Gyank climbed up to the ruins of the castle and sat on a short stone wall overlooking the river. Staring across the distant green hills, he wondered how far they had traveled, and how much farther they would have to go. His thoughts shifted to what brought him so far away from home; the stories of an old woman and the idea of discovering great powers.

Looking down the hill where the warm colors of the sky reflected off the river, he became aware of something sneaking up behind him. He hopped off the wall, spun around and drew his sword. Someone was standing in the shadow of a stone arch behind him. He couldn't see any distinct features, but he could tell that the shadowy figure wore a chain mail vest. With sword drawn, Gyank strained to get a better look at the dark image standing motionless and silent, but he didn't approach. He just stood ready and waited.

To his surprise, a soft feminine voice came from the shadowy figure. "Don't be alarmed."

Stepping out from under the arch was a strikingly attractive young woman with wavy, shoulder-length, chestnut-brown hair. In the light of the setting sun, her chain mail vest twinkled slightly as it conformed to the shape of her body and fanned out at the hips. A long sword hung by her side in a skillfully crafted metal scabbard, and a dark red cape was draped over her shoulders. A ruby amulet dangled from her neck on a gold chain, and her fingers were adorned with sparkling jewels. In addition to her stunning attire, a small hawk perched on her shoulder. Although dressed for combat, the impish smile on her face and the look in her dark eyes indicated that she was up to some kind of innocent mischief.

"Why were you sneaking up on me?" asked Gyank.

"I wasn't sneaking up on you. I was just watching you. I've been watching you and your friends all day."

"If you've been here all day, why didn't we see you?"

"I guess you didn't look in the right place." The smile never left her face as she toyed with him.

"Alright then, why were you watching us?"

"Just for the fun of it."

She tilted her head back slightly and shook it, causing her hair to stir. The hawk on her shoulder spread its wings to balance itself and then folded them back in place. Gyank had never encountered a girl who dressed like a warrior, yet acted so feminine.

In spite of her playful responses, Gyank remained serious. "Are you going to tell me who you are and what's your reason for spying— uh, I mean, watching us?"

"Can't you tell who I am just by looking at me?" When he didn't answer, she said, "Don't you recognize nobility when you see it? I am a princess. My name is Suraia."

"Begging your pardon," said Gyank politely, "and with no disrespect, you dress more like a prince than a princess. And if you are a princess, where are your guards?"

Suraia put her hands on her hips and leaned toward him. "Guards? Just because I'm a princess, doesn't mean I'm helpless. I can take care of myself. In fact, to prove it, I ran away from my father's realm so I could be on my own for a while." Suraia drew her sword and sliced at an imaginary attacker. The hawk took flight and circled above them. "One of my brothers taught me the art of fencing," she said while whipping her sword back and forth. "My skill equals the best of my father's guards."

Gyank kept one eye on the hawk while Suraia fought an invisible foe. When she put her sword back in its scabbard, the hawk returned to her shoulder.

"I'm sure that your hawk can do a fancy bit of fighting as well," said Gyank, putting his sword back in his belt.

"Tork attacks on my command."

"Is that the bird's name? Tork?"

"Yes, I named him myself."

"Tork the hawk," said Gyank with a smile. "That's clever. My name is Gyank. And I'd still like to know why you were stalking me and my friends."

"I just wanted to be sure that you weren't bandits, or men that my father might have sent out to look for me."

"If you're as well equipped for battle as you claim to be, then you shouldn't be concerned."

"To doubt my skill is an insult," she said as she drew her sword and approached. Gyank backed away while glancing up at the hawk, which took to the air. His attention was drawn back to Suraia when she pressed the tip of her sword against his chest.

"Hey, take it easy," he said.

"You should learn how to speak properly to someone of noble blood. Now, let's see some of your swordplay."

Suraia sounded serious even though she was concealing a smile. Not wanting a confrontation, Gyank backed up until he was cornered against a stone wall. It was obvious that she didn't want to hurt him, but in her playfulness, she brought the edge of her sword too close to his unarmored body. Gyank swiftly stepped aside and drew his sword. He blocked an overhead blow that came straight down toward the top of his head, and then deflected a sideways strike for his mid-section. Both of these blows came at him rather slowly, so they were easy to anticipate and defend against. Suraia stopped and lowered her sword. She seemed disappointed. "What kind of stance is that? Don't you know anything about fencing?"

Gyank relaxed and looked at his weapon. He thought back to the sword-fighting lessons with Notom, and although he had only practiced with a stick, he was confident in his ability. So rather than showing off his skill, he tried to see if he could learn something new from Suraia.

"I found this sword only a short time ago, and it's the first sword I've ever held in my hand."

Suraia shook her head. "Watch me."

She took her stance and began to demonstrate the fundamentals of fencing while Gyank mimicked her every move. A short time later, Otok came around a stone wall and caught sight of them standing side by side with their swords drawn. He stood there for a moment, and when they noticed him, he said, "What's going on here?"

"This is Suraia," said Gyank, "She's a lady of noble blood."

"I am a princess," Suraia declared proudly.

"Is that so?" said Otok, clearly not impressed. "I didn't know there was anyone else in these ruins."

"I didn't either," said Gyank. "Not until I met Suraia. She's pretty good with a sword."

Otok was suspicious of this flashy fighting girl, but he knew this was not the time to say anything. As if Suraia was not even there, he spoke directly to Gyank. "It's getting dark, and you were gone for a long time, so I came up here to see what you were doing. Apparently I interrupted a sword-fighting lesson. So I'll head back to camp. I'll see you there when the lesson is over."

Otok walked away, and Gyank said. "Come, let's go to the camp. We can finish this tomorrow."

"Your friend doesn't like me," said Suraia softly as if she was a bit hurt.

"Don't worry about Otok. He's a good man—the best in fact. Just give him some time. Let's go back to camp so you can meet our other friend."

The smile returned to her face. "That's fine. But first let me get my things." She pointed with her finger. "I stored them in that tower over there."

A short time later, Suraia was being introduced to Opus, and they got along right from the start. Then again, with Opus's cheery personality, he could make friends with just about anyone. Opus was intrigued by her pet hawk, and Suraia demonstrated how her avian friend would respond to hand signals as well as a variety of whistling sounds.

Otok was unusually quiet as he busied himself cooking a rabbit they had caught in a snare. By the time they finished eating, it was dark. Otok rolled up in his blanket to sleep while the others sat around the fire and shared stories until the once bright flames were reduced to a pile of glowing coals. Soon Opus nodded off to sleep leaving Gyank and Suraia huddled next to each other by the dying fire. As the moon climbed high in the night sky, they lowered their voices to a whisper. Staring into the dim orange glow of the embers, they spoke less until eventually they lay down next to each other and fell asleep.

~ ~ ~

The next few days were spent camped in the ancient city. Using the skills that Notom taught them, they lived off the land. The river provided fish, and there seemed to be a bounty of rabbits hopping about the maze of broken stones and brush. Although they worked hard on the raft, they also spent some time exploring the ruins and relaxing by the river. Suraia and Gyank stayed together most of the time and often could be seen in the midst of a sword-fighting lesson. Gyank's skill with his Serpent Blade was constantly improving, and without realizing it, he was blending the best components of Suraia's conventional form with Notom's unique style. During one of their play fights, Gyank made an amazingly fast and effective move to defeat Suraia.

"Where did you learn that?" she asked.

"It's a just move I picked up along the trail," said Gyank casually.

"You speak as if it was a daisy or a mushroom by the roadside. Let me see that sword."

Gyank handed her the Serpent Blade and she examined it. "Where did you get this sword?" she asked suspiciously while looking at him through the corner of her eye.

"I found it."

Suraia sprang into a stance and whipped the sword around her head. Startled, Gyank jumped back out of range. She flailed violently at the air and came to a sudden stop with a stabbing motion. "This is a fast blade," she said. "Perfectly balanced, incredibly light, and easy to handle. And it's made from a very unusual metal."

Gyank pointed to it. "Look at the snakes carved in the hilt, and the letters on the hand guard."

Inspecting the craftsmanship, she said, "I haven't a clue what the snakes signify, and the writing is strange to me. But there's no doubt—it's a special sword." Handing it back to Gyank, she added, "Now I know how you surprised me with that move."

"I guess it helps to have a good sword," said Gyank as dueling continued.

Suraia was convinced that the sword was the reason she was

defeated by a beginner. In fact, it was a combination of Notom's combat technique, Gyank's natural agility, and the qualities of the sword.

One afternoon, Otok and Gyank were working on the raft alone. It was the first good opportunity that Otok had to let his friend know how truly suspicious he was of Suraia.

"Something's just not right about her," said Otok.

"What do you mean?" asked Gyank.

"What's she doing all alone in a deserted place like this? There's something suspicious about it."

"What's so suspicious? Just look at us. We're out in the middle nowhere claiming to be looking for adventure."

"That's just what I mean," said Otok. "We're not merely seeking our fortune. We're after that book. And just like us, I think she's up to something that we don't know about. So what are we going to do when the raft is finished? We can't just take her along for the ride. We don't know if we can trust her."

"Why would she be teaching me how to use a sword if she was out to do us harm? I think it would be good to take her along. Look at Opus, we took him on."

"And that's another thing!" said Otok, getting agitated. "We both agreed to let him join us. You didn't even ask me about Suraia. You just decided on your own."

"You are right about that," said Gyank calmly. "I guess I should have talked to you first. But how could we stay in these ruins knowing that she's here and not invite her into our camp? If we take her along, we can part with her when it's time to part with Opus."

"Maybe by the time we finish the raft, she'll get tired of us and be on her way. Then again, the way she follows you around, she may never want to leave. Besides, you may not want her to go."

"What do you mean by that?" asked Gyank, obviously bothered by the comment. "I think you just don't like her."

"You're right!" said Otok in a harsh tone. "I don't like her!"

Gyank was about to go back at him when they heard Opus shouting from the top of the hill. They could see him waving his arms above his head as he stood on a short stone wall by the castle.

"Something's wrong," said Otok. "Let's get up there."

Their disagreement was instantly put aside and they ran up the steep hill. Opus saw them coming and climbed down off the stone wall. When they got to the top of the hill, Opus was waiting for them. "I found a passage," he said.

"Where?" asked Otok, all out of breath.

"On the other side of the castle. Follow me."

They hurried along a path that ran around a broken tower to the other side of the castle. Among a pile of fractured stone blocks was a hole that led straight down. Suraia was on her knees, peering into the darkness. She had brought a coil of rope from camp, and it was lying on the ground next to her. Opus picked it up and fed one end into the hole until it hit the bottom. "Who wants to go down?" he asked.

"Gyank, you're the best climber," said Otok. "You should go down."

"Alright," said Gyank.

After securing the rope to a huge stone block, Gyank carefully lowered himself into the hole. As he climbed down the rope, his eyes adjusted to the darkness, and he found himself in a large chamber made of giant stone blocks. The only light was a thick beam of afternoon sun coming through the hole above. The chamber was empty except for a few small piles of decaying wood that were once furniture. In the dim light, Gyank could see an old wooden door at the far end of the room.

Opus called down to him. "Do you see anything?"

Gyank's reply echoed in the chamber. "There's an old door down here."

"Where does it lead?"

"I don't know. Let me take a look."

Gyank went to the door. It was rotting and chunks of wood had broken off the bottom and lay on the floor. In the center of the door was a severely rusted iron ring. As Gyank took hold of it and tried to open the door, the rusty iron ring disintegrated and broke off in his hands. The hinges of the door were rusted solid. So he took a step back and gave the door a kick. His foot broke through the decaying wood, and after kicking it a few more times, he pulled at the crumbling wood with his hands to make a space big enough for him to fit through. Peering through the hole into the blackness, he could see absolutely nothing.

Gyank shouted up to his friends, "There's a passage down here. We're going to need a torch."

A moment later, Opus's voice echoed down into the chamber. "Otok is going back to camp to see what he can put together for a torch."

While Gyank waited, he broke more of the door away to widen the hole. Soon Otok was back with a makeshift torch and Gyank's tinderbox. Opus knelt down and called into the hole, "It might be dangerous following that passage. I think someone should go with you."

"I'll go with him," said Suraia.

"Opus, you found the passage," said Otok. "Why don't you go, and I'll stay here."

"No, that's alright. I'm not much for dangling on ropes. But both you and Suraia can go if you want."

Otok stuck the unlit torch in his belt and climbed down into the hole. When he reached the bottom, they lit the torch and bright flames illuminated the entire chamber. Holding the torch above his head, Otok approached the passage and gazed into the darkness while Suraia slowly lowered herself on the rope. As Gyank waited for Suraia to reach the bottom, he yelled up to Opus, "We'll be right back."

Holding the torch out in front of him, Otok stepped through the broken door and into a straight narrow tunnel of stone. Gyank and Suraia followed close behind to stay within the perimeter of the light.

A short way down the tunnel, they came to another wooden door. Protected from the elements, it was not rotted, and it had a heavy lock, but the door was slightly ajar. The rusty hinges squeaked as Otok leaned all his weight against the door to force it open. As he stepped through the door, the torchlight revealed a small stone chamber with an arched ceiling. Smashed wooden chests were scattered about the room, lying open and empty.

"This must have been a treasure room," said Suraia with excitement.

"It seems like we're a bit late," said Gyank as he bent down to examine a broken chest. "This place must have been discovered a long time ago. All the treasure is gone."

"Sure looks that way," said Otok.

"Maybe not—bring that torch closer," said Gyank, looking carefully at a small chest. In the flickering torchlight, he noticed a crack on the bottom of the chest that was not visible from the inside. "Otok, what do you make of this?"

Otok took out his knife and said, "Why don't we widen the crack and see?"

Gyank held the chest steady as Otok stuck his knife into the crack and pried back and forth. Suraia stood behind him holding the torch, her eyes wide with anticipation as the crack opened wider. Otok twisted the knife until the wood split, exposing a hidden space in the bottom of the chest.

"A false bottom," said Suraia, moving the torch closer to get a better look. "I should have known. My father sometimes hides his valuables in similar ways."

Gyank tilted the chest and a small piece of brown cloth became visible inside the crack. He gently tugged at it with his fingers and pulled out an old cloth rolled into a tube. Gyank opened it carefully, revealing several brightly colored crystals. Yellow, red, and green gems lay neatly next to each other in the cloth, sparkling in the torchlight.

"Let's check the other chests," said Otok, glancing around the room.

They searched all the other chests for similar secret compartments and found two other such hidden treasures. After examining their little pile of jewels, they put them in a small leather pouch that they found on the floor.

"We'll share it evenly between the four of us," said Gyank, tying the pouch securely to his belt.

His words suddenly reminded them of Opus waiting anxiously outside. Having lost track of the time, they quickly walked back to the chamber where the rope hung down from the hole above. The beam of light shining down into the room was considerably dimmer and they knew it was getting late. Suraia took hold of the rope and began to climb. Otok held the burning end of the torch against the stone floor and stepped on it with his boot, extinguishing the flame.

Gyank yelled up to Opus, "We're back. And wait 'till you see what we found. There was treasure down here in the passage. We have a handful of jewels."

Gyank waited for a response, and then shouted a bit louder, "Opus, can you hear me? Opus?"

There was no answer from above, and the smile on Gyank's face turned to an expression of concern.

"Something's wrong!" said Otok as he leapt straight up, caught hold of the rope and climbed as fast as he could. Gyank was right behind him. They heard the sounds of a struggle coming from above followed by Opus's frantic shouts, "Gyank! Otok! It's a trap!"

As Suraia reached the top of the hole, Otok looked up. He saw two pairs of hands take hold of her arms and jerk her out of the hole. Moments later, he reached the top and saw Opus with a man on each side of him holding his wrists and arms as they fought to restrain him. Another man was struggling with Suraia, but she was easily being overpowered. A fourth man came up behind her, pulled her sword from its scabbard and stepped back. Otok felt the point of a sword on the back of his neck and knew that he couldn't fight his way out of this one. With the touch of a sword on his back, he climbed out of the hole.

When Gyank poked his head up, Suraia was being held with one arm twisted behind her back and a knife pointing at her neck, while another man stood nearby with her sword. Opus had stopped struggling and was being held firm by two men. Otok had a sword at his back, and a few yards away was yet another man with an arrow against his bowstring ready to shoot. It wasn't too surprising that it was Norg who stood behind Otok with a sword. He had five men with him, all armed with bows.

Norg looked down at Gyank clinging to the rope and said, "Come up slowly."

Gyank did as he was told.

"Now drop your sword on the ground."

Gyank took the sword from his belt slowly and let it fall to the ground.

"And the hatchet, and the knife."

As Gyank took the hatchet out of his belt, he thought how easily he could kill Norg with one quick throw. Then he glanced at his vulnerable friends and dropped the hatchet and the knife on the ground next to his sword.

Norg poked Otok in the back. "You can drop your knife on the ground as well."

As soon as Otok did so, Norg walked over to Opus and said, "So you didn't like the way I was treating you. You wanted to be on your own." Norg suddenly became angry and his words were cold and harsh. "Now let's get one thing straight. I am your master. You will do as I say, and from now on you won't be given so much freedom." Norg threw a forceful punch into Opus's stomach.

Opus bent over in pain and slumped to his knees. The two men holding him pulled him back up to his feet.

"Do you understand me?" shouted Norg furiously.

Still hunched over, Opus gasped, "Yes ... yes."

"Good."

Norg stepped in front of Gyank and pointed the sword at his throat. "Now you will pay for your foolish bravery—just as I said you would."

With Norg's blade only inches from Gyank's throat, they stood frozen as they stared at each other. Neither of them flinched until suddenly Norg turned to his men and commanded, "Take them to their campsite." Then Norg noticed the pouch on Gyank's waist. "Wait. Didn't I hear one of you shouting about a treasure? Let's see what you have there boy." Norg ripped the pouch from Gyank's side and opened it. "How nice of you to be so generous to your friend's master."

Closing the pouch, he turned to one of his men and said, "Gather up their weapons."

The companions were shoved forward, and while they walked to their campsite, the man with the bow kept his distance so he couldn't be caught off guard. For the moment, they could do nothing to escape.

Once back at camp, it was obvious that Norg's men had searched through their gear and found it to be of little value.

"Tie them up," Norg ordered.

One of the men went into the stone building and came out with a coil of Gyank's rope. As he approached Otok, Suraia sprang into action. She was counting on something that the rest of the party had completely forgotten about, and ripping away from the man who held her, she gave a loud piercing whistle. The hawk perching quietly on the roof of the stone building took wing.

"Tork! Attack!" she shouted as she pointed at Norg.

The hawk swooped down with frightening speed, sinking its talons into the back of Norg's neck. He stumbled back and forth, trying to free himself as the bird flapped its wings violently. The man who Suraia had pulled away from seized her by the arm.

"Call off your bird!" he demanded.

This man happened to be holding Suraia's sword and he reached to pull it from his belt. Suraia grabbed his sword arm with both hands and bit down on his wrist.

Norg fell backward into the wall of the stone building. Tork let go and flew into the air. The man standing at a distance raised his bow and took aim at the bird. But before the arrow left his bow, Gyank bent for a stone and let it whiz through the air. The stone struck the man in the side of the face, and the arrow flew off his bow wildly as he hunched over in pain, clutching his jaw.

Opus took one big step backward and put his entire weight behind his elbow as he drove it into the stomach of a man standing behind him. The man bent over and crumpled to the ground while another man holding the Serpent Blade raised it high in the air to strike down on Opus.

The moment Otok saw the hawk swoop down on Norg, he scanned the ground for a weapon. By the ashes of their campfire was a long straight stick that was going to be used for a tripod. Remembering what Notom taught them about using a staff, he grabbed the end of the stick and swung it at the man who was about to strike down on Opus. He caught the inside of the man's elbow and redirected the sword down to the side. Otok held the staff across his body, ready to block or strike. The man thrust the Serpent Blade at Otok's belly. He stepped aside, and in the same motion, struck the man in the head with the end of the staff. The man was dazed for a moment and Otok took advantage of it. Holding the staff like an axe, he brought it down hard and fast on the man's wrist. The stick made a whooshing sound as it swept through the air, and the Serpent Blade fell to the ground. As Otok scooped it up, he caught sight of the man with the bow taking a bead on him. The stone that Gyank had thrown caused the man's lip to bleed, but he wasn't out of the fight yet, and he shouted, "Enough! Enough!"

The man's shrill voice caused everyone to take notice of him, and for a moment, they all froze. That's when they became aware of a new danger. Before anyone could speak, the silence was broken by a disturbing growl not too far away. It was the unmistakable voice of the wacoba.

Everyone was terrified as they watched the pack of black wolves moving among the ruins. There were too many to count, and they were systematically spreading out to close off any route of escape.

"We're in for the fight of our lives," said one of the men without taking his eyes off the wild beasts gradually moving closer.

"Don't make any sudden moves," said Gyank in a low and deliberate tone of voice as he stepped inside the stone building. Working frantically, he stuffed his stalking clothes and some other supplies into his pack, slung it on his back, and grabbed Otok's bow and quiver before going back outside.

"Here's your bow," he said, handing it to Otok along with the quiver. Without a word, Otok took them and gave Gyank his sword.

Norg's men had prepared their bows and were forming a half circle. With an arrow nocked against his bowstring, Otok joined the semicircle of bowmen while the others gathered behind this protective perimeter. Gyank scanned the area for a way to escape, or for a shelter of some kind, or at least a better place to make a defensive stand. Then he spoke in a low voice, but clearly so everyone could hear him. "If we want to survive this, I suggest we slowly start moving toward that wall over there." Gyank pointed to a relatively low wall not far away that was made of rough stone and easy to climb. The others glanced at the wall but did not answer.

In the same calm but deliberate way, Gyank said, "If we can get to that wall before they charge, we might have a chance. Standing out here in the open will surely get us all killed. If no one panics and starts to run, we just might make it."

With bows ready to shoot and swords in hand, the group started backing up toward the wall. They weren't even half way there when the wacoba charged in for the kill. As the first wave of black fur came at them, arrows flew. Many of the beasts were struck, and they twisted to bite at the arrow shafts sticking out of their bodies. The agony of the wounded didn't stop the others from charging.

The group kept moving toward the wall as fast as they could without actually turning and running. For if they did turn and run, they would be overtaken and ripped to pieces. They fired their arrows as quickly as they could reload, taking aim with every shot. Retreating as they fought, they quickly grew short on arrows, and the last shots were fired as they backed up to the wall.

"Up onto the wall!" shouted Gyank. "It's our only chance!"

Everyone turned, lunged at the wall, and climbed frantically. If they could get to the top, they'd be above the wacoba. Yet this wouldn't provide total safety because the wall was not very high. But maybe this was for the best because when they turned their backs to climb, the wacoba rushed in with great speed, crashing through brush and leaping over broken stone blocks. The group of terrified men scraped and clawed their way up the wall. Two of Norg's men were suddenly caught by the merciless jaws lunging up from below and screamed as they were dragged down. Even before they hit the ground, several other members of the pack were tearing at them, and they were engulfed in writhing, growling black fur.

The rest of the group barely pulled themselves onto the wall before the wacoba were jumping at their feet. For a moment, they just looked down at the wild beasts snarling and snapping up at them and were horrified by what happened to the men who didn't make it. These unfortunate men were already dead, and their remains were being pulled apart by the frenzied pack. But the moments spent looking at this gruesome sight were wasted. For instead of leaping uselessly, now the cunning creatures stepped away from the wall to take a running start. They came flying up the wall using their paws to grip the uneven stones and propel themselves upward.

All the quivers were empty and it was time for the sword bearers to fight the dreaded wacoba. Gyank knelt on top of the wall and used his Serpent Blade to fend off the beasts that lunged up at them. Suraia was by his side. Even Norg, desperate to survive, was slicing down at the black skulls when they came lunging up with teeth flashing.

One of the other men started to climb down the opposite side of the wall, but he was stopped by Opus. "Wait!" shouted Opus, grabbing the man's arm. "There aren't any of those ugly overgrown wolves on this side of the wall now, but it won't take them long to run to a spot where the wall is broken and come through." Opus pointed to a place where the wall had crumbled and there was a gaping hole.

The man looked up at Opus, and as he climbed back onto the wall, he began to panic. "Then we're trapped! We're all going to die!"

Opus quickly looked up and down the wall. They were truly in a bind, and as he tried to find a way out, the situation grew more perilous. The entire pack had gathered right under them, and many more were leaping up the wall, coming much closer to the top with fangs snapping. The three swords were not enough to keep them all at bay, and bows were used to desperately poke at the ferocious predators.

"We can't stay here!" shouted Otok. "Let's move! It's the only way to stop them from dragging us down!"

Otok ran along the top of the wall toward the castle, and everyone else followed in single file. The wacoba charged along the ground in pursuit, jumping up at the feet of their fleeing prey. The wall encircled the castle and was broken in many places. Otok looked ahead to see where it would lead, but it was clear that they were really running nowhere. Sooner or later, he would come to a break in the wall, and they would be in the same situation as before, or maybe worse. Perhaps the wall would be lower, or harder to stand on because of its crumbling condition.

As Otok raced along the top of the wall, he glanced down the hill, and through the trees he saw the river. That's when their only chance of escaping became obvious to him. Pointing down at the unfinished raft, he yelled, "The raft! The raft! Get to the raft!"

Otok charged toward the spot that would give him the shortest route to the raft and then jumped off the wall. It was all downhill. Perhaps too much so, for as they raced down the steep grade, they picked up too much speed and flailed their arms wildly as they tried to keep from falling or crashing into trees growing on the hillside. Yet as fast as they ran, it didn't seem fast enough. The wacoba would soon find the breaks in the wall, and the pack of ravenous animals would be in pursuit once again.

Otok was the first to get to the raft. Quickly slinging his bow on his shoulder, he planted his feet on the riverbank and pushed against the raft with all his might. Seconds later, Gyank was by his side and the raft slowly began sliding into the water. As they pushed, they looked back up the hill. Most of the others were not far behind, but Opus and one of Norg's men were still struggling down the hillside while farther up the slope one member of the pack had found a crack in the wall and was closing fast.

"Come on! Hurry!" yelled Gyank.

Opus lost his footing and slid a short distance before coming to a stop. He glanced back to see one of the wacoba charging down at him.

Gyank shouted up the hill, "RUN! Don't look back! JUST RUN!"

Opus bounced to his feet and bolted. The last of Norg's men was right behind him. One by one, the other men joined in the desperate effort to get the raft afloat. As it slid off the bank and into the water, Suraia came racing toward them and plunged into the river. She came up gasping, threw herself at the raft and clung to it. The rest of the men continued to push the raft away from the bank as they waded out into the river. Chest deep in the water, they began climbing aboard, but some of the logs weren't tied down and started to shift and come loose.

Otok and Gyank stood on the bank waiting for Opus as he bounded down the hillside. They looked back up at the wall, and to their horror, a wave of black beasts was covering the hillside as the wacoba poured down the slope in great numbers.

Opus reached the water and threw himself in, making a big splash. Otok and Gyank were about to dive into the river when they heard a desperate cry for help. Otok stopped and looked back. The last man had tripped on the riverbank and was overcome by the closest member of the pack. The large black wolf straddled the man as he lay on his back, trying to fend off the creature with Gyank's hatchet. The animal's jaws clamped down on the man's forearm, and the beast violently whipped its head back and forth, tearing his flesh and causing the hatchet to fall to the ground.

Otok didn't stop to think. There was no time to think. Something deep in his gut caused him to rush to the man's aid when he saw this terrible sight. He picked up the fallen hatchet and chopped at the back of the wacoba. The beast recoiled into a crouched position, and sprung at Otok, knocking him backward to the ground. The vicious animal snarled, exposing its teeth and gums, and with ears pointed back, it thrust its head forward, snapping at Otok's face. Otok instinctively pulled his head back and to the side while he caught hold of the wacoba's neck with his left hand. Locking his elbow, Otok's stiff-arm barely kept the creature's fangs from closing on his neck as it lurched at him. While Otok savagely chopped up at the beast with the hatchet, the man on the ground next to him scrambled to his feet and lunged into the river.

The wave of black wolves was almost at the bottom of the hill when Otok landed a blow to the creature's head. The hatchet sunk deep into its skull, and as Otok wrenched it free to strike again, the heavy beast fell limp on top of him. Drenched in the creature's blood, Otok started to push the dead animal off him. He looked uphill and caught sight of countless black beasts racing toward him. There was no time for Otok to get up. The wacoba would be on him in seconds. Suddenly, he felt a pair of hands slip under his armpits and clamp down around his chest from behind. With an unusual surge of strength, Gyank lifted his stout friend from under the dead animal and flung both of them off the bank and into the river. As soon as they hit the water, dozens of wacoba were splashing all around them as the wild animals poured into the river. Gyank released his friend, and they swam underwater as far as their breath would take them. When they surfaced, they were a safe distance away. The puzzled wacoba swam around in all directions looking for their prey, which seemed to have vanished. After a short time, the black creatures climbed back up on the bank, shook the water from their fur, and snarled at the raft as they ran along the bank chasing it downstream.

Otok and Gyank swam to the raft and climbed on. Logs that weren't tied down had broken free in the desperate struggle to escape. Even if the raft was complete, it was only designed to hold three or four people and their gear. Now the raft was extremely overloaded, and with all the extra weight, it was barely afloat. Water came up through the spaces between the logs, and no one was sitting on a dry spot.

For a while, no one said anything. They just sat or lay on the raft and rested. Norg had blood running down his back from the wounds inflicted by Suraia's hawk. The man who was caught from behind by the wacoba was gripping his forearm in an attempt to stop the bleeding, and none of the others were without bruises and scrapes. For the moment, they were safe. The black wolves ran along the riverbank after them, but they were clearly out of reach. It was just a matter of time before the wacoba gave up and disappeared back into the forest.

It was nearing dusk as the half-submerged raft drifted along, carried by the currents of the river. Shaken by their narrow escape from a horrible death, the exhausted group paid no attention to the river itself. After it was too late to change their course, they realized the river was moving them along at a great pace. The wide gentle river had narrowed and was getting much swifter. The waves grew and they went around a bend to find themselves helpless in a torrent of white water. As the rapids tossed the raft violently up and down, the man with his forearm ripped open couldn't hold on and he went sliding off into the water. The others quickly lost sight of him in the white foam of the river. They had no way to steer the raft, which twisted and spun out of control. It crashed into a boulder with a heavy flow of water spilling over it. The sharp jolt threw Suraia off, but she clung to the side of the raft as she was dragged along.

Gyank grabbed her wrist and shouted, "Climb back on!" The roar of the rapids was so loud that he could hardly hear himself. As Gyank leaned over to pull her up, the raft smashed against a huge rock sticking up out of the water. The impact was so great that it threw him head first into the powerful waves while cracking one of the logs in two. The raft bounced off the rock and spun in a circle as the rapids pulled it around the side of the boulder back into the main flow of the river. Otok scanned the churning foam for his friend. There were boulders everywhere, and the water splashed and pounded as it spilled through the maze of rocks. Neither Gyank nor Suraia was visible in the roaring water as it shot down river.

"Hang on!" yelled one of the men who was looking ahead.

The raft took such a dip that everyone was submerged in the turbulent water. When the raft bobbed back up to the surface, Otok wiped the water off his face and looked to see who was still hanging on. Opus and Norg had been swept off while the last two men were desperately clinging to the sides of the raft. Otok took a quick look at the rapids ahead and tightened his grip. The raft was thrown about and yanked from side to side. Otok didn't look up anymore. He flattened himself against the logs and hung on with all his might. He felt the raft hit another rock and he heard a loud crack as more logs splintered and pieces of the raft broke off. He held his breath as the remains of the raft submerged. When the raft surfaced, he took another gasp and held it. Moments later, he felt the raft plunge over a steep drop and crash straight down as it capsized. He still didn't let go. Holding on as the violent water swept him downstream, he worked his way to the surface and climbed on top of the cluster of broken logs. He was the only one still hanging onto what was left of the raft.

As suddenly as the river became rough and merciless, it calmed and Otok clung to the logs while the current slowly carried him into a small cove off the main flow of the river. Otok reached down with one foot to see if he could touch bottom. The water was only waist-deep, and with one leg hanging down to the rocky riverbed, he pushed the remains of the raft to the bank. Exhausted, Otok dragged himself onto the shore and collapsed. After a few moments, he looked up. He was on the other side of the river and figured that he was safe from the wacoba. The sky was growing dark. He tried to get up, but weakness overcame him and he fell back down. As he rested, he couldn't resist falling off into a deep sleep. He slept so soundly that the heavy rain that came down upon the Great Andelron River during the night did not wake him.

Chapter 7

GROK THE MIGHTY

When Otok awoke it was early the next morning. The heavy rain that came down during the night had left its mark on everything. The trees and vegetation were wet and drooping. The boulders along the bank were still damp, and small grooves were carved into the mud where water collected and ran off into the river. Yet the day after the stormy night was calm and the sun was bright.

Otok sat up, rubbed his eyes, and looked around. He was as lost as a person could be, but this didn't bother him in the least. His only concern was for his friends. He realized they could have been killed in the rapids, but he forced that thought out of his mind. Even so, they might be injured or on the other side of the river where the wacoba were, or both. Wherever they were, they were most likely separated and on their own just like him.

On the ground next to him was his bow, half sunk in the riverbank where the storm had packed sandy mud neatly around it. He was fortunate that it had stayed on his shoulder during the ride down the rapids. But his quiver was empty, and a bow with no arrows is no protection. Otok plucked his bow out of the mud, wiped it off, and stood up. He, too, was covered in dried sandy mud, and as he brushed himself off, he noticed Gyank's hatchet tucked in his belt.

Although the heavy rain would have washed away any tracks his friends might have made, Otok was going to find them no matter where they were. He knew they could have drifted past him as he lay on the bank exhausted, but since they fell off the raft farther upstream, that's where he would look first. As he searched, he scanned the boulders in the water as well as the opposite side of the river, but he saw no sign of his friends.

Otok had gone only a short distance upstream when he heard a groan coming from the woods. He stopped and listened. Moments later, he heard the groan again, got a fix on the general direction of the sound, and took off. The woods were swollen with vegetation, and he forced his way through as he fought with the underbrush. He heard the sound again, and even though it was very close, he couldn't see anyone.

"Where are you?" he called as he climbed over a moss-covered log.

Just then, Otok came upon a pair of bare legs sticking out from under a fallen tree. These short skinny legs obviously did not belong to anyone he knew. Otok walked around the tree to see who was trapped underneath. He found an old man lying face down with his hips pinned against the ground. From where Otok stood, he could see part of the man's wrinkled face and his long white beard, which was caught under his chest.

"Are you hurt badly?" asked Otok.

"I'm trapped. I can't move."

"Just wait a moment. I'll get you out."

Otok got down on one knee and put his shoulder under a heavy limb sticking out from the tree. He placed his hands under the limb with his elbows close to his body, and using his powerful legs, he tried to lift the tree. Otok grunted and strained, but his efforts were useless. He had to think of another way to get the man out. After a brief pause, he said, "I'll be right back."

Otok left the man and went looking for a long straight branch to use as a lever. There were many dead branches on the forest floor, but dead wood would break too easily. Otok would have to cut a limb from a live hardwood tree. The Forest of Elreia was many centuries old, and Otok found himself surrounded by mature trees that grew to enormous size. He noticed a gigantic tree with countless branches shooting off from the trunk in all directions. He climbed up to a thick branch that was relatively close to the ground, and sitting on the branch that he was cutting, he put Gyank's hatchet to use. Once the limb fell from the tree,

Otok jumped to the ground. The long hefty branch was not exactly straight, but it would do. He returned to the trapped man, placed the heavier end of the branch under the tree, and put a large stone under it so he could use it as a lever.

"Now, when I lift the tree, you pull yourself out from under it."

Lying with his face against the ground, the man shook his head. "Alright."

Otok pulled down on the branch slowly, applying more and more pressure until he was leaning on the branch with his feet barely touching the ground. The tree only moved a tiny bit when they heard the sound of cracking wood. The branch was bending to its limit and was starting to break. Otok realized this was not going to work, and he eased off slowly to avoid having the tree come down hard on the man.

"No," said the old man. "This is not going to work. I'm trapped here for good. It would take a team of strong horses to lift this tree off me."

The man was right, but his comment gave Otok an idea. "Perhaps we don't have to lift the tree at all."

Otok took the large stone he had used with the lever and wedged it under the tree close to the man's hips. "That will keep the tree from coming down any farther," he said as he started pulling dirt away from the man's hip opposite the stone. Soon he had dug a small trench next to the man. Lying on his belly, Otok reached under the man's hips to pull out handfuls of soil. "Try to wiggle out," he said.

The man slowly inched his way out from under the tree as Otok alternated between digging and gently tugging on his arms. Soon he was free and sitting on the ground next to the tree. He was covered with dirt.

"How do you feel?" asked Otok while the old man tried to brush the mud off his long white beard.

"I feel very lucky. If you hadn't come by, I would have laid there until I died. I owe you my life. If there's anything you want, just ask."

Otok ignored the man's offer. "How are your legs?"

"I can move them. I don't seem to have any broken bones. My back aches, but I think I can walk. Let's see."

Otok helped the small frail man to his feet. He was a bit shaky on his spindly old legs, and although he straightened up as much as he could, the curving of his spine over the years caused his long pointy beard to hang away from his body. He wore short pants made from tanned animal hide and a shirt woven from the bark of a stringy plant. His head was bald and his wrinkly face was that of a very old man. The only possessions he had with him were a bow made of wood and a leather quiver filled with arrows.

"How did you get yourself trapped under that tree?" asked Otok.

"I was heading home when I got caught in that heavy downpour. I threw myself to the ground, and there was a flash of lightning and a loud clap of thunder followed by the sound of cracking wood. I felt the tree come down on top of me, and I must have blacked out. When I woke, it was daylight."

"You threw yourself down before you heard the thunder?" asked Otok, thinking that this was a bit strange.

The man grabbed his beard up by his chin while looking at the ground. "Did I say that? No, couldn't be. I must have fallen to the ground when the tree came down on top of me. Yes, that's how it happened."

The man purposely did not look up at Otok. Instead, he kept his eyes fixed on the fallen tree. Otok was suspicious. He had heard correctly when the man said that he threw himself to the ground before the tree fell on him. Perhaps it was an insignificant slip of the tongue, yet Otok knew that if the tree had hit him while he was standing, it would have killed him.

"Well, however it happened," said the man, "when I awoke, I was trapped, and I just laid there until you came. Now I'm forever grateful. Whatever service I can be to you, just ask it of me."

"I don't suppose you would know where my friends are?"

"I'm sorry. Seasons go by and I see not a soul. But tell me about these friends you seek, and what brings you to this part of the woods."

"It's a long story, and I have little time. I must find my friends."

"If you wish, I'll help you look for them. I know the woods well. But come to my cottage first. I am weak and aching."

"I can't," said Otok. "My friends are lost in the woods here somewhere, and they may be hurt."

"Please, my cottage is not far from here, and I may be able to help you more than you think. Besides, your friends will be alright."

The man spoke as if he knew something that Otok didn't. There was a warm wholesome look in his eyes, and Otok figured a short trip to see that the frail old man got home safely wouldn't delay him long. After a moment of hesitation, Otok said, "Oh, alright."

The old man held onto Otok's arm for support, and he pointed the way as he guided them around fallen trees and moss covered boulders. He knew his way through woods and the walk was surprisingly easy considering the denseness of the forest.

"Do you live alone?" asked Otok.

"Yes."

"How does one so old come to live alone in such a dangerous forest?"

"To use your own words, it's a long story." Twisting his head to look up at Otok, he smiled. "Why don't we start with simpler questions? My name is Melnick. What do your friends call you?"

"My friends call me Otok."

"Tell me about the friends you're searching for."

Otok saw no harm in it, so he began by telling Melnick that he and his closest friend set out to seek their fortune. As he described their adventures, he was careful not to say anything about the book or the witch. Melnick listened intensely and with no change of expression until Otok mentioned that they had been attacked by black wolves.

Melnick's eyes opened wide with surprise. "You mean the wacoba?"

"I think that's what some people call them," said Otok. "They're as black as night and as dreadful as hounds from hell."

"That's them alright. Here in Elreia we call them wacoba. People from other lands refer to them as black wolves, or more often as Elreia wolves. Whatever you call them, they're my greatest fear. Not a creature large or small can withstand them. It's miraculous indeed that you survived the encounter. How did you escape?"

"We came down the river on a raft. That's where my story ends. Everyone was swept off into the rapids except for me. I have no idea where my friends are, or if they're hurt, or even dead. One thing I can tell you for certain, if they're able, they are searching for me right now."

At that moment, they came to a tiny clearing in the woods where Otok's eyes fell upon a most bizarre sight. There was a cottage built into the hollow parts of a living tree, a species of which Otok had never seen. Stringy moss drooped off crooked pitched roofs, and large round holes in the trunk served as windows. These holes were not cut into the tree but were instead natural knotholes where huge branches once grew. Indeed, not a single blow from an axe was struck against the tree in the process of building this peculiar home. Coarse gray bark enveloped the cottage as if the tree was trying to swallow it. A maze of intertwining roots sprouted from the base of the trunk and ran along the ground like hundreds of crooked fingers. The thickest roots outlined a winding path of slate leading to a door at the entrance. Above the cottage, twisting branches fanned out in all directions, and every root and limb was covered with fuzzy green moss. It seemed as if a giant creature that lived underground was reaching up with its many tentacles to engulf the cottage and pull it into the earth. Through breaks in the leaves above, beams of sunlight cast eerie patches of light and shadow upon the entire structure. There was a strange feeling in the air, as if the cottage was bewitched or haunted. It seemed to be the abode of mysterious powers and ancient witchcraft.

"This is my home," said Melnick.

"Now that you're home safe, you can rest, and I can go and look for my friends."

"Won't you grace me with your presence by coming into my humble cottage?"

Otok thought the strange tree house was anything but humble. And if he didn't know any better, he might have suspected that Melnick was an evil gnome trying to lure him into his lair. But the old man seemed so helpless that Otok was not at all afraid.

"I can't stay," said Otok. "I understand you need someone to talk to because you're lonely. But my friends might be in danger and I must go."

"My good man, you are mistaken. I do live alone, but that's not why I invite you into my home. The very thing that compels you to search for your friends is the reason I ask you to stay just a short time longer. I believe you are to be the chosen one."

"What are you talking about?" said Otok impatiently. "Chosen for what? I have no time for riddles. Besides, who are you to choose me for anything? You don't even know me."

"Please, don't get upset," said Melnick. "I may know you better than you think. Sometimes it doesn't take long to judge a man's character. Based on what you told me about your adventures, I can see you have many rare qualities. You've freed an enslaved man, escaped the wacoba, survived the Great Andelron, and now, lost in the forest and weaponless except for a tiny hatchet, your only concern is for your friends. A man of such character is rare indeed." Melnick looked at Otok and smiled warmly. "Please, let me tell you my story. You will not be sorry."

Otok wondered if Melnick really did have something important to tell him or if he was just a lonely old man. Or perhaps this was some kind of wicked trap. Whichever the case, Otok followed him along the slate path to the entrance of the tree cottage. As Otok stepped between the moss-covered roots protruding from the earth, he couldn't help but imagine that they might suddenly grab him. Otok had to duck his head to get through the door, and once inside, the ceiling was uncomfortably low. Yet for Melnick, it was just the right height. A bench made from a split log sat near a table in front of a large round window.

Melnick gestured with his hand and said, "Please sit."

Otok sat on the bench while Melnick pulled up a crooked, three-legged stool and sat across the table from him. Drawing in a deep breath, the old hermit began his story.

"Many years ago, Elreia was a place where evil thrived. Both men and beasts ruled the forest by might. Only the greatest fighters with the best weapons could survive. It was during this time that Grok was born into the world. All those who were unjust grew afraid, for the legend of Grok the Mighty was known throughout the land."

"This was many decades ago. Now Elreia is no longer plagued by war. But the many years of warfare destroyed its people and their culture. Great cities and kingdoms fell into ruin. I came to this land at the very end of that terrible age of bloodshed. I was traveling through the woods when I came across a lone warrior who was being hunted by evil men. His name was Lorgradan. He was a big, powerful man, and of the best fighters in the land. But he had been pierced by an arrow, and he lay wounded in the forest, waiting to die or to be captured. The enemy was closing in on him, and there were too many for Lorgradan to fight them all. His situation was hopeless, but he did not fear death. What he feared was that his soul would never rest for breaking a solemn oath that he and a long line of his ancestors had taken. One by one, they all had made the same vow, for Lorgradan was given a great honor and responsibility by his father. He was the wielder of the great battle-axe, Grok the Mighty."

"You mean to say that Grok is an axe?"

"That's right."

"But didn't you say that Grok was born into the world?"

"Yes, and in a manner of speaking, it's true, for Grok seems to have a life of its own."

Otok looked at him with utter disbelief. "Come on now—an axe with a life of its own? I may be young, but I'm not stupid."

"Let me finish before you draw a conclusion."

Melnick slowly grabbed his chin with one hand and ran it down his beard. "Grok, according to legend, was the greatest battle-axe ever forged. It was said that whoever wielded the mighty axe could not be defeated in battle. He could overcome any foe that stood against him. Incredible as it may seem, the legend states that Grok's power would actually increase when it was needed most. There was only one undesirable thing about Grok. Whoever had the honor of carrying the mighty axe into battle, also had the responsibility of keeping it safe. The warrior who had been deemed Wielder of Grok had to vow that he would protect the great axe from falling into the hands of evil men. He had to pledge his life to keeping this vow, and his soul would be cursed if he failed. Since it was forged, all previous wielders of the axe had kept their vow. Lorgradan was the last of a long line of great warriors who feared the curse of their ancestors."

"When I found Lorgradan, he was desperate. He was lying on the forest floor, clenching the axe as he bled to death. Gasping for breath and mumbling his last prayer, he grabbed hold of my foot when he saw me standing over him. He begged me to take the axe. He told me of Grok's power and of the great responsibility of having it. I took pity on Lorgradan, and so I relieved him of the axe." Melnick shook his finger at Otok to make his point perfectly clear. "But understand this—I took the axe as a keeper of it—not as a wielder of it."

Melnick paused and sat straight up in his stool. "Lorgradan was extremely grateful that I had removed this heavy burden from him, and thereby freed him from the curse. He died right there where he gave me the axe. Then I heard the pursuing enemy coming through the forest, and I fled."

Otok looked Melnick straight in the eye, and said, "I suppose you want me to take the axe. Why? So you could relieve yourself of the burden?"

"I only took the axe as a keeper of it. In this way, I was not bound to it. I took no vow, and I've never used the axe once in all my days.

I've kept it safe, but make no mistake—I am not a wielder of the great axe. It's not a burden to me and never has been."

"What makes you think that I would want it?"

"To answer your question, I must tell you the part of my story that I dread to speak of."

A passing cloud cut off the beams of light streaming through the trees, and the clearing in front of the cottage grew eerily dark. The old hermit leaned toward Otok, placing his elbows on the table between them. He peered out from under his heavy eyebrows while he spoke softly. "You asked me before, how did I come to live alone? I've been either blessed or cursed. I don't know which. But I live the life of a hermit not by my own wishes. Every place that I've gone to settle down, people eventually find out my secret and drive me away."

"You mean about Grok?"

"No," he whispered with emphasis. "My secret is far more powerful and dangerous than the axe." A wild fearful look came to his eyes, and he said, "I am a seer—a clairvoyant. I have visions of things happening far away, or things that will happen in the future. I have this gift, or call it a curse if you will, for most folks are deathly afraid of me. I've tried to hide it, yet in time, people always find out. I'm labeled a witch and driven away."

Melnick grew silent. He seemed to be waiting for Otok to pass judgment on him as if he was a criminal who had just confessed to a crime. Otok said nothing. He merely gazed at the old hermit in amazement. Then he remembered what Melnick had said about the falling tree, and just as Otok was about to speak, Melnick said, "Last night this power saved my life. During the storm, an urgent message flashed through my mind that told me to drop to the ground. I didn't stop to wonder about it. I just threw myself on the ground. This saved my life, for the tree would have killed me if I was standing."

Otok was stunned. Not only did this explain the incident, but Melnick spoke of it just as the thought popped into Otok's mind. Ignoring the surprised look on Otok's face, Melnick spoke as if he was absolutely sure of what he was saying. "In my mind, I've seen terrible things. A time of war and bloodshed is in the making. Grok has been dormant for ages. Now it has come time for the mighty axe to be held by a great warrior once again. I am far too old to take Grok on myself. I'm even too old to go in search of a man worthy of Grok. So I've been hoping that one day someone would come to me, someone who is worthy. You are young and strong, but most of all you are loyal. If you could have the same loyalty toward the destruction of evil that you have for your friends, then you are to be the new Wielder of Grok. But you must vow to use Grok only to fight evil in the world, and never to let it fall into evil hands."

Otok didn't believe a weapon could be cursed. He also didn't believe that an axe could give a fighter power that he did not already have. Yet he wondered if Melnick could really see into the future, or had old age and life as a hermit distorted his mind. Perhaps the incident with the falling tree was just luck. Wanting to separate truth from legend, Otok questioned the old hermit. "What terrible things have you seen in your mind? How do you know they're not just nightmares?"

"You doubt me. I'm not surprised. But let me tell you more. I can sense evil intensifying in the south. A dark and powerful secret may soon be uncovered in the Land of Shar, and war is in the making. Battles will be fought not over land, or food, or kings' realms. They will be fought over the power of knowledge. A mysterious and deadly secret that has been buried and long forgotten may very well resurface. And if wicked minds learn this secret, untold horrors will be unleashed upon the world. Evil will spread out from the Land of Shar, like a plague sweeping across the land."

Otok sat there in shock, his mind raced with questions. Could Melnick's psychic visions have anything to do with their quest? Could he have foreseen them finding the book? If so, might he know where it's hidden? Otok wanted so badly to ask these questions, but he held his tongue. Notom had taught him well, and he didn't have to learn the same lesson twice. He couldn't risk saying anything about the book.

"Go on," said Otok impatiently. "What else have you foreseen? Can you give me any details?"

"These visions are vague and foggy. Images flash through my mind, and I do my best to make sense of them. Of all my premonitions, the dark power that lies hidden is the most unclear. But I am certain that men are talking war. I don't know how fast the wheels of destruction are turning, but preparations are being made. Of this, I am certain." Melnick noticed the concerned look on Otok's face. "Why are you so worried? There's no immediate danger. It may be a while before any of this comes to pass."

Ignoring Melnick's attempt to put his mind at ease, Otok spoke with grave urgency. "Isn't there any more you can tell me? Anything at all?"

There was something about Otok's intense desire to know more that seemed to prompt a bizarre and frightful response from the old hermit. He sat up straight on his stool, his eyes became unfocused, and he appeared to look right through Otok as if he wasn't there. Melnick did not speak in his normal voice. Instead, his voice was strained and he spoke unusually loud as if he was no longer in the small room. He addressed no one in particular as the words came issuing out from his lips.

"Beware! Great battles will be fought and kingdoms will fall, but when it is all over, a far greater danger will arise. All will seem well in the world, but don't be fooled. All is not well. An evil force will grow and spread undetected, increasing in strength. It will follow you wherever you go. You cannot run from it. It must be faced by each man. Put aside selfishness, and unify. It is the only way to conquer this evil, for only in the hearts of good men can it be defeated. The battlefield is in your mind."

Otok sat listening in horror. These words did not seem to come from Melnick himself, but from some other mysterious source. Otok wasn't sure if he was more frightened by the message or by the strange way that it was delivered. Then just as quickly as Melnick fell into this eerie mode of speech, he broke out of his stare as if an invisible force had released him from its grip. Life came back into his eyes and he looked at Otok.

"What does it mean?" asked Otok, not realizing his question implied that Melnick was only the deliverer of the message.

"I'm not sure."

"Was this warning meant for me?"

"I believe it's meant for everyone. It applies to us all."

"What is this evil force?"

"I don't know. But I'm sure you'll agree most evil begins in the mind. And if it is defeated there, it cannot grow and spread. We must guard our thoughts as we guard our most precious treasures."

"Good things also begin as thoughts in someone's mind," said Otok.

"And so they do. But rather than trying to interpret this vague message, let me tell you what is clear to me. I've seen destruction in the Land of Shar. I don't know the exact circumstances, but I do know there are terrible forces waiting to be set in motion. This is why I tell you to take Grok. Even in the greatest of wars, one man's efforts can make a difference in the outcome of events."

Otok figured that if Melnick's prophecy had any truth in it, then it might be best to take the axe. "Alright," he said. "Let's see this great axe."

"Not so fast. First you must vow to use it only for the destruction of evil, and never to let it fall into the hands of evil men."

"I will do my best. I give you my word."

"Grok will serve you well, but remember, if you fail to keep your vow, according to legend, the ghosts of all the prior wielders of the axe will torment you from then on. The spirits of those great warriors will not allow you to rest—not in this life, and not even in the spirit world after your death."

These words were a grave warning, yet Otok wasn't concerned. He figured that such curses were the result of stories made up long ago to encourage loyalty. And as the years went by, the myth of the axe must have grown from legend into reality in the minds of gullible people. Just when Otok had reasoned it out with common sense, a thought that did not seem to be his own invaded his mind and he thought to himself, what if I'm wrong? Otok was suddenly jolted back to his current surroundings by Melnick's voice. "Your solemn vow is accepted."

Melnick stood up and climbed a short ladder leading to a small circular door by the ceiling. The door opened into what was apparently a hollow limb of the tree. Melnick crawled up into the dark tunnel and disappeared. Moments later, his feet emerged as the tiny man crawled backward onto the ladder, his long white beard slipping down out of the hole after him. In his hands was a long object wrapped in a cloth. He put it on the table and carefully unwrapped it. There, in the opened cloth, lay the great battle-axe, Grok. It was a single-edged weapon with a long handle. The head of the axe was forged from a strange gray metal, which was extremely strong, yet unusually light. It was skillfully hammered to create a large sweeping edge that curved up to a point above the top of the handle. The back end of the head curved slightly upward, but it did not form an edge or point. Otok wondered if it was fashioned that way for a specific purpose, or just for style. The handle was long to give a good full swing. It was made of a rare hardwood unknown to Otok, which had a smooth, close grain, yet it was not slippery and provided a good grip. This particular type of wood was extremely hard, yet flexible so it wouldn't break. There was no fancy engraving in the head or handle, and it was adorned with no symbol or crest of any kind. Although centuries old, Grok seemed timeless as its edge was still sharp and shiny, and the handle was in excellent condition except for a few battle scars. Apparently, the materials selected in making this weapon were the very best and chosen to last the ages. Grok was a durable tough weapon indeed.

After everything Melnick had said about the axe, Otok was somewhat disappointed. "What's so great about this axe? It looks just like any other axe."

"Yes, that's the beauty of it. Grok looks like an ordinary axe. It's the same with men; you don't know how special they are until you know what they can do."

Otok still believed the axe's power came from myth and legend rather than from its metal and wood. But he decided to take the axe because the old hermit seemed certain that he should have it. Besides, legend or no legend, Otok needed a good solid weapon.

As Otok sat there looking down at the axe, Melnick said, "In Lorgradan's day, I'm sure there was an elaborate ceremony to proclaim a new wielder of the mighty axe, but I know of no such ritual to pass Grok on to a new warrior."

"That's quite alright," said Otok. "We can do without it. Instead, maybe you can tell me more about the Land of Shar?"

"When you get there, keeping your vow will prove critical."

"What makes you think I'm going to the Land of Shar? Did you see that in your mind as well?"

"I didn't have to see that in a vision. I know simply by the way you've acted. I can also see that you have your doubts about the power of Grok. That's alright. I've seen enough to know that you'll do the right thing. And although you don't fear being cursed, you will be loyal to Grok's purpose. Any more about the outcome of things, I cannot say."

Otok looked out the round window at the moss-covered roots in front of the cottage. Of all the things the old hermit said, how much or what parts were true, he could not know. But he had no time to ponder about it. He picked Grok up out of the open cloth and said, "Thank you for the axe. But now I should be off. Time is passing."

As Otok headed for the door, Melnick said, "You will do the right thing."

"That's always my intention," said Otok.

The short experience with this wrinkled wisp of a man had been amazing, yet it resulted in only one thing that was certain, Otok had the axe named Grok, and at least to Melnick, that was important.

Chapter 8

THE BRINGERS OF EVIL

When Gyank opened his eyes, he was lying face up in a primitive hut made of sticks and leaves. He remembered falling off the raft while trying to save Suraia. After plunging into the swirling water, he managed to grab hold of Suraia as she went under. Gyank held onto her with one arm while he fought to keep both their heads above the violent water. Eventually, he dragged Suraia to the shore and then collapsed. That was the last thing he could remember.

Gyank put his hand up to his head and felt a big bump. Apparently, he had hit his head on a rock while struggling to get ashore. He slowly sat up and scanned the inside of the hut. It was empty except for the woven grass mat that he sat upon. He was alone and his possessions were gone. Outside the circular entrance to the crude shelter was a barefooted man standing guard, and from what Gyank saw, the man wore only a loincloth. Gyank wondered if he was a prisoner, or if he was being protected from the dangers of the forest. It seemed as if he was in a village because he could hear people talking and the sounds of children playing. Yet he could not make out a single word that was spoken.

He wondered where his friends were and if they were alright, but he didn't have much time to think about it because the guard noticed he was awake and shouted to someone in a strange language. Then he entered the hut and stood blocking the exit with his arms folded on his bare chest. He was deeply tanned and had red and black lines painted on his face that made him look fierce. He wore a necklace with teeth and claws of such great proportions that one would think the man had killed a monster in order to adorn himself.

The guard looked down at Gyank and didn't say a word. Moments later, he moved aside to allow an old man with stringy gray hair to enter the hut. The old man wore brown leather pants, crudely stitched together at the seams, and an open vest with colorful beads hanging from the front and back. He also wore a necklace with teeth and claws, but in the center was a small skull. The cord ran through the holes where the eyes used to be.ABut if he believed in such creatures, he would have sworn it was a tiny dragon skull.

The old man sat down and gestured with his hands, first pointing to himself, and then at Gyank. "I am Guda. I am headman of village. Who are you?"

Obviously, he did not speak the common language very well. He spoke slowly with many pauses, and he gestured with almost every sentence to help make himself understood. Even so, Gyank was pleasantly surprised to find someone who spoke his language at all.

"I am Gyank."

"What evils do you bring?"

"I don't bring any evils. I am a peaceful man."

When the headman spoke, the meaning of some of his hand gestures was clear. Other gestures made no sense to Gyank, but apparently, Guda was using a form of sign language along with his words.

"Witch doctor say … you are like evil men of the past. He say … you come here is bad sign."

"How can this be? I don't even know how I got here."

"Fishermen found you by river … bring you here. You … and others like you … are bringers of evil."

"Others like me? You mean you've found the others? Where are they?"

"One found dead … a man. One found alive … a girl … dressed as evil fighter from the past. She is hurt … she cries."

Before Guda finished moving his fingers down his cheeks, signifying tears, Gyank started to get up. "Where are they? I must see them."

"Sit!" demanded Guda, holding his hand out flat in Gyank's face. "You do as I say."

Gyank sat back down and Guda said, "Dead man was given back to river, for it was river that took his life. Witch doctor help girl." Guda paused, and then asked, "Why you come to our land? Why you bring evil to us?"

"We don't bring evil to you. We're just travelers. We fell off our raft and the river brought us here."

"You blame river?" said Guda, apparently upset by Gyank's comment. "River brings good things to my people. River does not bring evil."

"We're not evil," protested Gyank.

Guda made many hand gestures as he struggled with the language. "Old people of village ... remember old days ... days of men with light skin ... and stone shirts that shine like sun on river ... and stone masks with little holes ... so their warriors see us ... but we cannot see their faces. They were the evil ones ... and you are of their children."

Gyank realized that Guda was referring to men with helmets dressed in plate mail armor. Guda looked up at the guard and said something in their own language. The guard nodded his head and left the hut. Moments later, he came back with Gyank's pack and his sword.

Guda handed the sword to Gyank. "Is this yours?"

"Yes."

"Then witch doctor is right. You are a son of the evil ones."

"I found that sword in a pool farther up the river."

"Again you blame river for your evil!" said Guda sternly.

Gyank didn't respond. He realized that such superstitious people could not be reasoned with, and he was not going to change their minds about anything. Gyank was at Guda's mercy, and he knew that these people were going to do whatever they wanted with him and Suraia.

Lifting his gaze from the floor of the hut, Gyank looked at Guda and asked, "What are you going to do with us?"

"I do nothing with you. It is you that must do something."

Gyank didn't understand. Were they going to force him to perform some kind of deadly ritual task that would result in his execution? Afraid of what Guda might say, Gyank asked, "What do you want me to do?"

"Leave my people. Take your evil ... and go out of our land."

After wondering about what these people might do to him considering they thought he was evil, Gyank was surprised and relieved that Guda simply wanted him to leave.

"I will do that," said Gyank. "You are good people, and I will leave you in peace. But please let me speak to the girl that you found by the river. If she can travel, I will take her with me."

Guda led Gyank through the village to a small hut, and without a word, pointed to the entrance. Gyank bent down and went inside. A man dressed in a strange costume was kneeling next to Suraia. Yellow and white paint covered his face except for right around his eyes, which were painted black. He looked terrifying as the whites of his eyes were accented when he opened and closed his eyelids. His body was covered in furry animal skins, and long strings of beads and feathers dangled from his neck. On top of his head was a hat composed of shiny black fur and dagger-like canine teeth. An assortment of herbs in small stone cups were scattered about him on the floor, and he was waving a smoldering leaf over Suraia's body. One of her ankles was wrapped in mud and black leaves. She was awake, but she didn't move until she saw Gyank. Then she suddenly pushed herself up to a sitting position.

"Gyank! Are you alright? After we got to shore, you collapsed and I couldn't wake you. I hurt my ankle and couldn't walk. These savages came out of the woods and surrounded us. I was afraid they'd kill us both. I tried to talk to them, but they don't speak our language. They brought us here and I met Guda. But he thinks we're evil. And now this scary savage is waving things over me and chanting. What are they going to do with us?"

"Don't worry," said Gyank, trying to calm her down. "These are good people, and they're trying to help you." Gyank knelt by Suraia's feet and carefully removed some of the muddy leaves from her ankle. It was a dark blue and badly swollen. "I hope it's not broken."

Gyank looked up at Guda who was standing next to him. "Do you think you can heal her?"

"We must heal her. If not ... her evil will stay in village ... and haunt people. When she is well ... she must leave." Guda pointed at Gyank and spoke with stern authority. "But you ... must leave now!"

Gyank took Suraia's hand and said, "You're safe here. Let them work their healing on you. I must go, but I'll come back for you once I've found the others."

Suraia looked horrified. "Please don't leave me alone with these savages. Who knows what they'll do to me?"

Perplexed by her reaction, Gyank said, "These people have done nothing but try to help you. I must find Otok and Opus. They might be hurt like you, or maybe in a worse situation. I'll be back for you as soon as I can. I promise."

"No! Don't leave me!" pleaded Suraia as tears formed in her eyes and rolled down her face. "Don't leave me with these savages."

"Listen to me," said Gyank. "These people are not savages. How can you say that? They're trying to help you. Can't you see that? I'm going to find the others. I would take you with me if I could, but it's far better for you to stay here. It's safer and you'll have a chance to heal."

Gyank stood up and left Suraia crying. Once outside the hut, Guda said, "You say ... you go and find the others. How many others?"

"There were six. Two of them are my friends, but there were also four other bad men who came down the river. Your people found one man dead. I'm hoping it was not one of my friends. If there is evil coming, it will be coming with those bad men."

"It is how I feared," said Guda. "Bad times coming."

"There were only four of them, and now I'm hoping that it's only three. That can hardly mean bad times."

"You not understand. It is a sign ... bad times coming."

Gyank slung his pack onto his back and asked, "Which way to the river?"

Without a word, Guda pointed with his finger. Gyank looked at the sun to get his bearings and said, "Northwest. Good. That means the wolves are on the other side of the river. I just hope I don't run into another pack of them."

Gyank left the village and made his way through the woods. Soon he heard the sound of the rapids. When he got to the riverbank, he began to search downstream for any sign of his friends or the raft. He had not gone far when he came to a bend in the river where the trees came down to the water's edge. To his surprise, Otok was coming around the bend toward him.

"Otok!" he shouted.

Otok saw him, and they ran to meet each other.

"You're alright," said Gyank as he grabbed his friend by the shoulders. "I thought you might be dead."

"I'm fine. Have you seen anyone else?"

"Suraia and I were taken to a village by native people of the forest. She's hurt, but she'll be fine. I left her with them to look for you and Opus. Have you seen him?"

"No, I haven't."

"The natives found a dead man floating in the river. I'm hoping it's not Opus."

"I hope so too," said Otok.

They stood there quietly for a moment, trying not to think the worst. Then Otok broke the silence. "Are you sure the natives are friendly?"

"I think so. They're probably the people of the forest that Smilga told us about."

"She called them Erifs, didn't she?"

"That's right, and they sure have a strange way of looking at things, but I don't think they're dangerous."

"That's good, but we may have more trouble on our hands."

"What do you mean?"

"I've had a bit of an adventure myself this morning. Take a look at this." Otok lifted the bottom of his loose fitting shirt, which concealed the head of the axe.

"A battle-axe," said Gyank with surprise. "Where did you get it?"

Otok took Grok from his belt and showed it to Gyank. "It's a long story," he said. "Why don't we keep searching for Opus while I tell you?"

"Good idea."

As Otok put the axe back in his belt, he remembered Gyank's hatchet. "Oh yeah, I almost forgot, here's your hatchet," he said, taking it from his belt and handing it to Gyank.

"My hatchet! I thought I had lost it for good."

Otok looked upriver and said, "I was the only one to hold onto the raft until it came to calm water. From there I started searching upstream."

"And I've been searching downstream," said Gyank. "Since neither of us found him, our best bet is to look downriver from where you came ashore."

"That sounds reasonable."

As they headed down the river, Otok told Gyank about his encounter with the strange old hermit. He described everything from the eerie cottage to Lorgradan and the legend of Grok. But when he mentioned Melnick's frightening predictions, Gyank became concerned. "Sounds like trickery to me," he said. "Are you sure you didn't say anything that might have allowed him to guess about the book?"

"Absolutely not. I just listened. He came right out and said that a dark secret may be uncovered soon in the Land of Shar. I wouldn't believe any of his stories either, but I can't explain what happened with the tree. He would be dead for sure if that tree came down on him. And that's the only reason I take him seriously."

"Then why did you take the axe if you thought it was cursed?"

"I believe that Melnick had visions, but I don't believe in any curse. I also don't believe an axe can give a warrior power that he doesn't already have. That's just legend. I took the axe because I figured I'd need a weapon. Besides, Melnick seemed so certain that I should have it."

"That old hermit may be crazy," said Gyank. "Or maybe he was playing a trick on you. But if his prophecy is true, we don't want to unleash some mysterious dark power that we know nothing about."

"But Melnick's predictions didn't say exactly what would happen. He said evil would spread if wicked men learn the secret. Maybe we were meant to find the book, and it's up to us to keep it safe."

"There's no way of knowing, is there?" said Gyank. "We don't even know if we should believe any of it."

"The one thing Melnick was most sure of is that war is in the making. He said that men are talking war in the Land of Shar. But he doesn't know when it will happen."

"Otok, if kingdoms are at war, it will greatly reduce our chances of finding the book and getting home alive. We were hoping to go into the Land of Shar quietly, find the book, and leave without being noticed. If men are gathering for war, we may find ourselves in the midst of it."

"I know that," said Otok. "But I'm still willing to chance it. We've come so far. I say we keep going."

"I'm glad you feel that way," said Gyank. "I also want to go on, but I would never want to do it without you." Gyank patted him on the shoulder. "Well then, now it's a race. The sooner we get to the Land of Shar, the better chance we have of finding the book before war breaks out."

They went on talking about the old hermit and his predictions until they came to the spot where Otok had come ashore.

"That's where I finally came to a stop," said Otok, pointing to a tiny cove ahead of them. Parts of the broken raft were floating in the shallows, and most of the rope that had held the raft together was still draped around the logs.

"This is what was left of the raft when I came ashore," said Otok, standing next to the only chunk of the raft that was still somewhat together.

"Most of the raft is still here," said Gyank. "It's just broken apart. We can use the same logs and rope to rebuild it, but we'll have to do that later. Right now we must keep looking for Opus."

They searched until dusk without stopping, and by then, they were both were tired and hungry. They had come to a wide section of the river where the water was calm and tall trees lining the riverbank cast long shadows across the still water.

"It's getting hard to see," said Gyank, looking up at the sky. "We can't go on searching after dark. We might as well start looking for a place to spend the night. Tomorrow we'll get up early and keep searching."

They set up camp on a sandy bank and set out to find firewood. Gyank looked around the immediate area while Otok wandered farther downstream, hoping to find some dry driftwood. A short time later, as Gyank was reaching for his tinderbox, he heard Otok yell, "Gyank!"

Violent splashing disturbed the quiet river and echoed through the trees. Gyank looked in that direction, but the trees along the riverbank blocked his view. He pulled his Serpent Blade from his belt and ran toward the sound. Crashing through the brush by the edge of the water, he saw Otok swimming across the river as fast as he could. Gyank stopped and looked at where Otok was heading. Something was in the water on the opposite shoreline. He suddenly realized it was a man draped over a log that was hung up on some bushes leaning into the river. He tucked his sword back in his belt and splashing through the shallows, dove into the river. In the fading light of dusk, they raced across the calm water.

Gyank was the faster swimmer and he passed Otok just as they were getting to the other side. He stood up and ran the last few yards in waist-deep water. Grabbing the man by the shirt, he pulled him around to see who it was. Dead leaves and muck covered the man's hair and face. "It's Opus!" said Gyank.

Gasping for breath, Otok took hold of Opus's shoulders to keep his head above water while Gyank wiped the gunk from his face, revealing a large bump on his forehead with a clump of dried blood covering a gash.

"Let's get him to shore," said Gyank.

Holding Opus by the armpits, they pulled him to the bank. Gyank put his head to Opus's chest and listened. "He's still alive."

They shook him gently and called his name, but it was useless. Opus was out. Gyank waded into the river, took hold of the log that Opus had clung to and pulled it to the bank. "It's getting dark," he said. "I don't think it's a good idea to spend the night here. Those black wolves are on this side of the river. Let's use the log to float him across to the other side."

They carefully draped Opus over the log, and with one of them on each side, they steadied the log as they swam across. When they got to the sandy bank by their camp, they dragged Opus ashore, bandaged his wound, and got the fire started to warm him up. Soon the woods and the river were completely dark. But the fire was warm, and once Opus's clothes were dry, Gyank wrapped a blanket around him. "That's the only blanket we have left," he said. "It doesn't matter much right now, but wait until it starts getting cold. Things will be getting more difficult from now on. We lost most of our supplies back at the ruins."

"What do we have left?"

By the light of the fire, Gyank looked into his pack and started taking things out. "We still have some of my clothes. Most of all, I was able to save the stalking outfit. I think it's special in some strange way." Gyank held up the hooded shirt to admire it before looking into his pack to see what else he had. "We got one more coil of rope, but we lost the climbing spikes." Gyank reached down to the dark bottom of his pack. "Hey, I still have those smeatle leaves stuck to the bottom of my pack, and some wilted smeatle flowers too. But that's it. Oh yes, and I still have my little tinderbox."

"I still have the bow you gave me," said Otok. "If we find some good flaking stones along the riverbank, we can make arrows. We also have Grok with us."

"You talk as if that axe is a person."

Otok held the axe up and turned it slowly as he admired it. "Grok. I like the sound of it. Grok the Axe. Or as Melnick put it, 'Grok the Mighty.' Before the old hermit would even let me see it, I had to take a vow to protect it from falling into evil hands."

"You did what?" said Gyank as his interest suddenly peaked.

"I took a vow. It isn't a hard vow to take. Who would let their weapon fall into evil hands anyway? Curse or no curse."

"A vow is still a vow," said Gyank. "And now you'll have to stick to it."

"You're right. And I will. If I encounter evil men, I don't plan on giving my axe to them, I plan to use it on them."

Gyank smiled. "You sound confident for someone who never even held a battle-axe before."

"I'll learn how to use it. I just need someone to teach me. The same as you're learning how to use your sword. And that's another stroke of luck. You still have that sword you found, and your little throwing hatchet. We really aren't that bad off. The only thing I miss right now is food."

"I'm just as hungry as you are," said Gyank. "First thing tomorrow, we'll catch some fish and find some berries or edible plants."

As the fire burned low, they lay on their backs and stared up at the stars twinkling in the night sky.

"I hope Opus will be alright," said Gyank.

"I think he'll be fine. I just hope he wakes up so we can get on our way."

"As soon as Opus comes around, we'll head back to that cove and rebuild the raft. It's the best way to travel downriver, and even if Opus and Suraia are not completely well, we'll still be able to take them along."

"Yes, and taking them along creates another problem. Someday soon, we'll have to leave the river and travel by foot into the Land of Shar. We'll need to give them a reason why they can't go with us. Why don't we just leave tomorrow with Opus? Suraia will be safe with the Erifs, and this way we wouldn't be putting her in any danger."

Gyank turned his head to look at Otok. "Now, all of a sudden, you're concerned about her welfare. You just want to leave her behind because you don't like her. As soon as her ankle heals, the Erifs will force her to leave the village and she'll be on her own."

"She was on her own before we met her," argued Otok.

"I told her I would come back for her. I gave my word. I can't go back on my word."

"Fine, go back for her," said Otok, a bit perturbed. "And we'll drag her down the river with us. But when it comes time to part, how will you get her to leave? She likes you, and she's not going to want to leave. She'll come up with all kinds of reasons to come along with us. I just know it."

"Don't get all riled up."

Otok twisted onto his side to face Gyank. "Now you listen to me. We are going into the Land of Shar by ourselves. At least we know we can trust each other."

"Alright, I agree with you. But I must go back for her. When it comes time to part, I'll think of something to tell her, but it will have to be the same thing we tell Opus. Otherwise they'll know we're keeping something from them."

"We'll worry about it when the time comes. Right now, why don't we just get some sleep?" said Otok, rolling onto his other side to end the conversation.

~ ~ ~

The next morning, Opus opened his eyes and saw Gyank sitting next to him while Otok was squatting by the fire cooking breakfast.

"You took a bad ride down the river," said Gyank.

"Where am I?"

"We're on the other side of the river. Now you just rest. It's our turn to nurse you back to health."

"What do you mean, nurse me back to health?" said Opus indignantly as he sat up. "There's nothing wrong with me."

"You have quite a bump on your head," said Gyank. "Maybe you should just lay still for a while."

Opus touched his head and felt the bandage. "Nonsense, I feel fine. What happened to Norg and his men?"

"One of them is dead. I don't know who. As for the rest of them, we don't know. And if we never see them again, we'll be that much better off."

Glancing around, Opus asked, "Where's Suraia?"

"She's with the Erifs."

"What's an Erif?"

"They're people of the forest, and they're taking care of her. She hurt her ankle."

"How bad is it?"

"It's swollen up pretty good," said Gyank. "She won't be able to walk for a while, but we plan to rebuild the raft, so it won't matter too much."

"Well, let's get going," said Opus as he started to get up.

"Are you sure you can travel just yet?" asked Gyank, a little concerned, and also a little surprised.

"Of course. There's nothing wrong with me."

"Oh, you're real tough," said Otok jokingly. "Yesterday we thought you were dead."

Opus chuckled. "Nonsense. I just took a long nap, that's all."

"Well, if that's the case," said Otok, "have some fish for breakfast and let's get going."

Soon they were hiking along the river and sharing stories about their time apart. When they arrived at the cove, they started rebuilding the raft. Work went fast, and by late afternoon, they had completed the raft. Long poles could be used to push the raft in shallow water, but the river was deep, so paddles were a necessity. Gyank's throwing hatchet seemed to be the perfect tool for carving paddles from a split log, and soon the task was complete. Wanting to fill Otok's quiver, they searched along the riverbank for straight sticks that could be used for arrows shafts. Gyank found a good-size chunk of agate by the river that they flaked into arrowheads, and they found feathers to be used as fletching. While searching for these items, they discovered a cluster of wild berry bushes, which made a pleasant treat. As sunset approached, they were unraveling a length of rope so they could use the individual strands to fasten arrowheads and fletching to the arrow shafts. The longest of these strands were tied together and coiled neatly to be used as fishing line.

"It looks like we'll be ready to shove off before dark," said Gyank. "I'll get Suraia."

"Do you think we should go with you?" asked Opus.

"No, it's best if I go by myself. The Erifs might find something evil about you, and that would only give them something else to worry about."

Gyank headed through the woods and was greeted with smiles at the Erif village. He couldn't understand why until he was taken to Guda.

"I was wrong," were the first words out of Guda's mouth when he saw Gyank. "You not bring evil. The girl ... she is hawk friend."

Gyank was baffled. "Does this change anything?"

"Yes. She is daughter of great people ... hawk friends. Witch doctor say ... this good."

Yesterday, Gyank was accused of bringing evil to the village, and now he was greeted as an honored guest. Although this seemed ridiculous to Gyank, he was happy about it. A group of curious children followed him through the village as he was led to a hut where Suraia's hawk perched on a low branch nearby. Ducking his head, he went inside and found Suraia sitting on a pile of warm animal skins. She was surprised to see him. "You came back."

"Of course I came back. I said I would, didn't I? How's the ankle?"

"It's getting better. I don't think it's broken, just badly sprained."

"I found the others and we rebuilt the raft. We're heading down river. Do you want to come along?"

"Of course," she said with a big smile. "What did you expect?"

"After almost getting killed, I thought you might want to go back to your father."

"No," said Suraia, shaking her head. "I want to go with you. But I still can't walk."

"We only have to get you to the raft. And that shouldn't be a problem."

Gyank spoke to Guda who arranged for Suraia to be transported on a simple platform made of sticks and hide. She sat like a princess of the woods with Tork on her arm as four men hoisted her on their shoulders and carried her to the river. By dusk, they were back at the raft. Using hand signals, Gyank did his best to thank the men who carried Suraia. They seemed to understand, and gently petted the hawk before they disappeared into the forest.

"Suraia, how did you find your hawk?" asked Opus.

"I didn't find Tork. He found me. I kept whistling for him, and he finally came. From that moment on, the people of the village treated me like a goddess. I don't know why?"

"I don't know why either," said Otok softly under his breath so no one would hear his sarcastic remark.

"What did you say?" asked Suraia, not sure if she'd heard correctly.

"I said that it turned out for the best. So let's get started down the river."

"But it's almost dark," said Suraia.

"We'll be safer out on the raft," said Otok. "As long as one of us stays awake and watches the river, we'll be alright. It's better than sleeping here in the woods."

"Otok is right," said Gyank. "We'll just have to pay attention to the river and stay close to shore. If the current picks up too much, we can get to the bank quickly."

Secretly, Otok and Gyank did not want to waste any time, and they knew that much distance could be covered during the night on the raft. Under a dimly lit sky just after sundown, they boarded the raft. Opus sat in the center next to Suraia while Otok and Gyank stood up and used long poles to push the raft out into the main flow of the river. This part of the Andelron was wide and calm, and the raft barely moved. As they traveled silently down the moonlit river, only two of them knew they were actually in a race to complete a secret quest.

Chapter 9

BACKSTABBED

The night passed without incident, and the next morning found them miles away from the Erif village. They drifted down the peaceful river for days, stopping only to collect berries and cook the fish they caught. It was summer and food was plentiful along the river.

The raft would often float past an old castle on a steep hill overlooking the water. Yet these castles were always deserted, and not a soul was to be seen along the shoreline. The absence of people made it seem as if they were the first to explore this part of the forest, but the frequent sightings of tall, stone ruins was a grim reminder of the ancient cultures that once thrived there. In passing such abandoned fortresses, they thought of the wars that once plagued Elreia and the downfall of these great kingdoms.

Whenever they came within sight of a castle ruin, Opus would suggest they stop and explore. Yet each time, Otok and Gyank were able to talk him out of it because Suraia was in no condition to be caught in another wild adventure. This excuse soon became invalid because Suraia's ankle healed, and she was able to walk and run as well as she ever did.

Opus was becoming suspicious. His friends claimed to be seeking adventure, yet they let the raft drift past places that were begging to be explored. He had no idea they were focused on a faraway land and a power that seemed to draw them to it like a magnet.

One day, while they had stopped to collect berries and edible plants, Opus hollered, "Gyank! Otok! Come quickly!"

Moments later, the entire party was by a muddy bank looking down upon the man who had mistreated Opus all his life. It was Norg. His dead body lay partially buried in the mud with his legs sticking into the water.

"Look," said Suraia. "He still has the pouch of jewels on his belt." Kneeling down, she unfastened the pouch, opened it, and spilled the contents into her hand. The precious stones sparkled in her soft white palm. "We got the jewels back," she said.

Opus had a blank expression as he stood there in silence, staring down at the body.

"He will never abuse you again," said Otok.

"As bad as he was, I never wished that he would die," said Opus sadly. "So he's gone. Now what?"

"Now, we'll go on," said Gyank. "You'll start a new life—a better one."

Otok bent down and unfastened the scabbard from Norg's belt. There was mud caked all over it. Pulling the sword from its sheath, Otok washed both sword and scabbard in the river. Still dripping, he handed them to Opus. "Here, this is your sword now."

Gyank put his hand on Opus's shoulder and said, "Come on, let's get back to the raft."

They walked away in silence and shoved off. Opus was unusually quiet, but after a while, he was back to his old cheerful self. Suraia gave the pouch of jewels to Gyank, and it was reconfirmed that the gems would be divided evenly among the four of them.

They traveled for days without any difficulty, yet tension on the raft was building and everyone felt it. Otok and Gyank kept pressing onward even though Opus and Suraia wanted to stop and explore a castle ruin or a giant statue visible from the river. Opus was sure that these two friends had motives other than treasure hunting. If he could talk to one of them privately, maybe he could find out what they were up to. But on the small raft, there was little that one could say without everyone knowing about it. So the pressure mounted until arguments broke out, and it was almost certain that there would be trouble on the raft.

One day, as the sun approached the horizon, they came to a set of rapids. The river was nowhere near as fierce as before, and the raft came out of the white water intact and with all its passengers. Once again, they were in calm water. Only this time, unseen currents swiftly carried the raft along as the riverbed below them dropped down to dark unknown depths. The trees lining both shores fell farther to the sides as the great river became considerably wider.

"Look," said Otok. "There's a small island up ahead."

Squinting against the bright sunlight on the water, Opus pointed to a spot in front of the island. "It looks like something is splashing over there."

As the current pulled the raft toward the island, they realized it was the splashing of countless small fish jumping frantically out of the water. While the raft drifted over the disturbance in the river, the companions peered into the water with amazement. The school of fish moved in unison and was so tightly packed together that it appeared as one giant creature of which each individual fish was only a single scale. A surge of fish suddenly jumped into the air right next to Opus. He quickly grabbed a paddle and took a deep forceful stroke. "Those fish aren't jumping for joy," he said in a disturbed tone of voice. "Something's feeding on them—something big. We got to get to the island."

The rest of the party sprang into action as they began paddling toward the island. A short distance from the raft, the water broke again, first by many tiny fish fleeing for their lives, and then by a huge fin. The curved, triangular fin ran parallel to the raft and then slowly sank down into the water and disappeared.

"Look at that!" shouted Otok.

The sight of the giant fin struck them with fear and they paddled even faster. They could see a huge, dark shape moving under the water, circling around back toward them. Moments later, the fin briefly surfaced again, and as it submerged into the depths, it was followed by a thick tail with a single row of curved, triangular ridges running along its dorsal side. Everyone was paddling wildly, and the front edge of the raft was plowing through the water, yet they seemed to be only crawling toward the island.

In the light of the setting sun, the monster broke the surface of the calm river once again. This time, its head, perched on top of a long muscular neck, rose high up out of the water as gracefully as a swan. Water glided over its serpentine neck and dripped back into the river. Its thick, green scales were like overlapping shields pointing down the creature's body. Triangular ridges, like the ones on its tail, ran from the base of its skull down the back of its neck. The ridges increased in size to huge, curved fins standing along the creature's back. The head of the beast looked much like that of a dragon, and it had a long snout, which it lifted up to let a mouthful of fish slide down its extended gullet. Its powerful jaws snapped open and closed a few times while this prehistoric monster gulped its food. In doing so, the beast displayed its long pointy teeth that resembled curved daggers, sitting neatly in its jaw. Oddly, they were a clear blue that was almost transparent. Its bright green eyes with shiny black pupils were set under protruding bony ridges covered with scales. As the creature moved its neck, the setting sun reflected off its wet scales, making them shimmer.

"I think it sees us!" said Opus.

The raft was nearing the island when the monster submerged and darted through the water toward them.

Paddling frantically, Otok turned his head to see where the creature was. "Hurry, he's closing on us!"

The prehistoric head suddenly rose out of the water behind the raft and towered over them. With its long neck in a swanlike position and its gaping mouth dripping water, the creature hesitated while choosing which morsel would be tasted first. A gigantic webbed claw came up out of the water and effortlessly submerged the back end of the raft while lifting the front high above the surface of the water. Suraia's hawk flew off with a screech. There was no time to grasp weapons. The monster lowered its head, and paddles were thrust up into the snapping jaws. Wood cracked and splintered in the creature's mouth as the raft tipped to the verge of capsizing.

"Jump!" was blared out simultaneously.

Opus and Gyank dove off the end of the raft sticking up in the air while Otok and Suraia lunged into the water from the sides. They came to the surface swimming toward the island as fast as they could. The monster paused for a moment to capsize the raft, and then pushed it completely underwater. Moments later, the giant beast took off after its helpless prey.

Gyank knew he would be overtaken before he made it to the island, so he stopped and drew his sword to face his doom. He didn't stand a chance against the monster, but he just couldn't let himself be plucked out of the water like a tiny fish fleeing for its life. Otok and Opus came to the same conclusion. A deep instinct to survive forced them turn and fight when all seemed hopeless. And this is what saved them from certain death, for as they stopped swimming and turned to fight the sea serpent, their feet touched bottom. The water was only chest deep. The strong currents of the river had created a long sand bar that stuck out from the tip of the island.

Suraia was the closest to the monster and swimming as fast as her arms and legs could move her through the water. When she saw the others stop and stand up, she too spun and drew her sword. But there was no time for her. Just as she turned, the creature extended a claw and grabbed her. Like a doll, the monster lifted her out of the water and brought its snout down to meet her. Suraia's sword arm was pinned to her side by the webbed claw. The dreadful jaws opened wide to accommodate a large mouthful, but then the creature suddenly jerked its head back and let go a deafening roar that shook the forest. Gyank's hatchet had tumbled through the air and buried its head in the fleshy part of the monster's throat just below the jaw. The creature dropped its prey as a thick stream of blood flowed from the wound and ran down the underside of the monster's neck. Suraia splashed into the water and came up running. While the beast whipped its head around and wailed, the companions ran for the island. The water got shallower and progress became easier and faster. Yet, the great beast of the river was not defeated. It was not even badly wounded; it was merely shocked at being hurt, probably for the first time in all its long existence. Now the monster was enraged, and it came at them with a vengeance. As the creature chased them into the shallows, it revealed its tremendous proportions that before were hidden by the water. The animal awkwardly pulled itself toward the island by its giant claws and it twisted with each movement.

Opus took a quick look back, and yelled, "Run! Run for all you're worth!"

Glancing back at the beast, Otok said, "I can't believe the size of it."

The creature was as big as a whale, and its head perched on its long neck stood as tall as a tree. Its massive bulk was no longer supported by the water, and although the giant animal seemed clumsy struggling and thrashing in the shallows, it was still gaining on them.

The companions made it to the island. But the island was not what it appeared to be. The trees and vegetation made it look as if it was all a solid chunk of dry land. Actually, most of the island was submerged, and they found themselves in knee-deep water among slippery tufts of grass. But they could run no further. The creature had closed in and could now reach them with its long powerful neck. Exhausted and gasping for breath, they stood in the shallows and prepared to face the wrath of the river monster.

The head of the great beast hung high above the companions and looked down at them. Only this time, the creature was not feeding—it was preparing to do battle. It gave a loud roar and reached out its claw to grab Opus. He raised his sword to defend himself, but slipped on the muddy river bottom and fell backward. Otok fired one of his stone-tipped arrows. The fletching was wet, but the arrow flew straight and hit its mark. To their horror, the arrow merely bounced off the tough hide of the creature. Its scales were like armor plating, and the beast didn't even flinch as it pushed its giant claw down into the water and picked up Opus along with tufts of grass and mud. Otok fired again and again, but the arrows uselessly bounced off the river monster's scaly hide. Otok took aim at its throat, but the creature protected this vulnerable spot by keeping its chin down, even though Gyank's hatchet was still lodged in it.

Opus was lifted high in the air. His arms were free and he swung his sword back and forth at the giant snout coming toward him. The mouth of the creature opened wide and its long pointy tongue lashed out at him. All Opus could see was the bright pink flesh on the inside of the creature's mouth and the sharp rows of teeth closing on him. A wave of terror ran through his body and he desperately stabbed into the creature's gaping mouth. He struck the soft, pinkish-gray flesh of the slimy tongue and blood oozed from the wound. Opus was instantly jerked away from the huge jaws, and his ears shook when the monster roared. Then, as if to use Opus's body as a mallet, the beast violently slammed him to the water without letting go of him. There was a tremendous splash as Opus's head and arms were slapped against the water. Numb with shock, the sword slipped from his hand and fell into the shallows. Dazed senseless by the blow, Opus was like a rag doll in the creature's grasp. His arms hung straight down and his head was draped to one side.

Holding Opus's limp body in its claw, the terrible beast suddenly twisted its neck and turned its gaze upon Otok. As if the monster finally felt a pinch from Otok's useless efforts, it reached out with its other front claw and grabbed him.

Gyank rushed to his aid. "Let go! You fat serpent!" he shouted as he thrust the point of his sword at the giant claw, stabbing a thick webbed finger. The monster dropped Otok, recoiled its claw, and shook it up and down as if it was burnt. "So I was right!" Gyank shouted at the beast. "You are a fat serpent! And I have a pin that can prick you and burn you!" Gyank held up his sword and waved it as if he was daring the animal to attack him. "Meet the Serpent Blade!"

While the creature roared in pain, Opus seemed to come back to life and began fighting to loosen the scaly claw wrapped around his torso. But when the creature felt him wiggling, it tightened its grip, and Opus screamed, "He's crushing me!"

"Let him go!" yelled Gyank as he charged toward the beast, splashing violently as he lifted his knees up high to run through the water. But the river monster had many ways to defend itself, and before Gyank could get close enough to strike, the creature flung its tail around toward the front of its body and slapped the water, sending up a huge splash. Gyank was hit with a wall of water as the creature swept its tail through the shallows. As if swatting a fly, the immensely powerful tail knocked Gyank off his feet and sent him crashing to the muddy bottom. The Serpent Blade slipped from his fingers and disappeared in a cloud of muddy water. Before Gyank could take a breath, the beast seized him with its wounded claw and lifted him out of the mud.

With both Gyank and Opus helpless in its grasp, the monster turned its vengeful malice toward Otok, its head slowly lowering as if preparing to strike. While the creature's attention was focused on Otok, Suraia tried to sneak up on the mountain of scales and fins. It caught sight of her and spun its head around like a snake, hissing and dribbling blood from its mouth. As the terrible dragonlike head came down at her, she thrust her blade upward, but the giant jaws snapped shut, catching her sword in its teeth. The beast pulled its head back, yanking the sword from Suraia's hand as she fell forward. The creature opened its mouth and the sword tumbled down into the grassy water. Now, she too was helpless.

Gyank felt the crushing strength of the giant claw. Throwing his head back, he looked up at the monster's dreadful jaws and saw his hatchet still stuck in the creature's throat. The beast looked down at him with its cold merciless eyes, and suddenly Gyank had a glimmer of hope. With a desperate gasp, he shouted, "Otok! Shoot at its eyes! Its eyes!"

Otok took aim and shot an arrow at the big green eye. The monster ducked its head and the arrow flew between two of the ridges on the back of its neck. Just like a snake, the creature could move its head swiftly in any direction. Otok tried again, and the arrow flew past the creature's neck as it swiveled its head out of the way. Otok glanced at his friends. Both Gyank and Opus seemed to have the life squeezed out of them, and Suraia was stumbling in knee-deep water as she backed away in fear.

The hopelessness of the situation brought out a side of Otok that was otherwise dormant. Uncontrollable fury grew within him as he lifted his bow horizontally over his head and slammed it down into the water in front of him like a child throwing a temper tantrum. He ripped Grok from his belt and let go a war cry such as had not been heard in the Great Forest of Elreia for centuries. His cry was so loud and fierce that it echoed along the river and through the forest. Grok was alive again.

A surge of energy flowed through Otok's body as the great axe, Grok, set his legs in motion. "Take me, you ugly beast!"

The monster's snout, dripping with a mixture of water and blood, came down to meet Otok's challenge. Gripping the axe with both hands at the base of its long handle, Otok swung upward with all his might. Teeth and bone cracked as Grok cut deep into the monster's lower jaw. Blood poured from the wound like a waterfall as the creature recoiled its head and roared with intense pain. Otok wasted no time. The head was out of reach, but the enormous body wasn't. Splashing through the water, he ran up to the front of the creature and swung Grok as if delivering the last blow to fell a mighty tree. Giant scales broke and popped free as the axe sliced through the thick hide. A wide gash opened in the creature's flesh and the water turned red with blood. The bellowing roars of the great beast echoed in the forest as it writhed in agony, thrashing its tail and twisting its long neck. Otok stepped back to avoid the towering wall of scales as the creature's contorted body lurched toward him. Its claws opened wide, releasing Opus and Gyank. They splashed into the water, and clenched onto tufts of grass while they caught their breath.

Now with two free claws, the creature came at Otok to crush him to death. But Otok's rage had not subsided, and he prepared to meet the giant claws that had nearly killed his friends. As the monster reached down to grab him, he filled his lungs, and another war cry came from his lips like a blast of wind. Otok quickly shifted his weight and hewed off one of the massive claws at the joint. It was as thick as a tree trunk, yet the mighty axe cut through it, hide, scales, bone, and all. The monster recoiled its limb as the claw fell to the water, still twitching and grasping. Enraged and in pain, the creature whipped its tail around to crush Otok with one blow. But he dove out of the way as it pounded the water next to him. Otok jumped to his feet, and as he whipped his head to fling wet hair out of his eyes, the dreadful beast coiled its neck like a snake and lowered its head, preparing to strike. A gurgling hiss came from its gaping jaws, and the monster's dagger-like teeth snapped at him. Otok swiftly stepped aside as he swung the mighty axe in a big circle and brought it crashing down on top of the creature's head. There was a loud crack as the axe sank deep into its skull right above the eyes and stuck there. The huge river monster collapsed lifeless with a great splash, its long neck curled around on itself, and its dead hulking body spilling blood into the river.

Otok staggered backward, caught his balance, and glanced around. The sun had set and the sky was growing dark. His friends were scattered about the giant mound of flesh and bone. They were coughing and gasping for breath, but they seemed to be alright. Otok waded over to the dragonlike head of the beast. He put one foot up on the bony part of the skull behind the eyes and wrenched his axe back and forth until it came free.

Shaking all over and breathing heavily, he fell to his knees in the shallows. He looked down at the axe in his hands, and then at the gargantuan body of the beast he had slain. Otok could hardly believe what he had done. What strange power enabled him to face this dreaded monster? Perhaps in blind rage and desperation, he found strength in himself that he didn't know he possessed. Or was it something entirely different? Remembering the legend of the axe, he whispered to himself, "Maybe it is true ... I wonder."

Otok stood up and went to check on his friends. No one was seriously hurt and they were soon discussing their situation. The current had carried the raft toward the island and it was caught among the grass in the shallow water. It had been flipped over, but it was still in one piece. Their gear had been tied down in case they hit rapids; therefore, nothing was lost when the raft capsized. Once the mud stirred up by the battle had settled, the water cleared and they went looking for their weapons. Most of Otok's arrows were found floating among the tufts of grass, but in the fading light, it took some time to recover their swords. It was almost dark when Gyank removed his hatchet from the monster's throat, washed it in the river, and tucked it back in his belt. They gathered by the raft, and with some effort, flipped it back over.

"We can't afford to run into another giant serpent in the dark," said Gyank. "Let's tie the raft down so it won't drift away, and then search the island. If we can find a dry spot, I think it's best to spend the night here."

Everyone agreed, and once the raft was secure, Otok said, "Come on. Let's explore the island."

Gyank noticed Suraia walking toward the dead beast and said, "You go ahead. We'll be along in a minute."

"Alright, but don't be long," said Otok.

Opus grinned and said, "Don't fret—they can't get lost. We're on an island."

While Otok and Opus waded toward the main part of the island, Gyank walked over to Suraia who was standing by the carcass, staring blindly at its huge head.

"What's the matter?" he said.

Without moving or even blinking an eye, she said, "Do you know what the teeth of such an animal are worth?"

"I haven't the slightest idea."

"They're very rare. Some people would pay a handsome price for them while others would not want them at all."

"Well, I must be one of those people who don't see much worth in them."

"It's not that they don't see much worth in them. They simply wouldn't dare take the risk of having them. They fear such things are evil and bring bad luck. Some believe they have magical properties, and certain skills are needed to control their power."

"I don't fear the teeth of a dead animal. I just don't want them. Come on, let's catch up to the others."

Suraia ignored him. She seemed to be fixed in a trance as she gazed at the monster's teeth. "Look at the clear light blue color. They're like crystal daggers. Let's take them."

Suraia drew her sword and approached the animal's head. Gyank caught hold of her arm and stopped her. "You'll do no such thing. Leave well enough alone."

"Why? What are you afraid of?"

"I'm not afraid. I just think it's a bad idea. Besides, if anything is to be done with the creature, Otok should be the one to say. He killed it. And saved all our lives at that. Now let's go find the others."

As they walked away from the giant carcass, Suraia couldn't resist the urge to look over her shoulder at the monster one last time.

~ ~ ~

While Otok and Opus were alone exploring the dry part of the island, Opus said, "That's quite an axe you got there. You saved all our lives."

"We do what we must do," said Otok, making light of it. "I'm sure you would have done the same."

"Perhaps, but I've never had anyone risk their life to save me."

"We're friends," said Otok. "And friends look out for each other."

"I agree, and if that's the case, then why can't you tell me what you and Gyank are up to?"

"What do you mean?"

"Why do you insist on pushing the raft past places that are bound to be full of unexplored chambers? Are you in a hurry to go somewhere? Are you running away from someone? If you are, that's alright, you can tell me."

Otok didn't know what to say, and he stood there in silence. He was tired of deceiving Opus. Especially since he felt that Opus could be trusted with their secret, yet he had to hold his tongue.

"If we're truly friends," said Opus. "Then you can trust me."

At that moment, Gyank and Suraia came through the dark brush, and Otok breathed a quiet sigh of relief.

"The island looks safe to me," said Gyank as he approached.

"Yes, it does," said Otok. "I saw a good spot to set up camp back there a bit. Follow me."

After they had set up camp, Otok and Gyank went off alone to the far end of the island where a long sandy bank stretched out into the river. It was a dark, moonless night, and as they peered downstream, they could barely see the river turning in a big sweeping curve to the left. Beyond it was the forest, dark and threatening.

"I wonder what's out there," said Gyank.

"I don't know," said Otok, staring into the darkness. "But somewhere out there is the Land of Shar and an old leather bound book with a funny looking symbol in it. And if there isn't, then we're no more than a couple of fools."

"Whichever the case, let's hope our luck and skill are good enough to find out and go home to tell Smilga."

"You do realize that sometime soon we'll have to say good-bye to Opus and Suraia."

"Yes, I know. And I still haven't thought of a way to do it."

"I think we should decide on something soon. Opus hasn't said anything when we're all together, but when he was alone with me, he was pressing me for answers. He knows we're keeping something from him."

Gyank suddenly changed the topic. "Do you see anything out there in the dark?"

"No, where?"

Gyank pointed into the distance beyond the trees where the flow of water carved a turn in the riverbank.

"No. I don't see anything. All I see is a black night sky."

"It must be my imagination. Let's get back to camp and get some rest."

~ ~ ~

The next morning when Opus awoke, he was alone. He was usually up before anyone else, but this morning was different. He sat up with a jolt and looked around. The campsite was completely empty. The only blanket they had was given to Suraia, and it was gone. Gyank had used his pack as a pillow, but that was gone as well. There was nothing left behind by any of them except the cold ashes of their fire.

Could they have left without him because he probed too deeply about their secret? Was he stranded on this tiny island by himself? Struck with fear, he got up and ran toward the end of the island where the long sandy bank pointed downstream. Maybe he could catch a glimpse of them as they went around the bend. Opus was chubby, but he flew to the end of the island as fast as his legs could carry him. As he came charging out of the foliage, he saw Otok by the water's edge, looking down river. Relieved, Opus shouted to him, "Otok!"

Otok turned around to see his friend racing toward him. "What's the matter?"

"I'm so glad to see you," said Opus, trying to catch his breath. "I thought you had left me stranded."

"I wouldn't leave you stranded," said Otok, surprised that Opus would even think such a thing. "But what you say may not be too far from the truth. I can't find Gyank or Suraia."

"Do you think they might have left us?"

"I know Gyank didn't. But I can't say the same for Suraia. Last night, Gyank thought he saw something out there. It was too dark to tell, but look out there now." Otok pointed down river over the trees. Standing high above the forest in the distance was a single mountain peak. Covered with snow at the tip, it looked menacing in the eerie morning mist. "I wonder if it was the mountain peak that he saw last night."

"Who cares about a peak," said Opus. "We have to find out what happened to them. The island is not that big. If we haven't seen them, they must be gone."

"We know they haven't been here," said Otok. "The only tracks in the sand are from when Gyank and I were here last night."

"Something happened to them," said Opus, with urgency in his voice. "I just know it. We have to find them. Let's split up and search the island."

Otok started looking in the dense brush while Opus had another idea. He had to know if they were stranded, so he ran to the other end of the island to see if the raft was still there. He came charging out of the trees and into the shallows where he suddenly stopped and stood frozen among the tufts of grass. The raft was gone. For a moment, he just stared at the spot where the raft had been. Then he looked over at the giant creature still lying as it fell in the shallows. Gyank was sitting on a big lump of grass in the water next to the carcass. His back was turned and he wasn't moving. Opus ran toward him, tripped, splashed into the shallow water, got up and kept running. As he approached, he noticed that Gyank was crying. Tears ran down his face as he stared at the head of the creature. Its jaws and gums had been cut to pieces and its teeth had been hacked out. The animal's head was mutilated.

"I can't believe she would do this to me," said Gyank quietly.

Opus sat down next to him and asked softly, "What happened?"

"Last night, she told me the teeth of such an animal were very valuable. I told her to leave the creature alone." Gyank sniffed and rubbed his nose. "This morning, when I got up, she was gone. I thought she was just off in the woods. Then I noticed the pouch of jewels on my belt was gone. I couldn't believe she would steal them from us. So I came here to see if the raft was gone, and I found that she also took the creature's teeth."

"It's alright. Don't take it so badly."

"I feel like such a fool. I trusted her—and all the while she was just using me, waiting for a good time to spring her trap. Now look at the mess we're in. If only I had listened to Otok. He told me we shouldn't trust her. In fact, he didn't even want to take her along."

"It could have been much worse. She left us—so what? At least she didn't desert us when we were really counting on her for something."

"I guess you're right."

"You had to find out for yourself about her," said Opus in an understanding tone. "If Otok forced you to leave her behind, then you would never have known the truth about her, and you would have been angry with Otok. Consider yourself lucky."

"I really did like her."

"Yes, I know. I knew all along how you felt about her."

"And look at the mess it got us into. We're stranded here."

"So we don't have a raft, that won't stop us from getting off the island. We'll think of something."

After a long pause, Gyank said, "We have to go after her."

"What for? I know you don't care about the jewels or the teeth—neither do I."

"I have to know why she did this to us."

"You mean why she did this to you," said Opus. "You mustn't go after her. That would be a foolish thing to do. She is the way she is, and she won't change. It's best just to let her go." Opus paused. "Besides, how do you expect to find her? If she took the raft downstream, we'd have to build another raft to chase her. But we don't even know if she took the raft. She might have used it just to get ashore, and then set it adrift. Right now, for all we know, she could be heading in any direction on either side of the river. We're not expert trackers, and even if we were, would it really be worth it to go after her?"

Otok came walking up behind them. "She took off, didn't she?"

"Yes, she did," said Opus sadly. "And Gyank's taking it hard."

"It isn't all that bad," said Otok, trying to cheer him up. "A friend like that, you don't need."

Gyank sat there staring at the creature's bloody head. Otok saw that its teeth were ripped out, but he said nothing about it. Instead, he brought up a more cheerful topic. "Remember last night when you thought you saw something above the trees? Well, you did. It was the peak of a mountain."

Gyank looked up at Otok. "There's a mountain south of here?"

"Yes, come and take a look for yourself."

Gyank stood up quickly, and they hurried to the other end of the island where they saw the mountain far in the distance as clear as could be. Gyank looked at Otok and said, "Do you know what this means?"

"I think so," said Otok while Gyank fumbled in his shirt pocket. He took out the map and unfolded it. "Here's the Andelron," he said. "Look at the bend in the river. It takes a sharp turn southeast."

Exhilarated, Otok pointed to the map and said, "That peak must be part of the Uvannel Mountains. It's Mount Hemmetar! That's where Smilga said we should leave the river!"

In their excitement, they had dropped their guard and given themselves away. Opus gave them a puzzled look. "What are you talking about? Who's Smilga?"

Otok and Gyank looked at each other, and after a short pause, Otok nodded his head slightly, and Gyank knew they were thinking the same thing.

"Opus, it's about time we tell you," said Gyank. "As you probably guessed, we've been keeping something from you, and I hope you can understand why we couldn't tell you until now. We're on a dangerous quest. We planned to let you come with us only up to this point because now we'll be heading into the Land of Shar, and it's a deadly place."

"But you're my friends. If you must face danger, I'll go with you."

"You don't understand," said Gyank. "We have reason to believe that war is brewing in the Land of Shar. If this is so, the risk will be even greater."

"It is you who doesn't understand," said Opus firmly. "You've helped me escape from my hateful master. You saved my life, and shared all you have with me. I cannot let you go into a dangerous land without me. Three is better than two. And if I die as a result of my decision, then that's what was meant for me. You're risking your lives for this quest, so it must be important."

"Is this really how you feel about it?" asked Gyank. "I don't want you to regret this later."

"There are certain things that a man knows he must do, and this is one of them—even if it's to be the end of me."

"Then you should know the whole story," said Gyank.

They went back to their camp and told him everything about Smilga and the quest she sent them on. And so now there were three who knew of the secret book. Together they vowed to find it and bring it back to Smilga. Even if it came down to the efforts of the last man completing the task on his own.

Chapter 10

THE SHEPHERD GIRL

After analyzing their situation, the three companions realized they were not as bad off as they first thought. Since they were within sight of Mount Hemmetar, they had no more need for a raft. It was time to leave the river and travel on foot to the Uvannel Mountains. They could swim to shore, yet they feared another monstrous creature might be lurking in the depths. A raft would provide some protection, but it seemed a great labor to build a raft just to get ashore. So they waded out into the river as far as they could and began to swim. They stayed in a tight group as their arms and legs stroked rapidly under the surface of the water. No one dared to splash for fear that they might attract the attention of something lying quietly in the depths of the river. There was an ever-present feeling that they would suddenly be seized by huge unseen jaws from below. It was a great relief when they felt the riverbed below their feet, and they didn't waste any time getting to the bank, even though it was a hot summer day and the cool water was refreshing.

"We got through that alive," said Opus, wiping the water out of his face. "Now, which way?"

Gyank looked in the direction of the snow-covered peak. "According to the map, all we have to do is head for that peak and we'll soon be on the border of the Land of Shar. This is where Smilga said it would be most dangerous. And if what's ahead of us is any worse than what we've been through already, then we're in for the adventure of our lives."

With that thought in mind, they entered the forest and began their journey toward the mountains. The woods were so still and quiet that even their footsteps seemed loud and unwelcome, as if they were intruding and the eyes of the forest were watching them. Tall, dense trees blocked the sunlight, making the forest floor dark. Little vegetation grew among the huge tree trunks, and everywhere around them giant, twisted roots protruded out of the ground. They hiked in silence and kept looking behind them as they passed between the shadowy tree trunks.

Hours went by and the uneasy feeling still had not left them. Their eyes had grown so accustomed to the dim forest that when they saw beams of sunlight coming through the trees, they perceived them as something strange, something that didn't belong in that dark forest. They stood ready to grasp their weapons as they peered through the trees at the particles of dust sparkling in the beams of sunlight.

"I wonder what's over there," said Gyank in the softest whisper.

No one responded as they crept toward the light, staring as if under a spell. Otok was the first to step out from behind the base of a huge tree into the light. "It's just a road," he said, looking up and down the dirt path that wound its way through the dark woods.

"I wonder where it leads," said Opus.

"According to my map there's a castle nearby," said Gyank. "This road must lead to it or from it."

"We don't want any unnecessary dealings with castles," said Otok.

"I agree." said Opus. "But we can double our progress through the forest if we use the road."

"Opus is right," said Gyank. "We can move faster on the road, and it seems to be heading toward the mountain. I say we take the road, and if we see anything strange, we dodge into the woods."

"Alright," said Otok. "But we'll have to stay alert. With all the twists and turns, it won't be easy to see what's just ahead."

"I think it's worth the risk," said Opus.

"Then let's go," said Gyank.

As they walked along the road, straining to see around the next bend, they were also looking behind to see if anything was creeping up on them. All the while, they never lost the feeling that someone, or something, was watching them.

It was nearing dusk when they began to talk about what they would eat and where they would sleep. The forest, being uncomfortably still, forced them to keep their voices low. It was during this conversation that they heard the sound of many hooves approaching rapidly.

"Quick, into the woods," whispered Gyank as he darted to the side of the road.

They all ran in different directions, ducking behind wide tree trunks and dropping to the ground among the shadows of giant roots. They had gotten out of sight just as a troop of horsemen came galloping down the road. Dressed in chain mail armor, these soldiers carried large metal shields, and wore shiny helmets. Some had brightly colored robes that waved in the breeze, and each of them was equipped with a sword or a battle-axe. Otok poked his head up to get a better look. He could see the symbol of a tree on their shields, and one rider carried a long pole with a banner that bounced and waved as his horse galloped. About thirty riders in all, they passed quickly and were soon out of sight. The companions came out of hiding and gathered on the road.

"I wonder who they are, and why they're in such a rush," said Gyank.

"They must be on their way to a battle," replied Otok.

"If that's the case, then we're headed away from it."

"I don't think so," said Opus in deep thought. "I don't think they're on their way to or from a battle. I think there's a herald among them who's on his way to deliver an important message."

"What makes you think that?" asked Gyank.

"I could be wrong, but they seemed more like an escort than a battle group. My guess is that they're carrying a message, and the banner signifies the kingdom they represent."

Gyank pulled out the map and pointed to it. "There are two kingdoms on this side of the mountains, Derrim and Mellain. We must be between the two of them." Gyank looked up from the map at Opus. "You're right, that group was rather small. If a battle was going on, there would probably be armies of men marching through these woods."

Otok looked down the road where the horsemen had gone. "If they're an escort, I wonder what message they're carrying."

"I bet it's not good news," said Opus.

"Let's get off the road and find a place to sleep," suggested Gyank. "Tonight we're going to have to take turns standing watch."

They went a good distance into the woods and settled down at the base of a giant tree. There wasn't much of a camp to set up. It was far too risky to make a fire, and they had no sleeping gear. All they needed was a place to lie down. They found some edible plants and berries nearby that they shared, but it wasn't much. Otok volunteered to take the first watch, but as it grew dark, an eerie feeling came over them, and they all stayed awake for a while. The forest was completely noiseless, void even of the sound of crickets or leaves moving in the breeze.

The next morning, Opus was on watch when the sun came up. He woke the others and they headed back to the road. Gyank's map showed that the Valley of Vordar led through the mountains to Thorilleia. If they could find this valley, it would be a quick and easy way across the mountains, or so they thought.

By midday, the road led them to the edge of the dark Forest of Elreia, and they found themselves in a wide-open landscape separating them from the Uvannel Mountains. This magnificent mountain range stood tall before them and stretched as far as the eye could see. The companions stood in awe of the sheer size and scope of this string of vertical peaks, a barrier that seemed impossible to cross. Once again, they looked at the map and agreed that the only way across was through the Valley of Vordar. Reaching high above all the peaks around it was Mount Hemmetar, standing tall and alone with its snowy summit in the clouds. At the foot of the mountains were long green hills that rose and fell in shallow slopes, and scattered clusters of trees dotted the landscape and provided shade from the summer sun.

As they came out of the woods, the road ended and they made their own path across the grassy slopes. Numerous tiny streams flowed from the mountains and gently curved through the hills below. Stopping at the first little stream they came upon, they took a drink and wet their faces while listening to the soothing sound of water spilling between the rocks.

When they reached the top of the next hill, they looked back and saw a group of horsemen emerging from the forest. Out in the open with no place to hide, they quickly dropped to the ground and lay flat in the tall grass. The riders appeared to be the same group that they had seen the day before. Only this time, the horses walked at a leisurely pace.

"What are we going to do?" asked Opus. "They're coming this way."

Gyank looked down the hill behind them. "There's a small group of trees down there."

Lying flat on his belly, Otok turned his head to look down the hill. "Do you think we can get there before the riders get to the top of this hill?"

"It's our only chance of not being seen," said Gyank.

"Then let's go for it," said Otok as he began inching his way backward.

They crawled down the slope until they were far enough below the crest of the hill to be out of sight. Then they stood up and ran. Charging into the cover of the trees, they glanced back to see if the horsemen had made it to the top of the hill. Luckily, the riders were nowhere in sight.

"Quick, into the trees," said Gyank as he took hold of a branch and hoisted himself up.

They climbed quickly and were up into the thick leaves before the first rider's head appeared over the top of the hill. The horses moved at a slow pace, and it took a long time for them to pass by and disappear over the next hill. The three men hiding among the branches went unnoticed by all but one. A little girl was lying in the shade as she watched her father's sheep grazing on the hillside. She saw the companions race down the slope and scamper up into the trees, yet she made no sound or signal when the riders passed by. She stood there looking innocent and naive as they climbed out of the trees and for the first time took notice of her. Her dress was well worn, but she was clean and her long brown hair was well brushed.

"Hello," said Gyank in a kind voice. The little girl didn't respond. She just stared at the strangers. "Don't be frightened. We won't hurt you."

"I'm not afraid," said the little girl in a tiny soft voice.

"What is your name?" asked Gyank.

"Luta."

"Hello Luta. I am Gyank and these are my friends, Otok and Opus."

"Are you bad men?" she asked innocently.

"No, we are not bad men," said Gyank, glancing at his friends to get an idea of how they must look to this child. "Why do you ask?"

"You ran away from the king's men. You must have done something wrong."

"We didn't run because we did something wrong. We ran because we didn't want them to see us. We are strangers in this land and we don't know who we can trust. So we hide from everyone we see. This way we won't get into trouble. Do you understand what I'm saying?"

The little girl looked up at Gyank with her big, adorable, brown eyes, and said, "You have nothing to be afraid of. This is a peaceful land."

The companions looked at each other with surprise. Being closer to the Land of Shar, they expected to find more dangers and more wicked people. Perhaps Luta's comment was merely the perception of a child. Either way, they weren't going to risk being caught. Although

Luta was only a child, Gyank figured she might know the way to a mountain pass, or perhaps she could tell them something that would help them avoid a confrontation with armed men. Hoping that Luta would share something of value, Gyank spoke as pleasantly as he could. "I'm glad this is a peaceful land. Maybe you could help us find our way. I don't see a village or a castle around here. Where do you live?"

Luta pointed with her tiny finger across the shallow green hills at one of the smaller peaks. "At the base of that mountain is the castle of Mellain. You can't see it from here." Luta spun her head around to look up at Gyank, and in the cutest voice, she said, "But trust me, it's there. I live in the village near the castle."

"So we're within the realm of Mellain. And I guess those horsemen are on their way to the castle."

Luta began to skip around in a circle, and as she danced about, she sang playfully. "I'm riding my horse, I'm riding my horse, I'm riding my horse to Derrim."

"Oh, I've heard of Derrim," said Gyank. "Is that where the riders are from?"

Luta stopped skipping and looked up at him. "No, silly. They're from Mellain. Can't you tell by their crest? Lately, there have been many riders going back and forth across the meadows. They follow the road through the woods to a great castle, just like the castle of Mellain. I think they go to visit their friends in Derrim, and then come home again."

"Do the riders ever go through the mountains to visit anyone—maybe through a pass or canyon?"

"Why would anyone go into the mountains?" asked Luta with a confused look on her face. "The mountains are so very dangerous."

"My friends and I are on a journey, and we must get to the other side of those mountains. Do you know the easiest way to get to the Valley of Vordar?"

Luta's eyes grew wide with fear as if Gyank had suddenly

threatened her life. "No! You mustn't go there! You shouldn't even speak of such things! It is forbidden!" Luta took a few steps backward.

"Why is it forbidden?" asked Otok. "It's only a valley."

Luta backed away without taking her eyes off them as Gyank tried to calm her. "We don't mean any harm. I'm sorry I said that. I won't say it anymore."

Luta froze, and then sheepishly said, "I think I should get back to tending my father's flock."

"Please don't go," pleaded Gyank.

"It is forbidden! It is forbidden!" she said loudly as she turned and ran off.

The companions stood and watched as the little girl ran up a shallow hill where sheep could be seen grazing.

"At least we know we're near the castle of Mellain," said Otok.

Glancing around at the open landscape, Opus said, "More than that, we know riders have been traveling back and forth between kingdoms. It would seem that something urgent is going on. We also found out that Luta is deathly afraid of the Valley of Vordar. For some reason, it's forbidden even to speak of it."

Gyank looked in the direction of Mount Hemmetar. "Whatever is going on here, it would be best to steer clear of it. The sooner we move on, the better. Unfortunately, it seems that the only way across the mountains is through the Valley of Vordar. And apparently, that's a place to be feared. But we can't waste time looking for another pass that may not even exist. Whatever's in that valley, we must face it, or find a way to avoid it."

"Avoid what?" said Otok. "She's just a child. How do we know she wasn't told a bunch of scary stories to keep her from wandering into the mountains?"

"You could be right," said Gyank. "But whether there's something to fear in that valley or not, that's the way we must go." Gyank pulled the map from his shirt and looked at it. "We must pass the castle of Mellain to get to the Valley of Vordar. And for three strangers heading to a forbidden valley, Mellain may not be as peaceful to us as it is to Luta."

"You have a point there," said Otok. "Hopefully, we'll get to the castle by nightfall, and be able to slip past it while it's dark."

They left the cover of the trees and headed toward the peak Luta had pointed to. When they reached the top of the next hill, they had a good view of the surrounding landscape. They could see a herd of sheep grazing on a hillside and the tiny figure of a little girl walking toward a group of shepherds. As the companions hiked down the slope, Opus kept turning his head to watch Luta. He noticed one of the shepherds kneeling down in front of her as if he was talking to her. Then the man got up and began walking parallel to the companions.

"Gyank, I think we might be heading into trouble," said Opus.

"What do you mean?"

"You see that man over there? I saw him talk to Luta, and then he started walking in the same direction as us. It could be nothing, but if Luta told him about us hiding from the horsemen and that we mentioned the Valley of Vordar, he may be on his way to alert the castle guards."

Half-jokingly, Otok said, "We could angle toward him and make sure he doesn't get to the castle."

Taking the comment more seriously than it was meant, Gyank replied firmly, "No. We don't want to start creating trouble for ourselves. We'll just keep an eye on him and walk a little faster. If we can get to the castle before he does, we might be gone before he can alert anyone."

"We could pick up the pace to a trot," suggested Otok. "Then we'd surely beat him to the castle."

"I don't know," said Gyank. "We don't know what kind of runner he is. And we don't want to make him suspicious."

They kept moving along at a steady pace, and when the castle came into view, they found themselves at the foot of a mountain that was casting long shadows across the green hills. The shepherd was no longer in sight. He had disappeared on the other side of a hill in the distance. The sun had gone down behind the mountains, and the sky was lit by a bright orange sunset. The countryside grew dim and quiet. In a short time, it was dark.

High up on the lower edge of the dark mountain stood the castle of Mellain. Square windows in the walls and towers glowed with firelight, while the small, twinkling lights of the village stretched from the base of the castle out into the surrounding hills. From a distance, it was obvious that the quickest way past the castle was to cut straight through the village. Since all was dark and quiet, it didn't seem worth the extra time and energy to walk the perimeter just to avoid being seen. So they headed down the last slope leading to the village with the hope of passing unnoticed.

Although there were few people on the streets, light was cast from cottage windows either by fire or lamp, which made them visible to anyone who would care to take an interest in them. To avoid attracting attention, they walked through the streets as if they knew exactly where they were going. Gyank was a few steps behind his friends when he heard the sound of galloping horses approaching from behind. He spun around to face them, but saw only an empty street. By the sound of clapping horseshoes, he knew the riders were just about to turn the corner. "Hide!" he said as he darted off the road. The others had no time to react, and as Gyank pressed his back against the wall of a shop and disappeared in the shadows, a small group of mounted guards came speeding around the corner. From the darkness, he peered into the street where his friends turned to face the horsemen.

"Halt!" shouted one of the riders.

Opus and Otok stood still in the center of the street while Gyank glanced around and noticed an alleyway leading to the back of the shop. He heard a deep voice say, "Here are two of the spies from the Land of Shar." Then he quietly slipped down the alley and heard no more of the conversation.

Otok didn't reach for his axe or one of his arrows. Although he was ready to fight, he waited to see what would happen as Opus launched a harsh verbal assault. "What's the meaning of this?" he said in a demanding tone. "Is this how the people of Mellain treat tired travelers from Derrim? My lord will certainly hear of this outrage."

"Mind your tone. You're speaking to the king's guards."

Otok stood silent while Opus battled with words. "Did I hear one of you call us spies?"

"Three men were seen coming this way. It was reported that they're headed for the Valley of Vordar. You seem to—"

"Do we look like three men?" said Opus abruptly as he raised his voice. "Do we look like spies?" The guards did not come any closer, nor did they surround the two travelers. They were so shocked by Opus's reaction that they hesitated while he shook his fist at them. "Are you looking for trouble with Derrim? My lord will hear about this insult!"

"The two of you fit the descriptions reported," said the guard calmly.

"I don't care who we look like!" shouted Opus. "My lord will have your skin!"

"Is that so?" said the guard as he began to lose his patients. "Just who is your lord, may I ask? Or will you wave your arms and shout at me some more?"

Opus was stumped for a moment, and that was enough to give him away.

"Seize these spies for questioning!" the guard commanded.

Otok went for his axe and Opus reached for his sword while the horsemen sprang forward to surround them. Suddenly, there was a loud shout, the snap of a whip, and a horse whinnied from down the street behind the guards. A large carriage pulled by four horses came charging down the street with no one steering it.

Otok and Opus dodged to the side of the road while the guards fought to control their steeds as the carriage barreled through them. Behind the carriage was a small open wagon pulled by two horses. In the driver's seat was Gyank, hollering at the top of his lungs and snapping a whip behind the tails of the horses. He rode down the center of the street that had just been cleared by the carriage. As he passed through the crowd of guards, he slowed down and shouted, "Otok! Opus! Get in!"

They made a dash for the back of the open wagon and jumped on.

"They're getting away!" yelled a guard.

Gyank turned to see that both his friends were with him, and then snapped the whip and shook the reins. The team took off with a great jolt and sped down the road. Opus and Otok held on and moved toward the front of the wagon.

"We'll never outrun them," said Opus, looking back at the pursuing horsemen.

Gyank glanced over his shoulder and said, "We got to think of something quick!" He pulled on the reins and the wagon skidded around a corner and sped down another street. To their dismay, ahead of them was another group of guards on horseback who saw them and broke into a run. The wagon would have been trapped if it had not been for another crossroad part way down the street. Again, the wagon skidded into a turn, and this time it nearly tipped over. The two groups of horsemen merged as they joined the pursuit. Looking ahead, Gyank could see dark fields at the base of the mountain. They were coming to the other side of the village, but this was not a sign of relief because they would stand no chance of escape in the open fields.

As they raced past a line of shops with canopies held up by poles, Otok shouted over the roar of galloping horses, "Gyank, get closer to those shops!"

Otok pulled out his axe and leaned out of the wagon while Opus held onto the back of his belt so he wouldn't fall out. As they passed the shops, Otok chopped through the canopy poles and sent canvas and wood crashing to the street. Behind the wagon, horses fell and stopped short, causing riders to tumble into the pile of rubble.

"That slowed them down, but it won't stop them!" shouted Gyank as he took a quick look back to see what happened.

One rider was nimble enough to hurdle the broken storefronts and at the same time avoid bumping and colliding with the other horses. He was right behind the wagon when they came to the open fields and he sped up and came alongside them. To their left, the foot of the mountain stretched far out into the hills. Gyank made a wide sweeping turn and headed for the nearest cliff. The lone rider turned with them and drew his sword as he accelerated to come parallel with Gyank. As the rider raised his sword to strike down on Gyank, Opus grabbed a plank of wood lying in the back of the wagon and swung it horizontally, smashing the man in the chest. He fell backward off his horse as the wagon sped toward the dark, jagged cliffs jutting up out of the earth. Behind them, they could see the horses charging across the grassy field in the darkness.

Snapping the reins, Gyank shouted back to his friends, "Our only chance is to get up into the cliffs where they can't follow us on horseback! Get ready to jump off and climb as fast as you can! I'll let the wagon go on."

The horsemen were closing rapidly, yet the wagon seemed to disappear as it came within the deep shadows by the foot of the mountain. Gyank slowed down and pulled the reins so the wagon ran along the base of the cliffs. As soon as Opus and Otok jumped off, Gyank snapped the reins hard and leapt from the wagon as the horses lurched forward. He tumbled to the ground while the empty wagon sped away into the darkness.

Otok and Opus climbed fast and were soon a good way up the steep cliff. Gyank couldn't find a good place to start his climb and was still at the base of the cliff when the riders came upon him. He dove to the ground next to a flat boulder and stayed perfectly still. The first horseman raced by him in pursuit of the wagon. Gyank didn't move. He lay as still as a stone until all the guards had past. Then he got up and ran to the spot where his friends had climbed up. That's when the fastest rider caught up to the wagon and shouted, "They're not on the wagon! Search the cliffs!"

As several horses came galloping back toward Gyank, Otok whispered down to him from a dark crack in the cliff, "Hurry!"

Gyank climbed as fast as he could, but he was spotted and they heard a man yell from below. "There they go!"

Seconds later, a voice of authority shouted, "Dismount and go after them!"

Gyank looked up and saw a wide ledge just above him, but his friends had disappeared from sight. As he reached up to grab hold of the ledge, two hands came down out of the darkness and pulled him up the rest of the way. They stood up and ran along the ledge that ascended to a narrow crevice between two steep cliffs. Glancing back, they could see the guards were not far behind.

"Look, there's a path up there," said Otok. "It cuts right through those cliffs."

Opus was huffing and puffing as he ran. "I wonder if the men chasing us know about it."

"I wonder where it leads," said Gyank.

With a burst of speed, Otok rushed ahead, yet Opus was slowing rapidly as he pumped his arms and gasped for breath. On the steep incline, his chubby belly worked against him and he was lagging farther behind. He looked back and saw the guards climbing onto the ledge.

"There they go!" a man shouted while pointing up at Opus.

"Come on!" said Gyank in an urgent whisper as he stopped to wait for Opus. "They're gaining on us!"

From the narrow path between the cliffs above, Otok waved them on. "Hurry! It's all downhill from here!"

"Halt!" shouted one of several guards closing in from behind.

Gyank grabbed Opus's arm and started dragging him up the steep ledge as if towing a heavy cart. "Don't stop now," he said, tugging Opus along. "Just a little bit farther. Then it's all downhill."

The guards were only a few paces behind as Gyank and Opus

struggled to the top where Otok was waiting. One behind the other, they slipped through the crack in the cliff as they heard a man shout, "There's nowhere to run! You're trapped!"

On the other side of the narrow crevice was a steep slope of dirt and stone. Far below was a vast forest, so dark and dense it looked as if the slope led into a deep black pit. Neither the steep incline nor the dark foreboding forest caused them to hesitate as they plunged down into the valley below. Behind them, they could hear the shouts of the guards.

"They're going into the valley!"

"We can't chase them beyond the threshold!"

"Let them go! They're doomed!" Then a pause, and once again, "They're doomed!"

Chapter 11

THE FORBIDDEN VALLEY

They ran and slid down the long slope of earth and loose stone until they came to the bottom where they collapsed, gasping for breath. When the last bit of dirt and stone stopped rolling down on them, they realized the strange quiet of the valley. Their own breathing seemed to be the only sound in the vastness between the mountains. The silence made them realize they were no longer being pursued, and the shouts they had heard from the men behind them made it clear that they had escaped into the forbidden Valley of Vordar. The soldiers of Mellain, fully armed, would not chase them into this valley. So, for the companions, this was a sanctuary. But why did this place arouse such fear in men trained for battle? Certainly, it was justified by something, even if only by myth or superstition.

Otok was the farthest down the slope and covered by vegetation.

"Otok, you alright?" asked Gyank in a normal tone that pierced the silence as if he was shouting.

Sticking his hand up so the others could see where he was, Otok said, "I'm fine."

Gyank looked in the opposite direction. "How about you, Opus?"

Farther up the slope and in plain sight, Opus lay on his back, not moving. "I'm still with you," he answered between deep breaths.

Gyank stood up slowly and started down the last part of the steep slope. He stumbled on the loose stones, caught his balance, and continued. "Looks like we're safe for the moment. But did you hear what those men were yelling as we ran down the hill?"

"I sure did," said Opus as he got up and brushed himself off. "We are doomed. And if we were as fearful as the brave men of Mellain, then we would have died of fright before we reached the bottom."

Otok's voice echoed up from below. "You seem in good spirits for someone who's just descended into a forbidden valley."

Gyank stared into the dark forest lining the bottom of the slope. "I wonder what's in this valley that's so dangerous. I'm sure it's feared for a reason—probably a good one."

"I hope we don't find out," said Opus.

It was too dark to see the map, so Gyank didn't bother to take it out. He just spoke from memory. "According to the map, we'll have to travel the length of this valley to get to the other side of the mountains. If the map is accurate, Thorilleia is only a short distance north from there."

"Before we set out on another trek, why don't we get some sleep?" said Otok.

"I'm all for that," added Opus. "And it wouldn't hurt if we could also find something to eat. I'm starving."

The companions had traveled many miles that day and hadn't eaten much, yet they couldn't start foraging for food in the dark, so they lay down at the edge of the forest and went to sleep. They had planned to take turns sitting awake and keeping watch, but sometime during the night, one of them dozed off and they all slept soundly. The forest was still and quiet, and the next morning when the sun came up, as usual, Opus awoke first.

"Come on fellows. Time to get up. Seems like one of us couldn't handle his watch last night. But all is well, and it looks like a great day. Come on you two, get up."

Otok groaned and rolled over, but soon they were all up and on their way. They couldn't find anything for breakfast, so they traveled on empty stomachs once again. The forest was not as dense as it had appeared in the dark from the top of the slope, and hiking was easy. Opus's cheerful demeanor kept their spirits high, and his joking and laughter helped them ignore their grumbling stomachs. He had a way of making fun of their difficulties so that things didn't seem so bad.

Throughout the course of the day, they found a few berries and some edible plants, but it was nowhere near enough to satisfy their hunger. As evening approached, the forest quieted once again and the sounds of the travelers echoed loudly among the trees. Even their footsteps seemed uncomfortably noisy and unwelcome. Eventually they settled down to sleep for another night in the silent forest. It was decided that Gyank would take the first watch, and they agreed that although the previous night passed safely, it was dangerous for all of them to sleep at the same time. They promised each other that if the man on watch felt drowsy, he would wake one of his companions.

Otok and Opus had fallen asleep, and Gyank sat awake in the dark silence. There were no bright orange coals of a campfire to stare into. They couldn't risk advertising their presence in the forest by making a fire, so the campsite was dark except for the dim light that filtered down from the night sky through the trees. Gyank's eyes were well adjusted to the dark, and as he listened to the silence of the woods, he sat with his back against a tree trunk and looked up to see if he could spot the moonlit clouds through the trees. A large hand suddenly came from behind and seized him by the throat as if the tree had instantaneously sprouted a hand and grabbed him. How could something have successfully crept up so close to him without making any noise at all? Or was it by some evil magic that this thing simply appeared?

While Gyank tried to rip free, another hand came over his mouth. As he kicked his feet on the ground trying to wake his friends, he saw numerous dark shadows moving rapidly through the woods, encircling the campsite. These phantom shadows moved without a sound, and every black shape held the dark outline of a sword or axe. Gyank would have been certain they were the shadows of men, except that in the dim light, he could see they were covered with fur.

Gyank finally managed to kick Otok in the knee, and he awoke grasping for his axe. But it was too late. The creatures flooded the campsite, surrounded the companions, and made themselves visible. They were men dressed in animal hides that hung loosely about them. They were armed and ready for battle, but there was no uniformity about them. Each had their own style of weapon and their own way of carrying it. Some had knives strapped to their upper thighs or around their calves. Long swords, short swords, and axes of all kinds were in their hands. Scabbards of every shape and design dangled from their waists, and some had large sheaths strapped to their backs.

Otok sat up and twisted his head around to see how many there were, but several men pushed their sword tips into his chest, forcing him back down to the ground. He looked over at Gyank who had stopped struggling. One of the men gave Opus a nudge with his foot, and he awoke to see the hopeless situation. Words passed from one man to the next and the companions understood nothing. A slender but powerful man with long blond hair came forward, looked down at the captives, and spoke with a heavy accent. "Who are you?" His tone of voice carried authority. He was obviously the leader.

"We are travelers," said Gyank.

"Where are you going?"

"We're on our way to the other side of the mountains."

"Why?"

Gyank paused for a moment, and then said, "We're searching for riches."

"If you lie, we kill you," said the man. This wasn't spoken as a threat, but merely a statement of fact.

At that moment, neither Gyank nor the others understood how much of a fact it really was. For these men were not like other men of the world. They built no castles. They sought no great riches. They knew more about the woods and the mountains than was ever written in books. And above all else, they could fight like no other warriors in the land. Their ability on the battlefield surpassed the best-trained soldiers of the most military kingdoms. They were the great barbarians of the mountains that legends were built upon. The companions realized these men were the dreaded Vorak warriors that Smilga had warned them about.

The captives were bound by the hands and led off through the woods. Their weapons were taken and distributed among the men quickly and without the slightest quarrel. The Voraks had a fast pace and the companions had difficulty keeping up. Since their hands were tied firmly in front of them, they often lost their balance as they moved through the underbrush. Occasionally, one of them would trip and fall on his face only to be lifted up and pushed onward by a stiff hand. They traveled for miles through the night without stopping or even slowing their pace. The only sound to be heard in the forest was the heavy breathing of the captives and the noise made by their unskilled feet. The large group of barbarians trotting along with them made no noise at all. Gyank was completely baffled by this. He had always prided himself on his stalking ability, yet the way these men moved through the woods was uncanny.

After hours of the Vorak's grueling pace, the forest began thinning out. There were fewer trees and more brush, yet they were still in the woods. Then they heard a sound made not by them, but by an unseen creature. A long howl could be heard cutting through the dark silence of the night. It was followed by another similar howl that was much closer to them. The Voraks stopped and listened. Peering through the dark woods, the companions wondered if these were the wails of some horrible creatures similar to the wacoba, nocturnal beasts calling to each other, gathering for a kill. One of the Voraks put his hand up to his cheek and let out a howl that sounded exactly like the ones they had just heard. Then all went silent. The forest was filled with a dead, noiseless feeling.

Everyone stood motionless while a faint sound was heard off in the distance. It was hard to distinguish, but it grew steadily louder until everyone recognized it as the sound of a large group of men moving through the woods. The Vorak leader gave a hand signal to his men and they spread out and began to creep toward the noise. Two men stayed behind to look after the captives while the rest moved forward under the command of their blond-headed leader.

Mingled with the faint sound of advancing troops echoing quietly in the forest was an unfamiliar sound. Something very large was moving slowly through the brush. They could hear each time its foot lifted and stepped forward, crushing leaves and snapping twigs under its weight.

Suddenly, loud war cries echoed through the valley, and the silence was broken by the sounds of battle raging only a short distance away. The helpless prisoners thought of a way to escape. If they could free their hands and take care of the two men who stayed behind, they might be able to slip away into the forest before the battle ended. But soon all hope vanished. Voraks were charging back through the woods. Many were injured, including the leader, who was being helped along by two of his men. His thigh had been pierced by a long, black arrow, and the barbed tip was sticking out the other side of his leg. He was carefully lowered to the ground as his men crouched around him, looking for guidance. Their numbers were greatly diminished, but the fight was not over. The enemy could be heard in the woods not far away. From the sounds echoing through the trees, it was clear they were closing in to finish off the barbarians.

With blood streaming down his leg, the Vorak leader fought to stand up and pointed in a direction away from the sound of the advancing troops. Two men aided him as the small group began moving through the woods, pushing the captives along with them. After only a short distance, it was obvious that they were not moving fast enough and would soon be overtaken. Their wounded leader was slowing them down, but the men who could run faster and escape, did not. They would not leave their leader to the enemy. Gathering in a tight cluster, they prepared to make a final stand. The leader signaled one man to come close to him. He whispered into his ear, and then the man took off in a trot. The leader was either sending a messenger to get help, or merely to tell the story of what had happened to them.

Moments after the man fled into the darkness, countless soldiers came swarming through the forest. They were spread out in search of the surviving barbarians, and as soon as one of them spotted the

Voraks, he gave a yell and the rest of them came running. The barbarian leader sprang up in spite of the arrow stuck through his leg. He drew two swords from their sheaths on either side of his waist, and holding one sword in each hand, he stood to face the onslaught.

The companions hid in the underbrush with their hands tied and could do nothing but watch. They thought it strange that the Vorak leader fought with two swords and no shield. But when they saw his aggressive style of combat, the effectiveness of his technique became obvious. As the soldiers advanced, the Voraks stood their ground and showed superior fighting skill. Their leader's swords flashed in the moonlight, and although his movements were hindered by his wound, he slew two soldiers within the first few moments of battle. Yet, these great barbarian fighters were overwhelmingly outnumbered. Bodies piled up on the forest floor as the defensive circle of Voraks closed smaller. The soldiers were gradually winning the fight, but at a great cost. They seemed bent on killing their enemy to the last man as if driven by some berserk desire for battle. Meanwhile, the captives had no chance to escape. They were in the center of the Vorak's circle, and if they were to run, they would be mistaken for Voraks and slain.

In the midst of battle, a huge black shadow appeared behind the soldiers. The top of it loomed high above their heads in the shape of a human torso. The head of this ominous figure had a pair of long, slender horns that curved upward. The rest of the shadow was an indistinguishable dark mass. As it moved closer, two large red eyes became visible in the middle of the fearsome black shape, and it was clear that this terrifying silhouette was created by a monstrous creature being ridden by a cloaked man with a horned helmet. It was too dark to see any distinct features of the beastly steed. By the dim light of the moon, it seemed like some kind of giant prehistoric reptile with red eyes and piercing black pupils. When the dark figure saw that the Vorak leader was still standing and fighting fiercely, a hideous voice came from under the helmet of the rider. "Corrak, son of Cargon, you have seen your last day. By the hand of Lord Krotor, you will be slain."

With those words, a long, dark lance was raised up and pointed at the leader of the barbarians. The soldiers yielded, stepping back to leave the one called Corrak standing alone with a bloodstained sword in each hand. Shaking from the pain of his wounds, the great barbarian leader stood ready to meet his fate, while the few remaining Vorak warriors gathered by his side. Hidden in the undergrowth with their hands bound, the captives stayed still and quiet.

The eerie shadow of man and beast came charging forward, crashing through the forest. Corrak raised the sword in his right hand, and with all the force in his mighty arm, flung it at the rider. The sword did not spin as one might expect. Instead it flew from the great warrior's hand like a dart through the night air. It would have struck the rider in the chest had not a big, round shield come up from the shadows of the man's cloak and deflected the sword with a loud, echoing clank. Corrak quickly shifted the sword from his left hand to his right and stood ready to meet the sharp point of Krotor's lance. The last few Voraks ran forward to meet the charging monster and its evil master.

It was at this point that the captives saw their only chance to escape. Still bound at the wrists, they crawled over to a dead soldier lying nearby, his sword held tightly in his clenched fist. Otok took it and cut his friends' bonds. Moments later, they were all free and lying quietly under the thick vegetation on the forest floor.

While the prisoners were freeing themselves, Krotor and his evil creature crashed through the Voraks who came forward to do battle. They were knocked aside by the huge body of the warlord's steed and crushed under its mighty weight. The rider paid little attention to the barbarians who fell at the feet of his beast. His only intent was to destroy the man who stood alone before him. The point of the lance came straight for Corrak's chest. At the last moment, Corrak flung himself to the side with his good leg. The lance followed him down into the dark shadows. The force of the charging creature shattered the lance to pieces when it struck, and after the loud snap, no sound came from where Corrak fell. The shadow of man and beast spun around to look down on the slain barbarian leader. The creature's long tail followed behind gracefully as it moved like a giant black snake. An evil laugh cut through the silence of the forest and echoed among the trees in the valley.

Then another sound broke the silence, a sound that robbed Lord Krotor of his moment of glory. A soldier who had been scouting to the rear shouted as he ran toward his master with disturbing news. "Lord Krotor! There's a large number of Voraks coming over the next hill! They're moving fast and will soon be upon us!"

Lord Krotor tossed his shattered lance to the ground and twisted in the saddle to look at the dim outline of the hill behind them. He could see movement among the dark tree trunks silhouetted in pale moonlight. Pulling hard on the reins to turn his beast around, he said, "I will not waste myself on these men of the valley. Bigger things are at hand." Kicking his steed to lurch forward, the powerful warlord shouted a command to his men, "Make haste! And guard the prisoner closely. We must get him to Islar alive."

Lord Krotor and his troops disappeared into the darkness. The woods grew quiet as the faint sounds of movement diminished. Concealed by thick ground cover on the forest floor, the companions had gone completely unnoticed.

Otok stood up slowly and said, "I hope we never have any dealings with that warlord."

"I wonder who has had the bad luck to become his prisoner," said Opus, slowly shaking his head with pity. "What a poor unfortunate soul."

"Speaking of prisoners," said Otok, "if we don't get out of here fast, we'll soon be bound by Vorak rope again. As you heard, there are more of them coming this way right now."

Looking at the spot where Corrak fell, Gyank said, "We must first see if we can help him." He hurried over to Corrak's motionless body and knelt down.

"Otok rushed after him. "Are you crazy? He's dead! Besides, any time now, dozens of barbarians will be swarming all over us. Let's grab some weapons and—my axe!"

Otok spun in a circle as he scanned the forest floor. Bodies of the slain lay among the thick vegetation. Stooping over, he pushed brush aside as he frantically searched for his axe.

Opus paced back and forth not knowing which of his friends to plead with first. "Have both of you lost your senses? We've got to get out of here!" Standing over Gyank, he threw his hands in the air. "I can't believe this. Otok's looking for his axe, and you want to start tending to the wounded. We're going to be captured again!"

"Opus, listen to me," said Gyank. "You've seen how these men fight, and how they move through the forest. If we run, we'll only be caught again. Besides, we have to go in the direction they're coming from. Somehow we must make peace with them. And the best way I can think of right now is to see if there's anything we can do to save their leader."

"Their leader is dead! For all we know, they might blame us!"

"We must be sure," said Gyank, taking hold of a long piece of splintered lance sticking up from the ground. Pushing aside a large fern, he noticed the point of the lance did not impale the Vorak warrior. It had barely missed him, pinning his animal hide vest to the ground. Corrak had no wound from the lance, yet he lay in a puddle of his own blood. Aside from the arrow sticking out of his leg, he had suffered many minor wounds from axe and sword. When he dove to avoid the lance, he must have fallen badly because his head was twisted to the side next to a log. Maybe his neck had broken when he fell, or perhaps he was just knocked unconscious. Although he appeared to be dead, Gyank had to be certain. He put his head on Corrak's chest and listened for a heartbeat.

"He's still alive," said Gyank after a short pause. "We can't leave now. We must help him."

Gyank took off his pack and began using an extra shirt to bandage Corrak's most serious wounds. Otok found his axe among the bodies of the dead Voraks. It was tucked in a man's belt, and apparently had not been used during the battle. "I found Grok. Now let's get out of here."

"It seems like our partner has other plans," said Opus.

Otok walked over and looked down at the Vorak leader. "Come on Gyank, if we don't get out of here now, we'll be caught again."

"If we're able to save his life, we might get in good with these people."

"You've got to be joking. These are the Voraks—the evil race that Smilga warned us about." Otok pointed down at Corrak's limp body. "They'll kill us just as this man said."

"He said they would kill us if we lied. And I'm not going to lie."

"I don't know about this," said Otok, shaking his head. "But I hope you're right."

"So do I. As I see it, we don't have many other choices. If we run now, this man will die and we'll be just a couple of prisoners who escaped."

"As I said, let's hope you're right." Otok crouched down next to Gyank and helped him break the arrow shaft so it could be pulled out of Corrak's leg without doing more damage.

"I'm glad you two agree on staying," said Opus. "I don't like the idea but—" Opus looked up to see a large group of men running toward them. They made no effort to hide or move silently as they barreled through the woods.

"It looks like there's no more choice to be made," said Opus. "Here they come."

Unarmed, Opus stood ready to greet the men rushing toward him. He didn't know if they would understand his words, but he remembered the name that Lord Krotor used during the battle and he shouted, "Corrak has been injured and we're trying to help him!"

In no time, a crowd of men was standing around watching Otok and Gyank tend to the fallen Vorak leader. Opus was completely ignored as he was pushed aside so others could see. Glancing around, he saw other injured men being helped by their friends.

Then a burly warrior with a brown beard came through the crowd. Broad chested and powerful-looking, he stood a head taller than anyone else. The other men moved aside to let him pass. He knelt down next to Gyank and said, "I am Brombor, son of Cargon. This is my younger brother. What happened here?"

"There was a battle between your brother and a man called Lord Krotor. Your brother was brave and stood to face the challenge even though he had an arrow through his leg."

"Lord Krotor! Curse his name!" said Brombor with anger. "I will see my brother avenged. We will track that evil warlord and see that he pays for this."

"Your brother is not dead yet," said Gyank hopefully. "I think we might be able to save him."

"Then let's get him back to my village quickly."

Corrak and a few other surviving warriors were carefully lifted onto improvised stretchers and carried off. The dead Voraks would be brought back to the village so burial rites could be performed for them.

They traveled many miles westward through the forest before they came to the Vorak village, which was built on a wooded bank of a quiet river. Clusters of small, wooden cottages, which were connected by dirt paths, were scattered among tall trees. In the center of the village was a lodge consisting mainly of one huge room with a steep-pitched roof supported by massive logs. This was the Vorak place of counsel.

Although it was late at night, the village was alive with activity. Torches burned everywhere, casting an orange glow upon the cottages and the lodge. The smell of torch smoke hung in the night air. People ran from all directions to see Corrak being carried into the village on a stretcher. But the men carrying the wounded didn't stop. They walked straight to a cottage where old women skilled in the arts of healing could tend to the injured warriors.

The companions were taken to the main lodge where most of the villagers were gathering. As soon as they entered, their attention was drawn to the apparent disorder. There seemed to be no reverence in this house of council as Vorak warriors sat at tables with their weapons, ate sloppily and talked loudly. Brombor escorted them straight down the center of the lodge to the head table where several older men sat. These were clearly men of authority and distinction. Brombor stood next to the companions without moving or saying a word. One of the older men at the head table slowly raised his hand, and the room quickly grew silent. This man was obviously the chief, for the atmosphere instantly changed to one of great respect and admiration.

The Vorak chief had long, brown hair peppered with gray, and a heavy beard sat on his barrel chest. Although age lines showed on his face, he was a powerful man, both hefty and tall. His huge forearms rested on the table in front of him, and it was well known that to this day, no one had ever beaten him in an arm wrestle. The Vorak chief was not dressed like a man of great authority. He did not wear a crown like a king or have the expensive attire of a lord. He wore animal skins like the men who served under him, and no one would ever guess that he commanded the greatest fighters in all the land. It was not by what he wore, but by his rank among the Voraks that he was known throughout the Land of Shar.

Brombor broke the silence by addressing the chief. "Father, these are the men who were found with Corrak."

It was not surprising that Brombor was the son of the Vorak chief. They both had a similar physique, and there was a clear resemblance in the face.

The chief looked at the companions as if sizing them up and then spoke loudly and clearly. "I am Cargon, son of Baldor. Who are you that aided my son when he fell in combat?"

"We are travelers in a strange land who saw a man in need,"

replied Gyank.

Brombor interrupted before Gyank could say any more. "I was told they were prisoners taken by Corrak to be questioned. He suspects they may be spies."

"We are not spies!" said Otok in a defiant tone. "Why would we help your son if we were spies?"

"I can see this one is spunky," said Cargon, causing the men in the large room to chuckle and start talking among themselves. "Silence!" demanded Cargon. The room was instantly hushed, and the barbarian chief asked, "If you are not spies, then why do you come into this valley?"

Opus bowed his head and spoke in a calm diplomatic way. "If I may be permitted to speak, we were chased into this valley by the soldiers of Mellain who also accused us of being spies. It would seem that peaceful travelers are not safe in any land during these times. Has something happened to make every ruler think that spies are about?"

Clearly, Opus's tactful question was aimed at getting information about events going on in the Land of Shar.

Cargon leaned forward over the table. "Ah, it would seem that next to the spunky one stands one who is sharp-witted with his tongue. Know that in this house, a clever tongue will do you no good. We are people of honor and we speak only the truth. The penalty for lying is death."

This is what Corrak said when they were taken captive. And it was spoken with the same absolute certainty. Gyank wondered what they could say to get themselves out of this predicament. They certainly couldn't tell the barbarians about the book. And they couldn't get away with telling only part of the story because once they started, the chief would want to know all of it.

The companions remained silent and the chief spoke again. "I can see that you are thinking of what to say. I am a man of my word, and if you lie to me, I will find out. So think hard about what you say. You may be travelers, but I have yet to know a man who travels without a reason or purpose. What is your reason for coming into this valley?"

The entire room was still. All eyes focused on the companions, and after a long uncomfortable pause, Cargon spoke again. "Let me make it clear to you. I am the ruler of this valley, and everyone who enters or leaves must answer to me. Now I want to know where you are from and what are your intentions. And I want to know your names. Why don't we start with that?"

Standing motionless, Gyank stared down at his feet. Opus realized his friend had no intention of answering, and said, "I am Opus and these are my friends, Otok and Gyank. We entered your valley only to seek passage through the mountains, and we're—"

Suddenly, Gyank interrupted. "Cargon. You ask for the truth and you shall get it."

Otok and Opus looked at him in shock, afraid he might say something he shouldn't. If these barbarians ever got the book and its power, who knows what they would do with it.

Gyank took a step forward and spoke forcefully. "You threaten us. You promise us death if we lie but promise us nothing if we speak the truth." With absolute conviction in his voice, Gyank pointed at the floor in front of him and said, "But I would have you strike me dead right here before I break a promise I made to my friends!" As this phrase echoed throughout the lodge, Gyank composed himself. "You tell us that you're a man of your word—so are we. And we keep our promises. Therefore, I will tell you only what I can without going back on my word. We're on a dangerous quest. We've vowed to keep it secret, and to carry out the mission even if only one of us survives and must complete the task on his own. I can say no more without breaking my word. But I assure you that we mean no harm to you or your people and that we entered your valley only to find a passage to the Land of Shar. You, being a man of your word, should understand why I can say no more." Cargon didn't move or even blink as he stared into Gyank's eyes. It was a cold hard stare, but Gyank didn't look away. "You asked for the truth, and I have given it to you."

The lodge was filled with a tense silence. Cargon suddenly broke out of his stare and said with a lighthearted tone, "It seems we have quite a crew here. A spunky one, and one with a clever tongue, and one who's a man of his word—no matter what the cost."

The barbarian chief's demeanor became serious again. "I could kill you for not telling me what I want to know. Or I could force you to talk. But honestly, I would have said the same thing if I was in your position. I detest lying, and I respect a man for speaking the truth even when the consequences are grim. I also respect a man who keeps a vow. So I will be as fair as I can under the circumstances."

Cargon looked at Opus. "You want to know of things happening in the Land of Shar? War is in the making. And in such times only a foolhardy ruler allows men to travel his land unaccounted for. Even so, I will not ask you to reveal your quest."

Cargon grew silent, and everyone in the lodge could see signs of deep thought in his face as they awaited his decision. Then he spoke: "You helped my son when you could have run off and left him to die. But helping my son might have been a clever trick to gain our favor. I'm sure you realize we would have tracked you down before you escaped the valley. So your intentions are still not clear. For the sake of my people, your fate will be out of my hands. I will let it be intertwined with the fate of all things, as it ultimately is. If Corrak lives, then you will be given your weapons and you will be free to come and go in and out of this land for all your days. You will be regarded as friends, and my people will be in debt to you for saving Corrak's life. But if he dies, you will be charged with the responsibility of avenging his death, a duty that I wish upon no one. Only those closest to Corrak would take on this burden of their own choosing. For those that go are not expected to return. You will join the other warriors on this mission, and journey with them deep into the land called Sarilar. Far to the south in the Uvannel Mountains, there's an evil place called Islar where Lord Krotor reigns. You would have to travel a great distance through harsh lands and somehow get past the outposts of Islar, the ever-watchful dark towers. If you survive that far, then you would face the most difficult task of all—to kill a warlord of Islar. But not just any warlord—Lord Krotor! Even among evil men, his wickedness sets him apart. There's no opponent more feared, for he is not only clever and wicked, he's a great warrior. He does not need his guards around him, for he is the greatest fighter of them all. His fortress is perched high on the sheer cliffs of Islar, and who knows what black magic he may bring against you there. As you have seen, even as far north as the Valley of Vordar, he commands awesome beasts. Within the caves under his dark castle dwell unknown evil creatures. For your sake and for the sake of my fellow warriors, let's hope Corrak does not die."

The lodge grew deathly quiet. Merely thinking about Lord Krotor's dark fortress filled the room with a feeling of dread.

Gyank broke the silence with a request. "I would like to ask one thing of you. Since our lives depend on your son getting well, may we be permitted to help heal him?"

"Granted!" said Cargon loud and clear while slapping his hand on the table. "And now, while my son's fate is still in doubt, you will be my guests. Sit and eat."

The companions sat down at the table with Cargon and ate from the plentiful Vorak bowls and plates. They thought it was extremely odd that moments ago they were being questioned under threat of death, and now they were sitting at the chief's table, being treated as honored guests. What strange sort of people were these Voraks? Whatever the answer, the companions were overjoyed to be stuffing their bellies with good food. As they ate and talked, they were surprised that Cargon did not seem to be a cold, harsh ruler of fighting men. Instead, he was an amiable man who was well liked by his men. After the meal, they were shown to a tiny, one-room cottage that was to serve as their sleeping quarters.

Once the door was closed and they were alone, Otok said, "I don't like this one bit. I don't like the idea of having our lives depend on whether some overgrown barbarian can survive all those wounds."

"Be glad it's not worse," said Opus. "I think Gyank was right not to run. We stand a good chance of making friends with these people. Besides, we got a good meal out of it." Opus patted his stomach. "And I'll bet we'll be getting a few more meals at that."

"We still may be able to turn things our way," said Gyank, pulling out the smeatle leaves that were stuck to the bottom of his pack. "According to Smilga, this plant has great healing properties."

Otok pointed to the long slender leaves. "Hey, that's a good idea. I had forgotten about the smeatle. I just hope that plant can heal as well as Smilga claimed."

"The leaves are a bit wilted," said Gyank. "But they should still work. Isn't it strange, I never thought we'd be using this plant to save someone else's life, and in turn save our own. I always figured to use it if one of us got hurt or sick."

"I hope it works," said Otok. "But what if it doesn't? Do you have anything else in mind, or do you suppose we'll have to avenge Corrak's death?"

"I don't know," said Gyank, "but if we can cure him ... well, you heard what Cargon said. We'd be free to come and go as we please. Considering how much other men fear this valley, it would be the ideal refuge once we get the book. But if Corrak dies, we can always go back to your plan and try to escape."

"That's true," said Otok. "But if Corrak dies, they'd expect us to escape. They won't expect it while he's still alive. Right now might be our only real chance to get away."

There was a knock on the door, and they suddenly realized how loudly they were talking. They all froze and looked at the door, hoping their conversation was not overheard.

"Come in," said Gyank.

The door opened and a petite young woman stepped into the room and closed the door behind her. Although small in stature and younger than Gyank, she was no child. Her hair, which hung down to her shoulders, was a shade of light brown that appeared almost blond. A pair of beautiful blue eyes peered out from under soft bangs that barely touched her forehead. Covering her shoulders was a weather-beaten black cloak that hung loosely on her small frame and came down to her knees. The hood was pulled back and laid flat between her shoulder blades. Under her cloak, she wore a gray vest of soft wool over a burgundy shirt, and a pair of dark blue pants covered her legs. On her tiny feet were leather moccasins, laced above her ankles and well broken in from miles of travel. Despite her plain garb, she was strikingly beautiful, and she had a strange air of knowledge and wisdom about her. There was a moment of silence while the three young men stood towering over her, wondering if she had overheard them.

"Who are you?" Gyank finally asked.

"I'm Reesa," she answered in a soft voice.

"What do you want?"

"I want to help you," she said in a disarming way.

"How?"

"By helping you get out of this valley alive."

Gyank's response was rather pointed, but he spoke politely. "Why would you want to help us? You don't even know us."

"This is true," she said. "But I know you're not spies. I was in the house of counsel. I saw what went on. You are no more spies than I am. And I believe Cargon knows that."

"Then why doesn't he let us go?" asked Otok.

"Apparently you know nothing of the Vorak ways. Cargon cannot just let you go. He cannot allow you to defy his authority. No leader can afford to let that happen, especially not a Vorak leader. There is much honor among these people."

Gyank looked at her curiously. "You speak of the Voraks as if you're an outsider—as if you're not one of them."

"I'm not. I'm from Rimmellaineia, a land far to the north. I've made peace with these people, and I trade goods and knowledge with them for our mutual benefit. The Voraks have a bad reputation outside this valley, yet once you come to know them, you may also come to respect them. They have integrity, they are fair in all dealings, and they are truthful. I'm more wary of common folk. I've seen far too many of them get what they desire by deception instead of fair play and hard work. Strangely enough, it's these types of men who call the Voraks evil while making no effort to know them. I do know them, and I find they are more peaceful and honest than those who call them savages."

"Since you know these people, what do you think we should do?" asked Gyank.

"I suggest you hope that Corrak lives because to charge you with the task of killing Lord Krotor is almost as bad as sentencing you to death." A disheartening expression came over Reesa's face. "I've just come from the house where Corrak is being tended to, and he's not doing well."

Gyank picked up the smeatle leaves and said, "I was just about to make a trip over there to see if I could help him. I have a healing plant."

"I will go with you," said Reesa. "I have some knowledge of healing plants. Besides, you'll need someone to translate for you."

"Very well," said Gyank. "Let's go." Stepping out of the cottage, he looked back at his friends, and said, "Why don't you two get some sleep? I'll see what I can do for Corrak, and then I'll be back."

A few moments after the door closed, Otok asked, "What do you think of her, Opus?"

"She's very pretty—I must say that. I also think she means well."

Otok lay down on a bunk and looked up at the roof of the cottage with his hands clasped behind his head. "I must agree with you."

Although they kept thinking about their brief encounter with Reesa, they said no more about it. Exhausted and with full stomachs, they soon fell into a deep sleep. Even though they were prisoners, somehow they felt safe in the hands of the Voraks.

Outside the tiny cottage, Reesa led the way to where the elderly women healers tended to Corrak. As they walked along a dirt path through the trees, Gyank asked, "If the Voraks have their own language, why do some of them speak ours?"

"During the age of great wars, the Voraks learned the advantages of knowing their enemy's language. Besides the obvious, it's one of the first steps to making peace. Since that time, Vorak leaders have strived to learn the languages of other men. Not all the Voraks can speak our language, but most of them understand it, so be careful what you say in front of them."

"Isn't it dangerous for you to be telling me all this?"

"Not really," said Reesa casually. "They have nothing to hide. Besides, they know I would never betray them. So they not only trust me, but in the house of counsel, my thoughts and opinions are taken seriously."

Gyank smiled at her. "I suppose you have quite a bit of influence with the Voraks."

"Maybe," said Reesa modestly. "Although, up to now, I haven't had anything to contribute in the house of counsel."

"If you're a trader of goods, you must know your way around this whole area."

"I know the mountains pretty well."

"If Corrak lives and we can leave, would you consider being our guide?"

"To guide you, I must know where you're going. And you can't tell me that because of the secret nature of your quest."

"If we were to tell you, then would you guide us?"

"I wouldn't want you to tell me anything that you really shouldn't."

As Reesa spoke those words, they arrived at the cottage where Corrak was. Gyank used the smeatle leaves just as Smilga had described. He scored them with a knife so the juice would ooze out and wrapped them onto the wounds. With Reesa translating, he explained to the women healers that tea was to be made from the flowers and given to Corrak when he awoke. The son of the Vorak chief had lost a lot of blood, and he lay in bed with no visible sign of life in him. After Gyank had done what he could, he and Reesa walked back to the cottage where his friends were sound asleep. Reesa had to go a bit farther down the road, and she stopped just before they parted. "Good night, Gyank," she said.

"Good night."

"And, Gyank, don't run. I will help you."

"I thank you. You're a good person."

Gyank crept quietly into the cottage so he wouldn't wake the others, crawled into a bunk and fell asleep.

The next few days went by slowly. Everything that could be done for Corrak was taken care of by the elderly women healers. The companions made many trips to his bedside, yet all they could do was wait and hope. The smeatle plant proved to have great healing power, but it was still unclear if it would be enough to save Corrak's life. While they stayed in the Vorak village, they could roam free and no one asked where they were going or what they were doing. Perhaps the Voraks didn't expect them to escape or knew that they wouldn't get far if they did. Yet the way the Voraks acted toward them went far beyond the simple issue of escaping. At mealtime, they ate at the tables along with the Voraks, and no work was required of them. They were glad to be treated so well, but they were puzzled by it. Even if Cargon knew they weren't spies, to be treated as honored guests was beyond anything they would have expected.

Even though the Voraks had their own language, they took extra effort to speak in the common tongue so the companions could understand them. Those who couldn't speak the common tongue still took an interest in communicating. Someone nearby was always willing to translate so they would not feel left out of a conversation. By interacting with the villagers, it became clear that these people preferred to live in peace with those around them, regardless of their differences. Yet they were prepared to fight when necessary—and fight they did. At almost any time, one could see warriors honing their weapons or practicing their combat skills with each other.

During one of these training sessions, Otok noticed a Vorak instructor with a battle-axe tucked in his belt. This senior teacher stood back from the younger men who were practicing, and he would only occasionally interrupt them to demonstrate a fine point of technique. After watching for a while, Otok approached him. "I see you use an axe."

"It's my weapon of choice."

"I like the axe myself," said Otok.

Surprised that an outsider took an interest in his favorite weapon, the man went on talking about it. "I learned the axe years ago from one of the best axe men in all the Uvannel. If wielded with skill, it's the most devastating of all weapons. Most fighters know this and fear any warrior who can handle an axe well."

"I have an axe, but I haven't learned how to use it."

"Would you like to learn?"

"Would I?" said Otok, stunned by the offer. "Aside from Corrak getting well, I'd like nothing more."

"My name is Grimel," said the man, extending his hand to Otok who shook it enthusiastically.

"I'm Otok."

"We can start with the basics, but first you need an axe."

Grimel pulled the axe from his belt and handed it to Otok. But Otok didn't take it. Instead, he made a request. "Would it be possible for me to learn with my own axe? It was taken from me when I came to your village."

"Each axe is slightly different, and it would be best to learn with your own weapon." Grimel nodded in agreement. "Let's go get yours."

Although Otok made the request, he was surprised Grimel agreed. He was even more surprised when Grimel took him to a back room within the house of counsel where an amazing assortment of weapons and armament were stored on shelves and tall racks. Leading the way down a narrow aisle, Grimel pointed to a shelf. "Your equipment should be here."

Otok pulled Grok from among the other gear. "This is it."

"While we're here, let's start your first lesson."

"Here? There's not enough room to swing an axe."

"Exactly," said Grimel. "You must learn to fight in all circumstances."

Grimel swiftly slid the axe from his belt and thrust the butt of the handle toward Otok's chest, stopping only inches away. "See, the axe blade is not the only way to strike. You must know your weapon, and all other weapons as well. In combat, if you don't know what an opponent's weapon can do, one surprise could be the end of you."

Grimel began to point out one weapon at a time, explaining their usages, advantages, and disadvantages, as well as how they matched up against the battle-axe. Otok noticed the many different types of axes and asked about Grok. "I was given this axe only a short time ago, and I was wondering why the back of the head is curved up."

"That's for blocking," explained Grimel as he took Otok's axe to demonstrate.

"I thought it might be curved that way just for style."

"No, not at all. You have a very fine axe, and every part of it was designed for a reason. This curve, along with the curve of the blade, creates a pocket at the top of the axe that allows you to block and redirect a weapon to the side, then you can strike with the handle as I showed you." Admiring the workmanship of the axe, Grimel continued to explain. "Although almost any axe can be used with a shield, I can tell your axe was designed to be used with two hands and no shield. That's the fighting style I like the best. Using both hands, you get the most power into a strike."

As the lesson went on, it was obvious that Grimel was an excellent teacher. He was patient, he explained things clearly, and he also had great skill. Otok took a liking to him right away, and Grimel was glad to find a new student who not only took instructions well and learned fast but who embraced the learning process with a passion. After the lesson, Grok was returned to the house of counsel, and time was set aside for more instruction and practice the next day. Within a few short days, Otok had mastered the basics of Vorak axe fighting. Grimel's style was much more effective than the brute force, hacking techniques used by most. His form of combat was like a graceful dance where he was never off balance and moved fluidly without the restraints of armor or shield. The Vorak way of handling an axe was truly an art form, and Grimel took pride in how well Otok was progressing.

While Otok learned and practiced, Gyank and Opus spent much of their time with Reesa. She always had something nice to say and proved to be very good company. Her pleasing personality and calm demeanor were soothing, especially to Gyank, for his mind wrestled with worries. He had pulled his friends into this situation that depended on Corrak, and he kept wondering if he had made the right decision. In addition to this, many other questions were running through his mind. Was there really a book? If so, could they find it? And what mysterious, dark power did it hold? Reesa could tell that Gyank had many concerns, but she didn't pry into what was troubling him, not even to help. She was just always there to say a kind word.

The days went by. Finally, it was clear that Corrak was going to live. Cargon kept his word and declared them friends of the Voraks. The valley was theirs to enter or leave whenever they wished, and they would forever be regarded as honored guests. Cargon even went so far as to say that they had saved his son's life, for he attributed Corrak's recovery to the smeatle leaves.

They were given back their weapons and all the additional supplies they needed. Otok had Grok at his side, and now he was skilled in the Vorak way to use it. He also had his bow over his shoulder and a quiver full of Vorak arrows. Gyank once again had his special sword with serpents carved into the handle along with a beautiful leather scabbard that was found to fit it. He had his throwing hatchet tucked in his belt, and his pack was filled with all sorts of dried foods, climbing rope, spikes, spare clothes, and sleeping gear. Opus had his sword on his hip, and both he and Otok were fitted with Vorak packs filled with food and supplies. Since Gyank and Opus had no bows of their own, they were given beautifully crafted long bows of strong wood, and quivers full of Vorak arrows. The companions were prepared to continue their journey, but the one thing they wanted most of all they could not take with them. They wanted Reesa's guidance and companionship, but she had to attend to business elsewhere.

"It would be a great help if you could show us the way out of this valley," said Gyank, trying to talk her into going with them.

"I told you. I'm on the last part of my trading route, and I must meet my brother, Ramen. He'll be waiting for me at a predetermined place. If I'm not there, he will worry. I'm sorry, but I can't go with you."

"Then I guess we must say good-bye," said Gyank sadly.

"We'll miss you," said Opus as he gave her a hug.

Reesa turned to hug Otok, and then finally, as she gave Gyank a warm embrace, he said, "Yes, we'll certainly miss you."

The companions left the village. They had spent many days with the Voraks, and they feared time was growing short. The river that ran past the Vorak village was on Gyank's map, and they were told that it led to the other side of the mountains. They planned to follow it into the Land of Shar and then head north to Thorilleia. But not knowing what they would find when they got there gave them an uneasy feeling. Once again, they left a safe place to journey deep into a land of dangers and peril. Soon, the village was far behind them, and they were alone in a strange land.

Chapter 12

SELLOCK THE WIZARD

The river that they followed was created by melting snow that drained down from the mountains and flowed into the valley. The peaceful sound of gurgling water filled the woods as the shallow and serene river wound its way through the trees. They hiked along cheerfully although they were well aware that they would soon be looking upon the great walls of Thorilleia, and this is where their quest would become most dangerous.

That evening, they set up camp on the riverbank. The forest came down to the water's edge; this allowed them to sleep in the cover of the trees while listening to the tranquil sounds of the river. They were busy preparing supper when the sun went down and left them cooking in the dim light.

Sitting on a boulder, Gyank studied his map. "I wonder how long it will take to get to the castle of Thorilleia."

"Right now, why don't we worry about not burning our supper?" said Opus, poking the fire with a stick.

Just then, a dark shadowy figure stepped out from the cover of the woods. Otok saw it first and gripped his axe. Opus reached for the hilt of his sword.

"Relax, it's only me," said a soft familiar voice.

"Reesa!" shouted Gyank with delight. "What are you doing here?"

"I missed you fellows."

Reesa came forward and stood by the fire. She was dressed in her usual cloak and moccasins, but this time she was prepared for adventure. She had a pack on her back with a coil of rope dangling beside it, and she was equipped with a small recurve bow. It was not crafted in the Vorak style, but it was specifically made to match

Reesa's arm length, and it was just the right size for her. The quiver on her back and the arrows in it were also smaller in size and matched her bow perfectly.

"Supper smells good," she said.

"We're glad to see you," said Gyank. "But what changed your mind?"

"I didn't realize how much I'd miss you until you were gone. So I decided to come along and guide you out of the valley. The Land of Shar is a very dangerous place you know," she said with a teasing smile. "I'd hate for you to get lost in the mountains. Men with swords are not the only dangers."

"We're happy you're here," said Gyank, "but I thought you had to meet your brother."

"One of the Vorak scouts offered to meet him and tell him where I went. My brother will go to the Vorak village and wait for me there. When I get back, we'll leave for home. We have plenty of time before winter comes and the mountains become impassable."

"Well, sit down. Take off your pack and have something to eat," said Gyank who was absolutely delighted to have Reesa with them.

As they sat around the fire eating their evening meal, Gyank asked, "Aren't you concerned about traveling alone? As you said, the Land of Shar is very dangerous."

"Most of the time I'm with my brother and we look out for each other. But when I'm alone, I look after myself. I use my wits. Besides, I'm not so helpless. Don't judge me by my size. I'm a tough little girl," said Reesa half-jokingly.

"I suppose you are at that," said Opus. "At least tough in spirit."

Reesa smiled and casually spoke words of wisdom. "Being tough in spirit is the best kind of toughness. Wise men have said that defeat only comes after you've given up in spirit—and never before."

"I guess you're right about that," agreed Gyank. "I suppose you can never tell how tough someone is just by looking at them." As Gyank spoke, he looked at Reesa's pretty face and small frame.

Certainly, no one would think of describing her as tough. Gyank pointed to her bow and said, "Besides your toughness of spirit, I bet you're a good shot with that fancy looking bow of yours."

"Yes, I suppose," said Reesa modestly.

As the summer sky grew dark and the fire burned low, the four travelers went to sleep. They did not have to keep watch, for they were still in the Valley of Vordar, and still under the protection of the Voraks.

~ ~ ~

When they awoke the next morning, Gyank's map was taken out and looked at once again. It only made sense for the guide to know where they were going, and this didn't reveal anything about their quest. Hiking along the river was easy, and they covered much distance in a short time. By noon, they were approaching the other side of the valley. Mountains loomed up on both sides of them while the river and the forest stretched onward between the towering peaks. Sweaty from the summer sun, the party stopped to rest. They took off their boots and dipped their feet into the cool river.

Looking ahead at the mountains to the north, Gyank said, "The castle of Thorilleia must be somewhere beyond those mountains—at least according to the map."

"Your map is correct," said Reesa. She pointed to a mountainous ridge. "There's quite a castle on the other side of those cliffs."

"Do you think we'll get there by this evening?" asked Otok.

"Yes, if we really want to. But that may not be a good idea."

"Why not?"

"Well," said Reesa, "If I can, I prefer to look ahead before walking into a place like that. Heading north out of the valley, we should get there by nightfall. But whatever we find, we'll be in the middle of it."

"How can we see what's there before we get there?" asked Gyank.

"In order to go north, we have to cross this river sooner or later. If we cross it here, we might be able to climb up the ridge separating us from Thorilleia. From there we could probably see for miles in several directions. We might even get a view of the castle."

"That's an excellent idea," said Gyank.

"We'll have to climb the ridge," said Reesa. "And that might be risky."

"We can handle it," said Otok with confidence.

"There's one more thing," said Reesa. "It'll make the trip a bit longer, and I don't know how soon you have to be in Thorilleia."

"To tell you the truth," said Opus with a chuckle, "neither do we."

"It's better to take a little longer and be safe," said Gyank.

"I agree," said Otok. "It would be foolish to save a little time only to be captured."

Gyank sat on a rock, swirling his bare foot in the water while staring down at his toes. "How much can we expect to see from the top of a ridge? It still may not be safe even if we see nothing unusual."

"You're forgetting," said Reesa, "war is brewing; this is no time to be taking chances."

"You're right," said Gyank as he stood up. "Let's start looking for a shallow spot where we can cross the river."

It wasn't long before they found a place where they could wade across the river, and soon they were working their way up a steep ridge. It was almost sundown by the time they made it to the top, but there was no view of Thorilleia. On the other side of the ridge was a long rocky slope rising up to meet an enormous vertical wall of gray stone. This huge chunk of rock stretched far up to the sky, and looking up at it made them dizzy. At the top of the slope was a narrow gap in the sheer wall of stone.

"Maybe we can see something from up there," said Otok, pointing to the crack in the mountain.

With each step, rocks and gravel gave way under their feet, making progress slow and difficult. Only a short way up the slope, they stopped to rest. They were sweating and their legs were aching from the climb. Fortunately, a long shadow cast by the mountain shaded them from the rays of the sun. Once they had rested and cooled off a bit, they pushed onward to the top of the slope, and passing through the gap in the cliff, they came upon a magnificent view. Far below was a beautiful valley encircled by steep mountain peaks. The sun hung low in the sky behind silvery clouds, and broad beams of sunlight shone down into the valley, highlighting the jagged cliffs.

Scanning the rugged mountains surrounding the valley, they saw something among the cliffs that did not fit in with the natural scenery. Far to the east was a huge man-made wall spanning a wide gap between two enormous cliffs in the distance. The giant stone blocks of this ancient architectural wonder were weather-beaten and worn, yet they stood as an impenetrable barrier. The builders had quarried rock from the nearby mountains to create this gargantuan structure and so it blended in with the cliffs. It was much thicker at the base and narrowed as it rose up to the sky. Even so, the top of the wall was dense with heavy stones and it had a walkway wide enough to hold many troops. Huge, circular towers were built into the wall at evenly spaced intervals, and atop each tower were tall pointy merlons, like the teeth of some colossal monster yawning at the sky. Countless chambers and corridors within the wall served to house the thousands of troops needed to fortify it. Centuries old, this great wall in the cliffs was actually an immense fortress.

Although one would expect to see a giant gate opening to the east at the base of the wall, oddly enough, there was none. There were secret ways through the wall, but it was obviously designed to keep something in or out of the valley. Or perhaps its purpose was even larger in scope, for it divided the landscape, east from west.

"Will you look at that?" said Opus. "It's a giant wall. I wonder who built it and why."

"That's strange," said Reesa quietly to herself. "It's not supposed to look like that."

"What do you mean?" asked Gyank. "Are you familiar with this wall?"

"Yes, I've seen it often. But it's not supposed to look like that."

Reesa sensed something was wrong, but for the moment, she couldn't put her finger on it. She stood there, staring intensely at the ancient wall in the distance.

Her reaction was making Gyank concerned. "Reesa, if you know something, why don't you share it with us?"

"That's the great Wall of Thorilleia. It was built many, many years ago—long before the age of great wars. According to legend, the wall was built to protect the valley from the warlike peoples of Elreia. As you can see, it's in a strategic position. It closes off one of two entrances to the valley. The other entrance in the west is blocked off by the castle of Thorilleia—but you can't see it from here. With the wall protecting the east and the castle guarding the west, people could live here in safety, even if wars raged around them. They could grow crops, raise cattle, and get water from the streams that flow through the valley. Besides food and water, the valley is a source of wood, iron, stones, and other materials needed to wage war. In this way, Thorilleia could survive a siege indefinitely. They could never be starved into surrender by a foreign power."

While Reesa explained the history of the wall and its purpose, the last tiny piece of glowing sun disappeared behind the mountains. As the dim light of evening crept into the valley below, tiny specks of light became visible in the towers, and a troubled expression came over Reesa's face.

"What's wrong?" asked Gyank.

"There are lights in the towers."

"Why should that be a cause for concern?" said Gyank.

"Don't you understand? The wall is used to defend Thorilleia. In times of peace, there's no reason to have it fortified. For many years, it's been left unguarded—a reminder that war was dead in the world. My heart rested each time I came within sight of the wall and saw it dark and empty. If that's the torchlight of Thorilleian soldiers, then the rumor of war is true and the world will see another terrible age of bloodshed and death."

In the west, the warm colors of the sun lingered on the horizon, but looking eastward at the wall, the sky was deep blue, making it clear that the wall was alive with lights. Not only were there lights in the towers, the entire span of the wall was dotted with small torches.

"Does this mean the castle is under siege?" asked Otok.

"I don't know, but you can be certain that if the wall is fortified, Thorilleia is expecting to be attacked."

"Who do you suppose would attack Thorilleia?" asked Opus, as if Reesa had all the answers.

"It could be almost anyone," said Reesa, shrugging her shoulders while turning her palms up. "If I were to take a guess, I'd suspect a kingdom from Elreia because the wall defends against attacks from the east. If an army from Elreia wanted to attack Thorilleia, the only other way is through the Valley of Vordar. Neither way is easy, but you'd probably agree that most would rather try to take the wall. You know how much the Voraks are feared. Besides, if an army marched into the Valley of Vordar, the Voraks would see it as an invasion. They'd gather to defend their homeland, and that army would never make it through the valley."

"What about Lord Krotor and his men?" asked Otok. "They were able to get through."

"Lord Krotor is a different breed of man. Strange powers are at his command. Who knows what evil forces might have aided him through the Valley of Vordar. Besides, from what I heard, he didn't pass through the valley lengthwise from east to west. He only cut across it from north to south, and he only fought a small band of Vorak warriors. Even so, anyone else would rather fight Thorilleian soldiers at the wall than face the Voraks in the woods." Reesa paused to think. "It could be Mellain or Derrim at the wall. Yet neither is any match for Thorilleia."

"This is just great," said Otok sarcastically. "We've walked right smack into the middle of a war. And if the castle's besieged, there's no way we'll be able to get in there."

With a hopeful tone of voice, Opus said, "For all we know, it could be months before a siege actually starts."

"He's right," said Reesa. "Let's see if we can get a look at the castle before it gets too dark."

Heading west from the crack in the mountain face, they followed a wide ledge that gradually sloped downward and curved around a huge, vertical cliff. On one side of the path, the stone rose straight up to the darkening sky. On the other side, a precipice dropped straight down to the valley below. Turning a sharp bend in the cliff, they came within sight of the castle. Their eyes grew wide with amazement when they saw the size of it. As Reesa had said, the castle blocked the only other opening to the valley as its walls extended into the countryside. Looking down at the fortress from the side of the mountain, they could see countless archways connecting courtyards and battlements where layer upon layer of defensive wall reached out across the valley. Circular towers protruded from the walls, framing every arched gate, and atop these towers were catapults poised to hurl huge stones. The inner castle had slender towers with pointy roofs reaching progressively higher. It was protected by a deep dry moat facing the valley, while the back of the fortress was built into the face of a cliff. It was a castle whose origin went back hundreds of years. And for all those centuries, the Thorilleian builders had continuously added to its defenses. It was an incredibly strong fortress that grew stronger with age.

"How in the world will we ever get in there?" said Otok in disgust.

"If your quest lies within the walls of the castle, then you have even greater troubles." Reesa pointed with her finger. "Look to the river."

Beyond the castle, the Gubain River twisted and turned along the western side of the Uvannel Mountains. Broken into countless branches, it ran through the Marshes of Guglic, which stretched for hundreds of miles along the mountain chain. A good distance up the river was a fleet of warships anchored well outside of catapult range. The shoreline was dotted with bonfires, and men busied themselves felling trees to build implements of war. The frames of unfinished siege towers could be seen standing along the beach, partially lit by the orange glow from the fires. A huge tree trunk sat on a long slender wagon lined with heavy wooden wheels waiting to be pulled to the castle. Large axes had carved an enormous point where the roots had been, creating a formidable battering ram that stood ready to knock on Thorilleia's doors. All kinds of war machines littered the beach as catapults and ballistae were primed to fling stones and giant arrows at the castle walls.

"We've come all this way," said Gyank. "For what? To have our goal snatched away from us just before achieving it."

Otok stared down at the beach with the same hopelessness in his heart.

"Hey, come on," said Opus, trying to cheer up his friends. "We'll get in there somehow. We'll find a way."

"Opus, you have eyes, don't you?" said Gyank with despair. "Just look at the castle. Look at the men on the beach and their war machines. It would've been hard enough to sneak into that castle in peacetime. How do you suppose we do it while it's under siege?"

Opus didn't respond. He turned to Reesa, and asked, "Do you know who those men are on the beach?"

"I can't be certain, but to the best of my knowledge, only the Kingdom of Dlembar has a fleet of that size. They have the greatest navy on the Gubain. Their sailors are not only excellent seamen, they're also trained in the art of war."

Looking down at the fleet, Opus asked, "With all those siege towers and catapults, do you suppose they can take the castle?"

"It's hard to tell," said Reesa, doing her best to size up the situation. "They may stand a chance because Thorilleia is also manning the great wall to the east, so their forces are divided. Even so, if Dlembar takes the castle, it will be at a great cost."

Watching the dark images of men preparing for battle, Otok and Gyank silently contemplated their grim situation. If they were caught by Dlembar sailors, they would be mistaken for Thorilleians trying to escape, and if caught inside the castle walls, they would be accused of being Dlembar spies. Even if they could get inside the castle, they would still be faced with the task of finding the book.

Suddenly, Opus whispered a warning, "Everyone hide! Someone's coming!"

In the dim light, a robed figure was coming toward them along the ledge. The party ran back and found a rocky indentation where they could hide. Standing with their backs to the cliff, they waited in the shadows. Moments later, a man came trudging along the ledge. He was dressed in long gray robes and walked with a staff. His hood was pulled up over his head, and when they tried to get a glimpse of his face, they only saw the tip of his nose protruding from the darkness that concealed his features. In spite of his robes and hooded face, they could tell he was a spindly sort of man. As he passed, he didn't notice the dark figures hiding in the shadows of the jagged cliff. He disappeared around a bend on the ledge and Gyank whispered, "I wonder who he is. He certainly doesn't look like a sailor."

"No, he does not," said Opus quietly. "I'd like to know where he's going."

"There is a way to find out," said Otok. "Let's follow him."

No one objected, so they crept after him. To avoid being seen, they hugged the cliff as they watched the robed figure stop at the crack in the sheer stone and glance at the Wall of Thorilleia. The fearsome structure gave off an eerie glow in the distance.

The man turned, went through the gap, and started down the long rocky slope. They followed him, but had to stop at the top of the slope. They could not go any farther without being seen. Watching from the shadows, Opus lost his footing on the loose rocks and slipped, sending small stones and gravel tumbling down toward the dark figure below.

The man spun around and looked up. His eyes scanned the top of the slope, but he saw no one. Opus had fallen back into the darkness of the crack in the cliff and he lay perfectly still. His friends were also well concealed among the jagged rocks.

A deep voice hollered up the slope, "Who goes there?" The echoing question died and remained unanswered. "Show yourselves or face the wrath of Sellock the Wizard!"

This ominous threat struck the companions with fear. Since childhood, they had heard stories about the power wielded by such men, and his threatening voice made them wonder if he would use some kind of dark magic on them.

The shadowy figure spoke in a loud commanding voice. "Now suffer the wrath of Sellock the Wizard!" As he raised his staff, the words "Sellock the Wizard!" bounded between the cliffs in a long echo. But before he could utter another word, a desperate call came from above.

"Wait!" shouted Gyank, stepping into view. "We mean you no harm."

The others also showed themselves.

"Who dares to spy on me?"

"We are only travelers," said Gyank. "We're not spies."

"We will see," said the man as he began climbing back up the slope. As he reached the top, his hood fell back, revealing an old bald man with a wrinkled face and a gray beard. Although frail looking, he had an air of confidence and power about him. His piercing green eyes gazed at them from under his bushy eyebrows as if trying to detect what they were thinking. "You were following me. Weren't you?" he said calmly.

"We were surprised to see anyone outside the castle walls," said Otok, "especially alone and at night. We were wondering where you're going."

"So, you were wondering," he said as his eyes darted to the packs on their backs. "If you have some food to share, I will sit with you, and we will talk."

Between the towering cliffs, they sat and shared bread and dried fruit with Sellock. He obviously had not eaten in a while, for he gobbled his food like a ravenous dog.

"What are your names?" asked the wizard with a mouth full of food.

"I'm Gyank and these are my friends, Otok, Opus, and Reesa."

"You are kind to share bread. And I will share what I can with you. Ask a question, and I will do my best to answer."

"Who are you and what brings you here?" asked Gyank.

The old man spoke between swallowing large chunks of food. "I am Sellock. I serve as wizard for Derrim. I was visiting in Thorilleia, but it's no longer safe here, so I'm heading back to Derrim."

"The castle is under siege," said Gyank. "How did you escape?"

"That's a wizard's secret," said Sellock, peering suspiciously at Gyank. "Why do you want to know?"

"We have business within the castle. But obviously we can't get near it. If you were able to get out, perhaps you could you help us get in."

"I have the ability, but I also have a price. And I believe it may be too steep for you."

"Ask your price," said Otok.

"I must get to Derrim, but the great wall is shut. All passages are locked and guarded. By decree of the king, no one is to pass in either direction. Anyone attempting to do so will be suspected of being a spy. The only other way to the east is through the Valley of Vordar. And to pass through that valley is a great task indeed—even for a wizard." Sellock rubbed his beard and said, "You ask what my price is? My price is safe passage through the Valley of Vordar."

Knowing they could do this, Opus's eyes lit up, but he kept silent as Gyank proposed a bargain. "If we agree to see you safely through the valley, would you help us get into the castle?"

"I would. But once I've helped you, what guarantee would I have that you'd keep your end of the bargain?"

Gyank responded as if he was insulted. "I'm a man of my word. I'll keep my end of the bargain."

In spite of Gyank's confident response, Sellock was still leery. "And just how do you propose to do that? Nobody can get past those evil men in the valley."

"If I say we can do it—then we can do it," said Gyank.

The wizard glared at him suspiciously. "I'm not so sure."

Agitated by Sellock's distrust, Otok said, "I'm not so sure you could get us inside that castle."

"You doubt the great Sellock?" The old man sat up straight and declared loudly, "I am a wizard—nothing's impossible for me!"

Otok snapped back at him. "If that was the case, you wouldn't be asking us to help you through the valley!"

To prevent the argument from escalating, Reesa interrupted in a loud and commanding voice. "Listen to me!" Surprised at how forcefully she demanded their attention, they remained silent while she continued in a normal tone. "Why don't we all stay calm? I'm sure we can come to an agreement that will suit everyone. Sellock, we've made peace with the men of the valley. As long as you're with us, they will not harm you. Now that you know our means, why don't you tell us yours? Perhaps then we could come to an agreement."

Sellock thought for a moment. "Alright," he said. "I'll tell you. There's a secret passage that leads under the castle." An expression came to the wizard's face as if he had just divulged a critical secret, and then it faded.

Sellock crossed his arms. "And now that we know each other's means, how can you take me through the valley when your business is here in the castle?"

"I have an idea," said Reesa, looking to the others for approval. "You don't need my guidance anymore. Sellock could show you the entrance to the passage, and you could head into the castle while I take him to the Vorak village. If I speak on his behalf, I'm sure Cargon will allow him safe passage through the valley."

Not wanting to put Reesa at risk, Gyank said, "Thorilleia is at war. Wouldn't it be better if you waited here for us to return so we could go back together?"

"No!" said Sellock. "The passage is unsafe. We could not wait for you because you may never come out. And if I were to say anything about it, I'd urge you not to go. I've just come from down there. You're certain to be captured, and then you'll be tortured to death. Is this what you want? Why don't you come back with me to Derrim, where it's safe?"

"No, we must get into the castle," said Otok firmly.

"Then it's settled," said Reesa. "I'll take Sellock back while you go on."

Gyank looked at Reesa. "I'd feel better if we went back together."

"I'm sorry, there's no other way," she said.

"Then let's go," said the wizard. "We're wasting time. I'll show you the passage, and I wish you luck. Although I know how futile it is to venture into that dark place."

Sellock led them along the ledge. The moon shined through thin wispy clouds, casting dim shadows upon the sheer stone stretching up into the night sky. On other side of them, the cliff dropped straight down into what appeared to be a dark abyss where unseen jagged rocks pointed up at them from below. Even though the ledge was wide enough for the five of them to walk abreast, none of them stepped too close to the edge. As they descended, bright moonbeams pierced through a break in the clouds and revealed their dark shapes moving along the cliff. Then a cloud drifted in front of the moon, and they were concealed in the shadows. Down they went, closer to the threatening castle where torchlight glowed from every tower, and the top of each wall was illuminated as it stretched out into the dark valley. Specks of light from bonfires on the beach in the distance fell out of view behind the castle walls.

Appearing around a curve on the ledge ahead were two columns of men in uniform coming toward them. Round metal shields were strapped to their arms, and on their belts hung scimitars with shallow, graceful curves. They did not wear the heavy plate mail armor of knights. Instead, they were clad in leather armor studded with large metal beads that glistened in the moonlight. Their light, flexible armor was designed for ease of movement in battle and for working the rigging of a ship. These were Dlembar sailors.

Before the companions could do anything, one of the sailors pointed at them and shouted, "There! Up ahead! Thorilleians are escaping!"

They turned and ran back along the ledge, but it was useless. The sailors would soon overtake them. Gyank, Otok, and even Opus might have been able to get away, but Reesa's legs were too short and she could not keep up the pace. Sellock was even worse off than Reesa. In his old age, he could run surprisingly fast, but he was no match for the pursuing sailors. After a short burst up the ledge, he was falling farther behind and would soon be caught.

"Help me!" he shouted frantically. "Don't let them take me!"

When the companions heard his cries, it didn't occur to them that Sellock was their only chance to get inside the castle, yet they stopped and turned to help him. They simply could not run away while he desperately called for help. They pulled their bows from their shoulders and prepared to fire a round of arrows into the crowd of men charging up the ledge. Sellock fell to the ground just before the sailors got to him. The companions released the Vorak arrows, which flew over Sellock's head and found their marks in the group men. Another round was fired into the crowd, forcing them back as they shielded themselves.

While the sailors yielded and fell back to hide in the jagged wall of the cliff, Sellock quickly got to his feet and ran. The battle was far from over, for the sailors had archers among them as well as swordsmen. Taking shelter along the ledge, the companions pressed their backs against the rocky cliff as several Dlembar arrows whizzed past them. Standing closest to the sailors, Otok was the only one who could attempt a shot without stepping away from the cliff. But whenever he stuck his head out to take aim, an arrow would come his way and he would pull back. He had no chance to fire, and the sailors advanced each time they forced him to duck back into the shadows. With their opponents pinned, the sailors were able to leapfrog each other so that one archer was always ready to shoot. Soon the Dlembar sailors would be upon them, and there wasn't much they could do.

The time had come for Reesa to reveal that she was much more than a guide. She worked her way past the others so she could get back to where Otok was pinned down. Once next to him, she took charge of the situation. "Otok, step back and let me get to the front."

"Reesa, there's too many of them, and they're getting closer."

"I'm a smaller target than you are," she said as she slipped past him and got down on one knee. As compact as she was in this position, she still could easily handle her bow without the bottom end of it hitting the ground. "Stand close behind me, but stay next to the cliff," she said as an arrow whizzed past her shoulder. "Stay hidden so they can't see you. I'll shoot first and take out the next man who shows himself. The others will try to advance while I reload. That's when you can lean forward and take a shot at a man while he's in the open."

Reesa made it sound so easy, and Otok responded in a frustrated tone of voice, "Reesa, they don't show much of themselves, and as soon as I draw back on my bow, they shower me with arrows."

Reesa paid no attention to him. She just knelt there waiting, her pretty blue eyes peering out from under her blond bangs. A determined look came over her soft, girlish face. Reesa meant business.

"Get ready," she said as she leaned out just enough to see past the rock she knelt behind. An archer hugging the wall with only his arm and half his face showing pulled back on his bowstring. Reesa drew back on her bow and released an arrow all in one quick motion. It flew along the cliff, only inches from the stone. As it twirled, the fletching brushed the rocks before it struck the man just below the armpit. The point of the arrow sunk between his ribs and pierced his heart. His hand released the bowstring, and his arrow flew off wildly toward the dark abyss. Reesa's shot was an amazing demonstration of skill. But in the dim light, the only one who knew of it except for Reesa was the man who fell dead on the ground.

"Now, Otok! Shoot!" she cried softly.

Otok leaned away from the wall and saw two men advancing. He quickly took aim at one of them and fired. The arrow pierced the sailor's leather armor and stuck in his chest, causing him to drop his bow and stumble backward. The second man flattened himself against the cliff and disappeared in a dark crevice. Otok and Reesa pulled their heads back as two other men fired at them.

"I don't know how you did it," said Otok. "They haven't given me a big enough target to shoot at until just now."

"It worked once, but they'll be ready for you the next time I shoot." Reesa quickly pulled another arrow from her quiver and nocked it against her bowstring. "I'll take out another one. This time, you must aim and shoot faster, or they'll stick you with an arrow."

Reesa poked her head out for a quick look and pulled back. She caught a glimpse of three men taking aim at her. The one who had just advanced to a dark crevice and two others who were copying her strategy as one knelt and the other stood over him. She had the best shot at the man kneeling directly in front of her. Drawing in a quiet breath, she suddenly leaned forward and shot with incredible quickness. The man's bowstring was pulled back ready to fire, but Reesa was too fast. Her small arrow flew right down the man's line of sight, and traveling along the arrow shaft still in his bow, it struck the eye that was peeking around the rocks. Reesa did not see him go limp and collapse to the ground. She jerked her head back as an arrow hit the cliff next to her. Otok leaned forward to shoot, but without releasing the bowstring, he forcefully threw his body back against the cliff as an arrow flew past his chest. "That was close!" he said.

"Yes, and this isn't going to work much longer. There are too many of them taking aim, and I can only get one at a time."

"It's a mystery to me how you can get a shot off at all—let alone hit anything."

Otok knew that Reesa had killed two men with two shots, and this alone impressed him. Yet he did not see just how deadly accurate she was with her little bow. Reesa was indeed an exceptional archer, but not even she knew the extent of her skill. She had never been in an archery contest, nor did she realize that her blue eyes were more than just beautiful. She had exceptional vision and could see at a distance far more clearly than most people. This certainly enhanced her ability, but whatever the reason, when Reesa took aim, she simply did not miss, even the smallest of targets.

While they stayed hidden for the moment, Gyank got their attention. "Come on," he whispered. "We can move farther up the cliff. By the time they realize we're gone, we'll have put a good distance between us. We'll look for an easier spot to defend. Maybe we can catch them in the open."

So, they quietly moved up the ledge, staying hidden in the dark shadows of jagged stone. Trailing the others, Reesa and Otok kept glancing back to see if they were being chased. After Reesa demonstrated her skill, the Dlembar sailors were sure to hug the cliff. Even so, Reesa could see dark shapes moving among the rocks in pursuit. Yet, she couldn't stop and wait for an opportunity to take a shot because she would fall too far behind.

Unfortunately, there wasn't a good place to make a stand on the ledge. Soon they would be coming to the gap, and beyond that was the rocky slope where they certainly wouldn't stand a chance. Something had to be done to change the situation. And this is when everyone looked to Sellock.

"Do something," whispered Gyank urgently. "Work your magic. Use your staff."

"We must find a better spot," said Sellock. "Quickly! Around the next bend."

Sellock led the retreat back to the sharp bend where they had first caught sight of the castle. For the moment, they were safe.

"Come on Sellock!" urged Otok. "They'll be coming around the bend after us. Cast a spell on them. Do something!"

"Give me a minute," he said. "I must cast a spell that will work quickly, and that will work on all of them at once." Clutching his staff in both hands, Sellock crinkled his brow as if concentrating.

At that instant, the sailors came around the bend. They had not expected the fleeing party to stop and were surprised to suddenly come upon them when they turned the blind corner. Too close for bows to be of use, swords were drawn and the battle began. Gyank's Serpent Blade flashed blue in the moonlight as he stepped forward to engage the sailors. Opus was right by his side with his sword, and Otok began to swing his axe with confidence. Besides her bow, Reesa only had a small hunting knife under her cloak. She had no weapon for this kind of combat. Even if she did, her size and strength would leave her at a great disadvantage. So she kept an arrow nocked against her bowstring and slipped back along the ledge to get a clear shot if her friends yielded. At the same time, she continued urging Sellock to help them. "Why don't you do something?"

Sellock stood back against the cliff while the three young men tried to hold off the sailors. Terribly outnumbered, they would have been easily overcome had they not been fighting on a ledge that they could block off by standing side by side. Even so, they couldn't hold back the Dlembar sailors for long. These soldiers were disciplined, well-trained fighters, and were better equipped for battle. Each time Gyank tried to inflict a crippling wound, a large round shield would come up and a loud clank would echo in the mountains. Otok's battle-axe was denting the Dlembar shields, but he couldn't strike a debilitating blow either. As they stepped back to avoid being struck, the sailors advanced and forced them back even more.

Gyank was the closest to the edge, and as he yielded, he stepped too close to the precipice. Stones gave way under his foot and he fell, dropping his sword on the ledge while his momentum dragged him over the edge. He clutched the rocky surface with his fingers spread wide apart as his legs dangled in the air. His hands slid along the stone as his chest, shoulders, and then his head went over the side. He finally came to a jolting stop when his fingers got a grip on the edge of the ledge. There he hung, dangling by his arms over the sharp rocks far below in the darkness. His feet waved free as he tried to find a foothold. But there was none.

Opus glanced at the precipice. The pair of hands clinging to the edge began to slip as the stone crumbled. Little bits of rock and dust fell down into Gyank's hair as he struggled to climb up. The thought of watching his friend fall into the dark abyss gave Opus a surge of strength, and he swung his sword at the man in front of him with all his might. The sword knocked the man's shield aside and sliced through the leather armor on his shoulder. The sailor gasped and fell back on his shipmates. Opus dropped down on one knee and reached for his friend. He caught the back of Gyank's wrist just as the stone broke. The sudden jolt yanked Opus down, and he threw himself flat against the ledge to avoid being dragged over. Gyank's free hand instantly grabbed hold of Opus's wrist. The entire weight of Gyank's body now hung on Opus's outstretched arm.

With Otok by himself next to the cliff, the sailors rushed forward to strike down on Opus. One of them raised his sword, aiming for the back of Opus's neck. Suddenly, the man froze. An arrow from Reesa's bow had pierced his neck. He fell to the ledge and his limp body slipped off into the darkness. Reesa went to nock another arrow, but there was no time. The men of Dlembar charged forward to stab at their vulnerable foe. Lying on his stomach, Opus was exposed and helpless, so he hung onto Gyank with all his strength as he rolled onto his side in order to get his sword arm to face the onslaught. In this position, he awkwardly slashed at the legs of a sailor, causing him to jump back. Another arrow flew from Reesa's bow and struck the man in the chest. He dropped his sword, fell to his knees, and grasped the arrow sticking out of his body. Gyank still could not find a foothold to push himself up. He clung to his friend's outstretched arm, which shook back and forth as Opus tried to fend off another sailor by chopping at his feet. Reesa loaded another arrow, but it was too late. Opus's sword was pushed aside, and he was slashed across his upper back just above his pack. The blade severed one of the straps and the pack flopped to the side as the man quickly drew back and struck again, stabbing the point of his sword into Opus's shoulder.

"Ahhhh!" cried Opus while clinging tightly to his friend, refusing to let go. Another arrow flew from Reesa's bow, killing the man who stabbed Opus and causing him to topple off the ledge. But several more sailors rushed forward to slice at him. He rolled onto his back and raised his sword to defend himself. In doing so, his arm twisted around painfully as Gyank was spun sideways. Blood ran down Opus's arm and dripped onto his friend dangling below.

Suddenly, he heard a forceful grunting sound like that of a wild beast. Opus was stepped on and tripped over as men tumbled off the ledge and fell past Gyank into the darkness. Screams came echoing up the cliff and ended sharply when the men crashed onto the jagged rocks below. Otok had held his battle-axe horizontally across his chest, and using his powerful thighs, he had driven four sailors off the ledge like a giant mountain ram. He sent one crashing into the other while he used the long handle of Grok to knock them into the abyss.

With one mighty shove, Otok had cleared the ledge next to his friends, and when he turned to face the rest of the Dlembar fighters, he felt a surge of strength come over his body just as he did when he faced the river monster. Standing alone on the ledge with his back to his fallen companions, it was as if he was suddenly transformed. He planted his feet in a wide stance, and holding Grok at the end of its long handle, he swung the mighty axe back and forth. With each forceful blow, a grunt escaped his lips. Otok's reach swept from the wall of the cliff on one side to the edge of the precipice on the other.

The passage that had taken three of them to block was now being held by Otok alone.

But holding them at bay was not enough to satisfy his rage. With the senseless fury of a madman, Otok went at them. And as he did, Dlembar sailors fell to their death on one side while others were smashed between the head of Otok's axe and the cliff. Grok cut cleanly through leather armor and bashed through metal shields as if they were made of straw. Otok kept advancing at the cost of the sailors as he stepped over the bodies of the men who fell at his feet. No one could withstand the fierce onslaught of Otok and his axe. The remaining sailors fled back down the ledge. As they ran, they shouted cries of a fearsome demon with the strength of ten men.

Otok stopped his attack and fell to his knees exhausted. His heart was pounding and sweat covered his blood-spattered body. Behind him, Reesa helped Opus pull Gyank up onto the ledge. Opus lay there bleeding while Reesa quickly dug into her pack, looking for bandages. Only now did Gyank become aware of Opus's injuries. When he saw the gaping cuts leaking blood from Opus's back and shoulder, the full impact of what had happened hit him hard. "Oh, Opus," he groaned. "They cut you all up—and you still didn't let go of me."

Opus moaned quietly from the pain. Sitting next to him on the ledge, Gyank was clearly shaken. "You didn't let go—you hung onto me."

Reesa realized how badly this was affecting Gyank, and she gave him a word of reassurance. "He'll be alright, Gyank. It looks much worse than it is."

"Are you sure?"

"Yes, don't worry. I have everything under control," said Reesa confidently.

While Reesa worked quickly to stop the bleeding, Gyank sat there watching her. He was in shock, and at the same time amazed that his friend held onto him, refusing to let him fall to his death.

Chapter 13

A DIFFICULT DECISION

By the dim light of the moon, Reesa tended to Opus's wounds. Gyank looked around and noticed that Sellock was gone. "Where's Sellock?" he asked in a startled tone of voice.

"He must have fled during the battle," said Reesa while pulling a long, thin cloth around Opus's torso.

Otok was farther down the ledge, still trying to catch his breath. Gyank hollered over to him. "Otok, are you alright?"

"I'm fine."

Gyank got to his feet. "There's only one way Sellock could have gone, and I'm going after him."

He started running back along the ledge. In his haste, he forgot to pick up his sword. The sight of Opus's wounds angered him, and he ran dangerously fast along the winding ledge. He came to the gap between the cliffs where they had first seen the Wall of Thorilleia. Breathing heavily, he scanned the slope, but the robed wizard was nowhere in sight. He spun around and looked across the valley at the wall in the distance. It was glowing eerily with the light of hundreds of torches. Gyank looked away so his eyes could readjust to the dim, moonlit cliffs. Glancing to the right, he spotted the dark figure of a man dressed in robes running along the top of a short but steep slope. Gyank took off after him. By the time he got to the top, he was gasping for breath, and Sellock had disappeared. There was a narrow ledge running along a vertical cliff, and it was the only way the wizard could have gone, so Gyank dashed along the ledge through the darkness.

As he came around a sharp corner, he was struck in the stomach with the heavy end of Sellock's staff. The clever old man had been hiding there waiting for Gyank to come to that blind spot. Gyank bent over, clutching his stomach, while Sellock brought the staff down on his back with a crack. Gyank fell to his hands and knees by the edge of the precipice and rolled onto his back just as the bottom end of Sellock's staff came down at his head. The wizard's staff had a long metal point attached to the end of it to provide better grip for hiking, but it also made a good weapon. Gyank quickly twisted his head to one side, and the metal point struck the stone right next to his ear. He grabbed the staff with both hands and hung on so Sellock could not lift it up and stab down at him again. The wizard knew he had to do something quickly before Gyank could catch his breath. So he braced his back against the cliff, bent his knees, and used his feet to push Gyank toward the edge of the precipice. Lying on his back, Gyank slid toward the vertical drop. He clung tightly to the staff, holding its point against the stone while it scraped along the ledge next to his ear. Pebbles and sand being pushed by Gyank's body fell off the cliff to the jagged rocks far below. Gyank had no way to stop himself from sliding, and Sellock's legs were steadily straightening out. Before the wizard's knees would lock, Gyank would be off the edge of the cliff. But when the metal point of the staff slipped off the precipice, the force of Gyank pulling on it jerked Sellock forward. With his opponent off balance, Gyank quickly shifted his grip an arm's length farther up the staff and yanked down hard. The old man fell on top of him and the staff went tumbling down into the darkness. It took a seemingly long time before the faint sound of the staff striking the rocks far below echoed up to them. As they grappled on the ledge, Gyank shoved Sellock toward the wall of the cliff while flipping over on top of him. Straddling the old man, Gyank tried to wrestle him into submission.

"Alright, my great and powerful wizard, who are you really?"

Sellock didn't answer. He continued struggling until Gyank pulled out his knife and pointed it at the wizard's throat. Gyank got up slowly and put his back against the cliff. "Now, get up," he said harshly.

Afraid of being shoved to his death, Sellock lay motionless on the ledge, his fearful eyes gazing up at Gyank.

"I said, get up!"

Sellock pushed himself away from the edge, and with a terrified expression on his face, he clutched the wall of the cliff as he slowly got to his feet, all the while keeping his eyes on Gyank.

"We're going back the way we came, and don't try anything, or I'll carve you up real quick. This little knife is very handy. Now move!" Gyank gave him a poke from behind, and they started back along the narrow ledge. When they came to the gap in the cliff, they could see three figures coming toward them. Otok had one arm around Opus helping him to walk while Reesa carried Opus's pack along with Gyank's sword. As soon as Otok lowered Opus to the ground, it was clear that his rage had not completely subsided. He grabbed Sellock by the front of his robes and practically lifted him off the ground. "Alright, you coward! We know you're not a wizard! So who and what are you?"

Sellock said nothing. Otok paused for an instant and then shook him violently. "Look here mister, our lives are at stake, and I'm not going to be led into some kind of trap. So you better start talking. And this time I want the truth."

Sellock still did not answer. He just looked at Otok, and a slight smile of defiance came to his lips. Otok let go of Sellock with one hand and smacked him across the face. The smile disappeared. Otok's big hand came back the other way and his knuckles struck Sellock's face, causing his nose and lips to bleed. Otok kept smacking him so that his head whipped back and forth. Then Otok threw him to the ground and shouted, "I said talk!"

"I'll talk," said Sellock in a spiteful tone. "I'll tell you everything you don't want to hear. Your quest for the book is over! The book's been found!"

The companions were shocked. How could this man know about their quest?

"What are you talking about?" said Otok.

"I know what you're here for, and why you want to get into the castle. You're after the great book of Seregon, aren't you? Well, you're too late. It's been found." Sellock's voice grew loud and desperate. "It's been found! Don't you know what this means? We're all going to die!" Sellock kept repeating as if he was a crazy man speaking to himself in a fit. "It's too late ... too late! You'll never get it. Never! The book's been found! Found, I tell you! We're all too late!"

Otok grabbed Sellock and pulled him to his feet. "Who are you? What do you know about the book?" Then he shouted into his Sellock's face, "Talk!"

Otok shook him while he tried to speak. "The b-book ha-has been-been fou-fou-found."

"I've had just about enough of you," said Otok as he held Sellock still for a moment. "Now, who are you, and why do you claim to be a wizard?"

Sellock went on mumbling incoherently, and Otok shook him once very hard to get his attention. "Those men from Dlembar will be coming back soon with reinforcements, and we don't have time to waste on you. If you don't tell us what we want to know, you will die right now."

Otok threw him to the ground again. He was dizzy and his face was a bloody mess.

"Alright. Enough, enough," said Sellock between gasps. "My name isn't Sellock, and I'm not a wizard. It's all just posturing. Sometimes I use the title 'Sellock the Wizard' to gain respect, and to get people to fear me."

"Then who are you?" asked Otok impatiently.

"My name is Toger. I'm a wanderer. I travel from kingdom to kingdom. I sing and dance and tell stories for the men of the courts. I juggle and I play musical instruments. I'm a court jester, that's all. I'm just an old man who acts silly to make the nobility laugh."

"Fine. Now tell us how you know of the book," demanded Otok.

Toger wiped blood from his lips with the back of his hand and said, "Many years ago, I came across a dark hallway deep in the castle. It led to the dungeon, and to the door of a cell where a man was held captive. In the quietest whisper, he told me he had found a book that held the secret to immense power, and that he was thrown into the dungeon because he wouldn't give it to Rocor."

"Who's Rocor?" asked Otok.

"He's the king of Thorilleia." Toger stopped to collect his thoughts. "The prisoner hid the book before he was captured, and King Rocor told him that he would stay in the dungeon and rot until he revealed where the book was hidden. The king is quite clever, for he told no one of this prisoner or the book. He kept it all very secret while he had his men search. I'm sure these men didn't even know what they were looking for. Rocor probably told them he wanted to find a book about his family history that was lost in the castle years ago. But it's hard to keep secrets buried within castle walls, and in time, someone must have figured out what Rocor was searching for. Word got out that the legend was true—that the great book of Seregon really did exist. Secretly, men came from all over to spy on Thorilleia and to search for the book. But no one could find it."

Toger suddenly stopped talking, and Otok took a step toward him. The old man had a look of horrible dread on his face. But he was not responding to the threat of Otok's punishment. His eyes were focused far off in the distant darkness as he continued to speak. "Then finally, word of the book reached far into the south and fell upon the ears of the most wicked of all men. Deep in the southern realms, beyond the land of Sarilar, Lord Krotor of Islar learned about the book and the man who knew where it lay hidden. Craving the power of the book, the evil warlord came north with a terrible force of man and beast."

Lying on the ground, bleeding from the mouth and nose, Toger pointed his bony finger up at them and spoke as if giving a grave warning. "Mind you, that warlord is clever as well as powerful. He had a group of his best warriors dress as peasants and hide in the fields. Then he attacked from the other side of the castle with the bulk of his men. He made sure that his troops were seen far in the distance. This way, the castle doors would stay open long enough for all the people of the village and those working in the fields to get inside. While Thorilleian soldiers ran to defend the walls, Krotor's secret force went into the lower levels of the castle undetected. They found their way to the inner corridors and chambers of the dungeon, where they forced a guard to lead them to the prisoner who had found the book. The men of Islar took the prisoner and escaped the castle. The siege outside lasted only long enough for the task force inside to do their evil work. When it was all over, the men of Thorilleia found that the prisoner was taken and they knew the purpose of the attack. Everyone feared what Lord Krotor would do if he ever wielded the power of the book. So the king had no choice but to send his soldiers after him. They were terrified of passing through the Valley of Vordar, but the thought of that evil warlord getting his hands on the book forced them to go. If you ask me, it's not likely they will retrieve the prisoner or return to Thorilleia alive."

The companions listened in horror. Toger could be lying, but it did not seem likely. They had seen Lord Krotor in the Valley of Vordar. And more than this, the words of the evil warlord echoed clearly in their minds: "Guard the prisoner closely. We must get him to Islar alive." This was the phrase they remembered hearing in the dark forest of Vordar, and a wave of fear ran through their bodies.

There was a long silent pause. Something just didn't make sense to Gyank and he asked, "If the book is hidden somewhere in Thorilleia, why would Lord Krotor take the man who knows where it is all the way back to Islar?"

Toger looked up at him. "Lord Krotor can't stay here. In the forest or in the open countryside, he can't defend himself against a powerful castle like Thorilleia. Only a small fraction of his warriors came with him while the rest of his mighty army stayed in Islar. Otherwise, it would have looked like an invasion. Thorilleia would have known Krotor was coming well in advance, and he wouldn't have been able to steal the prisoner. Lord Krotor planned this out very well. He will take the prisoner to his fortress in Islar and torture him until he finds out what he wants to know. In that horrid place, they have methods of torture that you or I could never even imagine. Krotor will get his answers—he will. You can bet on it."

"But if the book is still here, then we can find it," said Otok.

"Fools!" snapped Toger. "You are all fools! Don't you know that men have searched for years trying to find the precious book, but no one has succeeded—including me. For years and years, the search has gone on!"

The companions looked at each other bewildered.

"You'll never find the book in time," said Toger. "Lord Krotor will be back as soon as the prisoner talks. Then there will be a battle such that the world has not seen in ages."

Gyank pointed at the Wall of Thorilleia glowing in the distance. "What of the wall being fortified, and the ships in the river, and the fires on the beach? There's much more going on than you tell us."

"I told you!" said Toger with a desperate tone of voice. "Word of the book got out, and other kingdoms want it for themselves. They offered ransom money for the prisoner. They raised the price to incredible sums, but King Rocor knows how valuable the book is and would not let the prisoner go. So Derrim formed an alliance with Mellain, and they're about to attack the Wall of Thorilleia while Dlembar is preparing to attack from the river. Thorilleia will be fighting on two fronts. Think about it. If the Wall of Thorilleia is breached, then Derrim and Mellain will come through the valley and attack the castle from that side. If they take the castle, they'll defend it from Dlembar. Or Dlembar could take the castle first. But here's the worst part of all this—these kingdoms think the prisoner is still in Thorilleia. They don't know about Krotor's secret attack, and they wouldn't believe King Rocor if he told them the prisoner was stolen. They would think it was a trick to end the siege, or buy time. Only after the castle is taken will they realize the prisoner is not there, and then who knows what will happen. Perhaps by that time, Lord Krotor will be back to claim the book, and the other forces will be too weak to resist his army. I dread to think of it."

"What are we going to do?" asked Opus, ignoring his wounds for the moment.

"I don't know," said Gyank. "But we must decide quickly. We have little time. The Dlembar sailors will be coming back soon."

"Somehow we must make them believe the prisoner has been taken," said Otok.

Toger wiped the blood from his lips with the back of his wrist. "You must be joking. They would never believe you—or me. We can do nothing. Nothing!" Once again, Toger began talking as if in a fit. "We're all doomed! Lord Krotor will get the book and conquer the world. We are witnessing the end of the world and the beginning of Krotor's wicked rule. It's hopeless! We'll all be tortured and enslaved! An era of darkness is upon us! And to think I could have had the book all for myself. I could have wielded great power and proved to the nobility that I'm not just a fool. All the lords and kings would have looked up to me, and they would have to jump at my whim. I would have been all powerful."

While Toger rambled on, Reesa seemed to be in a world of her own as she stared off into the darkness with an amazed look in her eyes. Suddenly, she blinked and came out of her trance. "I can't believe my ears. I thought the book of Seregon was only a myth."

"Reesa, what do you know of the book?" asked Gyank.

"I've heard rumors of such a book while on my trading route, but I thought it was just a tall tale—folks retelling an old legend. I never dreamed it was real."

"Well, obviously it is, and we have to make a decision," said Gyank.

Toger was still mumbling to himself like a crazy man, his head only inches from the ground as he knelt there completely oblivious to what the others were saying.

"We must go after Krotor," said Otok.

"Yes, but how?" said Gyank. "It's been a while since we saw him in the Valley of Vordar. We could never catch him before he gets to his fortress in Islar."

"I know a way," said Reesa. "But it's very dangerous."

Gyank looked at her with surprise. "We can't drag you along on a hopeless mission."

"No. You can't drag me. But you won't have to—because I must go."

"Why?" said Gyank. "This doesn't involve you."

"Yes, it does," said Reesa firmly. "It involves all free people. Don't you understand? You don't want to put me in danger, but if Krotor gets the book and learns of its power, I'll be in danger anyway. He'll conquer the world and make slaves of us all." Reesa pointed at Toger kneeling on the ground. "I hate to say it, but this man's assessment of what will happen if Lord Krotor gets the book is not far from the truth. Then again, there's no telling what Derrim or Dlembar will do if they get the book. The only way to be safe is to stop the book from falling into the wrong hands. I'm willing to risk my life in order to protect us all from the evil that might soon be unleashed. You must let me go with you. I may be small, but don't underestimate me."

Gyank looked at her and said, "After seeing how you handled yourself on the ledge back there, I'll never underestimate you."

"I'm going with you," insisted Reesa.

Otok glanced back at the ledge. "We better get out of here. Let's go down into the valley; then we can decide what to do."

Gyank looked at Opus sitting on the ground. "Do you think you can make it back to the valley?"

Opus was hurt badly and he didn't know how far or how fast he could go, but not wanting to slow the others down, he spoke with confidence. "Sure. You bet I can make it. It'll take more than a couple of sword wounds to stop me."

As they gathered up their gear, Toger was still on the ground groveling and mumbling to himself about the book. Otok got Gyank's attention and asked, "What about him?"

"I don't think he'll do us any more harm. I bet he's searched a long time for the book. He desperately wants it. Now he realizes that if anyone gets the book, it won't be him. He seems rather pitiful to me."

"Pitiful?" exclaimed Otok. "He looks like he's gone insane."

As they walked away, each of them couldn't resist looking back once more at the Wall of Thorilleia. All lit up and alive with soldiers; it marked the beginning of terrible bloodshed.

They went back the way they had come, and even though it was all down hill, Opus needed help getting down the slope. Once they got to the bottom of the ridge by the river, they sat down to talk about a plan. Gyank started the conversation with a question. "First of all, are we all willing to go after Lord Krotor and try to rescue the prisoner?"

"It's quite clear how Reesa and I feel," said Otok. "But what about Opus? I wouldn't blame him if he didn't want to go. He's all cut up."

"It isn't that bad," said Opus. "I'll live through it. And if you're considering leaving me behind, you can forget it."

"There would be no shame in it," said Gyank. "You could stay with the Voraks. You know as well as we do that this would be the safest place for you. They'll care for you, and you'll have a chance to heal."

"I'll heal soon enough. We're in this together and I'm not giving up now. Besides, I took a vow."

"Under the circumstances, no one would hold you to your vow," said Gyank.

"No! I'm going with you," said Opus emphatically.

Sitting on a boulder next to him, Otok said, "If you want to come that badly, then we'll take you along if we must carry you."

"I'm coming with you, but you won't have to carry me." Opus smiled in spite of the pain. "It just might take all four of us to put a dent in Krotor's plate mail."

"Alright then," said Gyank, "we need to come up with a plan. Reesa, you said there's a way to catch Lord Krotor."

"I don't know if we'll catch him, but there is another way to Islar, and it may be quicker, but it's extremely dangerous. Lord Krotor will take the prisoner to the Towers of Islar. That's his stronghold, a tall, dark castle perched on a sheer cliff overlooking a river. I've never been there, but I've heard stories about that evil place. They say it's impregnable. It's surrounded by barren, rugged mountains, and there's no vegetation anywhere near the castle where you could hide, only stone and sharp rocks. In fact, the entire realm of Islar is encompassed by jagged, mountain peaks, and the border is guarded by two small fortresses on either side of a narrow canyon. Those ever-watchful towers are known as the outposts of Islar. It's clear that we won't catch Krotor by following him though Sarilar. Even if we did go that way, we'd have to go through the canyon, and we'd never get past the outposts without being seen. Most folks would agree that the canyon pass is the only way to the Towers of Islar, but there is another way. It's not a secret, but it's so dangerous, nobody would even consider it." Reesa paused and gave them a serious look. "The only other way is through the Marshes of Guglic. These swamplands are so vast and so perilous that nobody would dare enter them, let alone try to traverse them. An army could never make the journey, but we are only four. With a small boat, we just might be able to make it. Once through the marshes, we'll be on the other side of the Towers of Islar. This doesn't mean getting into Krotor's castle will be easy. I don't even know if we'll be able to climb up to the towers, but I can say that we'll be undetected. Krotor would never expect anyone to come by way of the swamps. The sheer cliffs rising up out of the river on that side of the castle prevent any kind of large-scale attack. But we are only a few, and stealth will be our ally." Reesa hesitated for a moment, and then said, "This is a drastic course of action, but it's our only chance against Lord Krotor. I can see no other way. We may never make it through the marshes. We may catch sickness or get lost in the endless winding waterways, but if we try to get through the canyon, we will surely be caught."

"If you say this is our best chance, then I'm willing to try it," said Gyank.

"The choice is made," said Otok. "The marshes it is."

"What are we waiting for?" said Opus in agreement.

"First we need a boat," said Gyank. "And I think I know where we can get one. Dlembar has an entire fleet out there in the river. I don't think they'd mind if we borrowed one little boat for a while."

"Then let's get going," said Otok, as he stood up and reached down to help Opus to his feet.

Throughout the night, they hiked along the quiet river, following it out of the Valley of Vordar to where it joined the Gubain River. Turning northward toward the castle, they followed the banks of the Gubain until the forest abruptly came to an end. The trees and underbrush had been chopped away by the axes of men. Stretching in front of them was a long, open beach of sand, dirt, and rock. The forest had been decimated so the beach and the river could be watched from the castle towers. The barren space between the river and the castle's outermost wall provided a protective barrier through which there was no way to approach without being seen.

From the edge of the forest, they could see Dlembar warships anchored farther up the river. The hulls of the ships were dim shadows under the cloudy night sky, but the white sails neatly wrapped against the booms were unmistakable. Along the beach, men worked on the construction of war machines by the light of tall, blazing bonfires.

"How will we ever be able to get past all those men?" asked Reesa.

"I have an idea," said Gyank. "If we wade into the river up to our necks, we should be able to get by the men on the beach. They're busy with their work, and they're looking into their fires. They'll be blind to anything moving in the darkness of the river. If we can swim up to the ships, we might be able to cut a small boat free and drift away with it into the darkness. Or perhaps, we can take one from the shore without being noticed."

"You make it sound so easy," said Otok. "All they have to do is see us, and we'll have an entire navy on our backs."

"I know, but we need a boat, and I don't see any other way to get one, although you are right about not letting them see us. We'll have a better chance of that if some of us stay here. Since we have to come back this way, Opus could wait here for us. He's in no shape for a midnight swim. Reesa, you wouldn't mind staying here with him. Would you?"

"No, of course not. We'll stay in the cover of the forest and wait for you to come back with a boat."

Gyank took off his pack and pulled out his dark stalking clothes. "These should come in handy tonight," he said as he sat down on the riverbank next to Otok and began taking off his boots. "I guess this task is up to you and me. We'll have to leave all our gear behind except for our knives. They'll do just fine for cutting rope."

"Yes, and let's hope that's all we'll need to cut with them," said Otok, pulling off his boot.

Soon, they slipped quietly into the cool, dark water. They waded out to their chests and bent their legs so only their heads were above the surface. Being careful not to make waves or splashing noises, they moved parallel to the beach as they walked along the muddy river bottom, creeping silently toward the blazing bonfires where men were working and talking. Small boats that were used to transport sailors to the beach lined the shore. Flames jumped skyward and sparks flew everywhere while busy sailors worked on assembling a heavy catapult. The entire area was illuminated by the tall stack of burning logs.

Gyank whispered, "What do you think? Can we get one of those boats, or is there too much light?"

"The men standing watch on the ships have a good view of the shoreline. If the men on the beach don't see us, the men on the ships will."

"You're right," said Gyank, turning to look at the warships anchored parallel to the shore. "Let's head to the ships, and hope we find better pickings out there."

Within a few steps, their feet could no longer reach the muddy bottom and they began to swim. Afraid to risk even a tiny splash, they used slow underwater strokes to propel themselves through the dark water. They approached one of the ships from the bow so the men standing watch on deck could not see them. A thick anchor rope came down from the bow and disappeared in the depths of the river. They swam up to it quietly and hung on to rest.

Gyank whispered ever so softly, "See any small boats?"

"No. Wait a minute." Otok let go of the anchor rope and swam a few strokes so he could look along the port side of the ship. Then he swam back to the anchor rope and nodded his head. "There's a small boat on that side."

"Perfect. The ship will shield us from the men on the beach."

"There's only one problem," whispered Otok. "The boat's not in the water. It's up by the deck on winches. We'll have to get up there and lower it down."

"It's still better than trying to take one from the beach. Did you see how many men were on watch?"

"I only saw one, but I heard others."

"We can't let them call out. Let's go."

Gyank reached up and took hold of the thick anchor rope. He pulled himself out of the water with his arms and wrapped his legs around the rope slowly and silently. Water from his wet clothes ran down his body onto the rope as it trickled into the river, minimizing the dripping noises as he climbed. Otok was right behind him, using the same technique. They inched their way up the rope and peeked under the railing of the bow. A sailor on watch was looking at the beach. Toward the center of the ship, three other men stood talking. While Otok and Gyank wondered how they could get up there without being seen, one of the three men walked down a few steps into the cabin and closed the door behind him.

Gyank gave his friend a single nod of his head and then quietly climbed onto the deck. He crawled behind a large ballista mounted on the bow. As Otok started to pull himself up, he made a slight noise that caught the attention of the man standing watch nearby. But the man couldn't see them because the ballista blocked his view. As he slowly walked around one side of the ballista, Gyank crept around the other side to keep out of sight. The man saw Otok inching his way onto the deck and reached for his sword. Gyank lunged from his crouched position and grabbed the man from behind, wrapping one arm around his throat while cupping a hand over the sailor's mouth. The sword had just cleared its scabbard when Otok rushed forward and seized the man's sword arm. They wrestled the sailor to the deck and quietly knocked him out with the hilt of his own sword.

Otok held onto the weapon as they crept along the deck toward the stern. Hiding behind one of the masts, Gyank used his hunting knife to cut a length of rope that was hanging free. The other two men on deck were talking as they faced the beach.

"When do you think we'll be moving our siege towers up to the castle?"

"I'm not sure, but progress is going well on the—"

The length of rope Gyank had cut was now tight around the man's neck. The sailor reached up with both hands trying to relieve the pressure while the other sailor had Otok's powerful forearm wrapped around his neck. Though they struggled, they soon lost consciousness and fell quietly to the deck.

"The boat," Gyank whispered while pointing to the lines holding the boat over the water. As they grabbed the ropes that controlled the pulleys, they heard the sound of a door opening and froze. Without hardly breathing, they listened intensely. They couldn't see anybody, but they could hear footsteps heading away from them. Apparently, whoever came on deck didn't notice the men lying unconscious. Perhaps he came out a door that faced the other way. The footsteps ceased and they silently started to untie the lines holding the boat. Unfortunately, the man who had come on deck noticed the marks made by two pairs of wet bare feet, and he ran along the deck following the footprints while shouting, "All hands on deck! All hands on deck!"

As they frantically tried to untie the lines holding the boat, they heard a thump and something hit the wooden deck nearby. Otok groaned quietly in pain, and his legs gave out from under him as he collapsed onto the deck, grasping the back of his thigh. Blood streamed out of Otok's leg where a crossbow bolt had pierced his hamstring, passing completely through his leg and embedding itself in the wooden deck. The bloody bolt sticking out of the deck pointed up at the crow's nest where a man with a heavy crossbow was stationed on the mast.

Gyank rushed over to Otok, crouched down next to him, and looked up at the crow's nest. While the man reloaded his crossbow, the sailor who had noticed their wet footsteps charged across the ship with his scimitar in hand. One of the men lying unconscious nearby had a bow. Gyank picked it up while pulling an arrow from the man's quiver. He nocked the arrow, quickly drew back on the bowstring, and fired up at the man in the crow's nest just as he was taking aim. The arrow struck the man in the chest and he fell from the mast with a scream that ended in a thud. The man with the scimitar was now only a step away and ready to strike. Shifting his grip on the bow, Gyank swung it like an axe, aiming for the man's head. The scimitar came up to meet it and sliced off the tip of the bow. The taut bowstring snapped and the bow wiggled violently. Gyank swiftly thrust the cut end of the bow into the man's face. It struck his mouth and slid up into his nose, tearing his upper lip. The man's hand instinctively covered his face as he fell back against the railing. Gyank threw the bow down and turned to help Otok. But Otok's eyes grew wide and he shouted, "Gyank, look out!"

The man with the scimitar was not finished yet, and he went to stab Gyank from behind. Gyank spun around just in time to throw himself against the railing as the thrust went past his chest. He caught the man's extended arm and yanked him downward while driving his knee up into the sailor's chin. Dazed, the Dlembar fighter collapsed to the deck.

"Here!" said Otok as he slid his sword, handle first, across the smooth wooden deck. Gyank scooped it up and dealt a final blow to the man. By this time, doors and hatches had opened all over the ship, and armed men came from every direction. Otok fought to stand up, and Gyank rushed over to help him.

"Quick! Over the side," said Gyank as he helped Otok hobble to the rail. Otok threw himself over and plunged into the river with a loud splash.

A husky voice shouted above the commotion, "They're going over the side! Stop them!"

Standing next to the boat, Gyank raised his sword and slashed the lines attached to the pulleys. The boat lurched nose down as the lines came free and then crashed into the dark water with a huge splash. Gyank threw the sword at the man nearest to him and dove overboard.

"Otok! Where are you?" were the first words out of his mouth when his head popped above the surface of the water.

"Here," said Otok's voice nearby in the dark.

"Grab onto the boat."

A voice from above cut through the night. "Where are they? Get some lanterns over here!"

Otok was floundering in the water, trying to keep his head up. Gyank pushed the boat over to him and he caught hold of the gunwale. Gyank swiftly pulled himself into the boat and stepped over to where a pair of hands was gripping the side. He grabbed Otok by the wrist and pulled hard, leaning back so the boat wouldn't tip over. As Otok came up over the side, Gyank grabbed the back of his shirt and he plopped into the boat like a played out fish. He lay on the bottom of the boat gripping his leg in an attempt to stop the bleeding while Gyank scrambled to get the oars in the water.

"There they are!" a voice shouted as lanterns were held over the side of the ship.

"Archers! Fire!"

The oars had just dug in for the first stroke when the loud twang of arrows hitting the wooden boat reverberated in the hull. Several arrows barely missed Gyank as they stuck up out of the seat next to him. He stroked as hard as he could to get away from the ship and into the darkness of the river.

"That was close," said Otok, looking at arrow shafts embedded in the hull on either side of him.

"It's not over yet," said Gyank as he pulled on the oars to steer the boat away from the fleet. Otok took out his knife and cut his pants above the wound. Lines of dark blood ran down his thigh and dripped onto the bottom of the boat. While he did his best to use the bottom part of his pants to bandage his leg, Gyank was urged to pull harder on the oars by the sound of arrows whizzing into the water behind the boat.

The alarm spread to other ships and to the men on the beach as captains shouted and horns were blown. In the light from the bonfires, a fleet of small boats could be seen racing from the shore, while other chase boats were lowered from the ships.

The boat they had stolen was light and narrow, and it cut nicely through the calm water, but it was no match for the well-manned boats that pursued them. Otok knew he had to help row, so he finished with his leg and took out another set of oars. Together they pulled on the oars for all they were worth. Not far behind, many boats could be seen with a lantern perched on the end of a sailor's outstretched arm.

"Archers, stand ready," commanded a voice in the darkness. "They're headed downstream."

Otok and Gyank did not let up. They kept rowing as fast as they could because, in spite of the chase, they had to make a stop.

~ ~ ~

Watching from the edge of the forest, Reesa and Opus saw the tiny lights of the chase boats flickering off the dark water in the distance. Yet they could not see the boat being chased.

"They're coming," said Reesa. "Let's get all the gear and wade out into the river."

Opus was feeling weak, but he knew this was going to be a narrow escape. He waded out into the dark water, slipping on the muddy bottom and fighting to stand up. Reesa was by his side, laden with all the gear, and doing her best to hold it up out of the water to keep it dry. Standing chest deep in the river, they peered at the specks of light twinkling off the water as the fleet of chase boats came directly at them. But there was no sign of their friends. As the glowing lanterns approached, a fleet of black hulls with men rowing in unison became visible. Finally, they heard the sound of oars splashing close by, mingled with the huffing and puffing of their struggling friends.

"Gyank, over here," said Reesa in a quiet but distinct voice.

Otok and Gyank stopped rowing and let the boat coast. "Reesa, Opus, come on, get in," said Gyank as he turned his head to see where his friends were. The boat glided alongside Reesa and she tossed all the gear into the boat. Then she grabbed on as the boat coasted past her, and she was pulled off balance.

"Opus, grab on," said Gyank, dropping his oars to help Opus into the boat.

Reesa was still draped over the side with her legs and hips hanging out when Otok and Gyank started rowing again. She pulled herself in and plopped into the boat. Reesa took one look at Otok's bloody leg and cried in a whisper, "Otok, your leg!"

"Never mind!" he said. "Grab an oar!"

The chase boats had closed in on them, and they were in danger of being seen. Reesa sat next to Opus on a bench and each of them took an oar to balance out their efforts. The dark outlines of Dlembar chase boats were right behind them, and since they faced the stern to row, they could see the distance between them diminishing. They would soon be in sight, and then the arrows would come in unavoidable waves.

Reesa looked to see where they were going. In the dim light, there appeared to be nothing ahead of them but forest. "Pull more on the right or we're going to hit," she said.

The others turned their heads to see a line of black trees spanning from one side of the river to the other. It seemed as if the river ended abruptly in a wall of dense vegetation. The boat took a turn as they pulled the oars harder on one side and slid past a cluster of brush sticking out over the water. Only after making this turn did they realized that the river split into countless branches, both wide and narrow, where the water snaked its way through the forest.

The companions pulled hard on the oars and slipped into the cover of the trees. Reesa was in the bow and kept turning to look ahead where the waterway forked and curved sharply as it weaved through the woods. She made quick decisions each time the river split as she guided the little boat through the towering trees. Soon the sounds of chase boats diminished. The glow of lanterns was blocked by the dark forest, and the party glided onward through the calm water. There were so many forks in the river and twisting offshoots that even if their pursuers split up to search every alley of escape, they could not cover all of them. Although they were safe, they did not stop rowing for a long time.

Eventually, the silence and darkness reduced their fear until it vanished altogether. They were now on their way down the Gubain River, which led into the Marshes of Guglic—a place where no men lived, a place where men would not even think of going, for the dangers of the swamps are great.

Now their quest had taken on a new, more important, purpose. Rather than merely finding the book and returning home with it, the companions were setting off to save the world from a tyrannical ruler. In order to do that, they would have to first rescue a man they didn't even know from the most feared warlord in the land.

*This ends the first part of the Dragon's Dust story. The second part is called **Prisoner of the Dark Fortress,** which tells of the recovery of the Book of Seregon and what happens to those who learn the powerful secret that it holds.*

Made in the USA
Middletown, DE
01 February 2017